RELIGIOUS RIGHT RELIGIOUSLY WRONG

A MODERN DAY PARABLE

PAUL SWEARENGIN

Religious Right Religiously Wrong: A Modern Day Parable
Copyright © 2023 by Paul Swearengin All rights reserved.

No portion of this book may be reproduced in any form without written permission from the publisher, Paul Swearengin, 2037 W. Bullard Ste. 257, Fresno, CA 93711 www.pastor-paul.com
Library of Congress Control Number: 2019904098
https://lccn.loc.gov/2019904098
Swearengin, Paul R. Religious Right Religiously Wrong: A Modern Day Parable / Paul R. Swearengin; [edited by] Paul. Fresno, CA : Paul Swearengin Pub., 2019.

pages cm
ISBN: 979-8-218-25633-3 (alk. paper)
Printed in the United States of America
ISBN 13: 979-8-218-25633-3 ISBN 10: 8-218-25633-3

Graphic design cover and internal pages by
Toby Delaney, Delaney Matrix Inc & Jeffrey Scott Agency

FOREWORD

Is Jesus a conservative and a supporter of the right wing of American politics? It might be an odd question to ask. A better question might be to wonder if Jesus supports the conservative political stances so prevalent in the American Evangelical Church today.

I find it fascinating to imagine if Jesus were to set foot on American soil, what would he say to our churches and religious leaders? In the biblical story of Jesus' first century visit to earth Jesus seemed more apt to challenge long-held, engrained, religious beliefs rather than embrace them. Would Jesus join in with the Evangelical Church's continuation of its decades-long partnership with conservative politics and ideology or would he have a "give to Caesar what is Caesar's" type admonishment?

In this book, Pastor Saul Thompson is a leader of a politically conservative Evangelical church in a politically conservative Evangelical town. When a mysterious character shows up and begins to critique the religious leaders of the town, Saul is forced to deal with these questions. Will he join in a response similar to that of the Biblical first century religious leaders who decided to dispose of the miracle-worker who made them look bad? Or will he consider a more heavenly way to look at politics?

The Evangelical Church has been a major factor in my life since birth, and, for the most part, has had a positive impact on my life. Today, however, I see a Church ("Big C" for the church, collectively, not particular individual churches) that needs to wrestle with some tough questions concerning political power, beliefs in conspiracy theories and the hope put into institutions, like the Supreme Court, to set the world right again. In a large portion of the Evangelical Church, there's a prevalent mindset that Christian faith compels a particular political bent from its believers. Is this mindset in agreement with Biblical guidance? Let's just go right at the "elephant in the room" question - Is God a Republican and ideological conservative? What do you think?

The desire is that this book serve as a conversation starter. It is not a definitive answer. For some, parts of this discussion are understandably difficult in the challenge of some long-held, sacred beliefs. But the questions are too important to allow this challenge to stop any reader from considering them. Don't take the journey of this book alone. You can be part of an ongoing conversation about the ideas and hard questions put forth at www.Pastor-Paul.com. Please don't allow a hard spot that challenges you to cause you to put the book down. Let's think together.

The characters in this book are as real to the author as any everyday acquaintance. While the stories in the book are very much related to actual events and people, no character is fashioned after any one person. Each character, however, is an amalgamation of real people. These aren't just characters in a book, but are people who live around us in culture today. Saul Thompson is a good man with a heart's desire to make a difference in the world. He'll face a challenge to his tactics for pursuing that purpose. Many of us need the same challenge to truly "take every thought captive" in order to understand if we have "eyes to see and ears to hear" the truth in our day. Jesus' accused the religious leaders of the Bible of taking away people's ability to think and to receive grace. Does the American Church do the same today? Or has some of our pedagogy taken away the benefit of legitimate discussion of ideas? Let's be set free from any presuppositions and think anew about the role of the Christian faith in culture today. I believe God will not be mad at us for challenging ourselves. For those who are not Christians, I hope this story gives you some insight into the heart of followers of Christ and how they're interacting with our culture today. For all of us, there might be a better way if we understand one another.

I love the journey we are about to go on together in this story. I hope you love it as well.

—Paul Swearengin, Author

TABLE OF CONTENTS

FOREWORD 5
PROLOGUE 9
Chapter 1: THE MARRIAGE RALLY 11
Chapter 2: BEKERING POLITICS 16
Chapter 3: SEEING JOSEPH 20
Chapter 4: AN UNEXPECTED GUEST 23
Chapter 5: POLITICALLY INCORRECT CONVERSATION 28
Chapter 6: A LIFE-CHANGING COLLISION 32
Chapter 7: ISAAC'S QUEST 41
Chapter 8: TELLER OF A DIFFERENT STORY 45
Chapter 9: SAUL AND HIS SERMON 55
Chapter 10: MIGRANTS, MUSLIMS AND MIRACLES 60
Chapter 11: SAUL CAUGHT SPYING 65
Chapter 12: A PASTOR AND THE MAYOR 73
Chapter 13: MEMORIES PACKED AWAY 79
Chapter 14: A RADIO SHOW AND A STRAW MAN 82
Chapter 15: THE RADIO HOST 91
Chapter 16: FISHING FOR ANSWERS 95
Chapter 17: A GALA EVENT 100
Chapter 18: BEKERING, WE HAVE A PROBLEM 105
Chapter 19: BEKERING'S PAST AND FUTURE 109
Chapter 20: THE OTHER SIDE OF THE RELIGIOUS WAR 114
Chapter 21: THE STRESS OF BEING MAYOR 124
Chapter 22: THE PASTORS' MEETING.. 132
Chapter 23: DON'T CALL HIM A PASTOR 135
Chapter 24: A FATHER-SON CLASH 141
Chapter 25: ANGST AROUND THE FUNERAL 149
Chapter 26: A SURPRISE FUNERAL GUEST 154
Chapter 27: HEALING A MOTHER'S HEART 162
Chapter 28: LOSING A SON AND LOSING CONTROL 167
Chapter 29: CHANGES IN BEKERING 172
Chapter 30: A CHANGE AT THE DAY OF PRAYER 176
Chapter 31: JOSEPH'S COMEUPPANCE 180
Chapter 32: LOVE THINE ENEMIES... 187
Chapter 33: A FRUSTRATED DRIVE 191
Chapter 34: SAUL'S SEARCH FOR ANSWERS 194
Chapter 35: A HARSH GOD 197
Chapter 36: A NEW SERMON 204
Chapter 37: THE BOARD MEETING 212

Chapter 38: NO LONGER A PASTOR 216
Chapter 39: TWO REPORTERS AND AN IDEA 220
Chapter 40: THE VOTE 223
Chapter 41: A DRIVE TO THE PAST 230
Chapter 42: TIME TO CHANGE THE WORLD 234
EPILOGUE 239
ACKNOWLEDGEMENTS 241
About The Author–Paul Swearengin 243

PROLOGUE

The wind of Eastern Oregon came through the car's window, gently brushing the driver's long, curly hair as a yawn tried to escape his bearded mouth. It had been a long drive and he was relieved to finally be approaching his destination.

"Bekering – 20 MILES" announced the white road sign.

The car's driver was Joseph, and although he still didn't know why he was drawn to Bekering, he felt a familiar sense of anticipation as his light-blue Mercury Cougar coasted past the sign. Purpose; that was the feeling he sensed with each heart thump.

As Joseph's yawn was about to fully manifest, the car filled with exhaust as a rusty, red pickup roared past.

"Whoa! What the… Heaven!" Joseph shouted as his Nike clad right foot mashed the well-used brake pedal. The pickup had abruptly veered back into Joseph's lane to avoid the two-lane highway's oncoming traffic. The two vehicles barreled forward in the westbound lane of Highway 95, an Eastern Oregon roadway seemingly built for such daredevil driving.

Joseph rolled up his window and used the collar of his blue plaid shirt to wipe stinging tears from the tops of his cheeks. As the fumes, and thus his eyes, cleared, Joseph's attention was drawn to the weather-beaten pickup tailgate.

"AMERICA, LOVE IT OR LEAVE IT," declared a bumper sticker.

"DO YOU UNDERSTAND THE MEANING OF THE WORLD 'ILLEGAL' IN 'ILLEGAL IMMIGRANT?'" declared another of Mr. Pickup's tattered stickers.

"Oh, for heaven's sake," Joseph sighed as he rubbed the dark brown hairs of his short beard. His striking brown eyes grew wide as they continued their tailgate tour.

"THEY CAN PRY MY GUN FROM MY COLD DEAD HAND!" These words were hovered over a picture of a white-robed man with a long white beard and sporting a holster with a gun on each hip. "GOD IS PRO SECOND AMENDMENT" the sticker continued in bold, red letters. Joseph moaned.

"I wonder where he finds that in the New Testament."

The grimace on Joseph's sun-tanned face wasn't just a result of reading the bumper sticker, but even more bothersome was the silver fish—the symbol of Christianity—affixed to the pickup's bumper. Joseph rightly assumed the pickup driver, like so many Christians Joseph had recently encountered, believed the Christian faith represented by that fish compelled him to hold the other beliefs emblazoned on his tailgate.

"Spirit of Heaven, we have a lot of work to do," Joseph said aloud. "Is this what brought me here?" Joseph became lost in his thoughts and no longer noticed the tailgate or the passing countryside.

"Christian people don't seem to know any other way to think anymore," Joseph spoke to the empty passenger seat beside him. He found he couldn't be angry at the pickup driver. Mixing politics with Christianity was now standard procedure for the Christian people Joseph encountered in his travels. "I hope Bekering can hear another way."

As the pickup accelerated, leaving Joseph behind, the sign Joseph had been looking for came into view: "Bekering, Oregon – Population 122,017" said the white lettering on the green background. He'd made it.

Next Joseph saw a larger, wooden standard holding several advertisements for Bekering churches including one at the top, much larger than all the others, that read, "WE WELCOME YOU TO OUR CITY WITH OPEN ARMS - THE PEOPLE OF THE BEKERING CHRISTIAN CENTER." The be under grin faded a bit.

"I wonder if this greeting will prove true once they've met me."

CHAPTER 1:
THE MARRIAGE RALLY

Pastor Saul Thompson sprung his long, thin legs up the steps of a temporary outdoor stage erected at the North Bekering Shopping Center. Saul's desire to keep his hair "TV Ready" was made difficult by the ongoing gusts of breeze on this bright Bekering morning. That full head of hair had begun to gather a few flecks of grey but Saul still displayed a youthful appearance even after crossing the half century threshold three years prior.

Once on the stage Saul leaned on his elbows on a support railing, letting his trim body a rare moment of relaxation. This offered him an open view across the massive shopping complex. The shopping center was an asphalt labyrinth of large parking lots situated in front of big box, national chain retail stores that Saul hoped would provide visibility to draw a large crowd to his event. Saul was the Senior Pastor of the Bekering Christian Center, otherwise known as BCC, having served in that role for the past twenty-two years. BCC was the city's largest church, and today's pastoral duties had Saul rallying people against Oregon's new law that legalized gay marriage and strengthened protection for the rights of Oregon's burgeoning LGBTQ+ community.

"It's a big day, Saul," he said to himself, reaching up to adjust his tie and patting his hair once again. The stage sat on an erector set frame which boosted Saul several feet above the blackened parking lot. Large black, square pieces formed the stage's deck beneath Saul's feet. The stage was tucked in the corner of the northernmost parking lot and came as close to a community gathering place as could be had at this location. The shopping center was clearly built for commerce, not civic engagement as indicated by the cars circling the nearby roundabout. Saul winced with discomfort of blatant capitalism as the event's backdrop just as much as the large plastic banner that spanned the back of the stage.

"The Defense of Marriage Rally," the banner read in bold, black lettering on a yellow background, "organized by the Evangelical Republicans of Eastern Oregon." Saul had served as spokesperson for this group for much of the past two decades and was regularly its Master of Ceremonies. He was preparing to cinch up his Republican-red power tie—part of his uniform for such events—when a voice in the distance interrupted his train of thought.

"We want love, not hate!"

Saul peered across the lot toward the voice and felt a familiar burning sensation in his reddening ears. He spied the multi-colored rainbow flag of The Love Coalition, a group seemingly always protesting Saul's events.

"You're heartless, Pastor Saul," shouted a glaring protester standing with a group near the flag. Saul attempted to center himself as his breath suddenly labored.

"You're fifty-three years old and a big boy, Saul," he self-scolded. "You can take a little critique." Saul's strong stance on cultural issues consistently drew the ire of this group, but Saul wasn't about to temper his belief. In fact, he'd spoken of this exact issue last Sunday at BCC in his weekly sermon.

"People try to say homosexuality is natural," Saul had preached from his perch behind the top-of-the-line acrylic pulpit given to him as a fiftieth-birthday gift. The pulpit had control buttons allowing Saul to advance his PowerPoint presentation displayed on two of the three huge video screens at the front of the BCC sanctuary. Saul himself was always visible on the middle screen, to be easily seen by the nearly three thousand attendees divided amongst three services held each Sunday.

"Listen to me, now," he continued. "In Romans 1, the Bible says the very act of homosexuality is not only a sin, but abnormal to humanity."

Saul had paused dramatically as he recited the passage oft-misused to condemn queer people. He looked around the room as if to connect to ever eye. "Someday, if God doesn't punish America for this sin, he'll have to apologize to Sodom and Gomorrah."

"You suck, Pastor Saul!" Another taunt from across the lot brought Saul back to the present. "I thought pastors were supposed to care about people." The protester flashed a middle-fingered gesture in Saul's direction. Saul gave a short tug on his yet unbuttoned collar.

"Don't let them get to you, Saul," said Patty, Saul's wife, who had just topped the stairs onto the stage. Her medium length blonde hair waved back and forth and her modest blue dressed swished around her legs as Patty's short heels clacked across the checkerboard platform, closing the gap between the two. She leaned in and gave her husband an encouraging kiss on the cheek.

"Oh, I'm not worried about me, Pattz," he said. "It's you and Isaac I worry about."

"Oh, baloney," she smiled, pointing at Saul's chest. "Those words hurt your heart, Saul. I know it." Saul turned back to look out at the group in order to avoid his wife's knowing stare. This allowed him to noticed the arrival of the group's leader, Elsa Kratt.

"I wish they knew the good I'm trying to do for us all," he said. He turned back to Patty as the sound of her hand rummaging through her purse caught his attention.

"It's hard to make people think you're fighting for them when they believe you hate them," she responded, pulling a plastic case of breath mints from the bottom of her bag. She popped one in her mouth and offered the round plastic case to Saul. He stared incredulously at Patty for a moment before breaking into a smile.

"My wife is never one to mince words, is she?" He took a breath mint, figuring she might be offering it for good reason. "You know I don't hate them."

"I may know that," she said before pointing at the group, "but they clearly don't. Honestly, Saul, I don't blame them. Our side can be downright mean and hypocritical."

Saul looked back to the protesting group. He could see Elsa was having an animated discussion with the young man who'd made the obscene gesture towards him. Elsa was a large woman, tall with short styled hair. She cut an imposing figure in her t-shirt and ripped jeans and Saul was sure the young man was intimidated. Saul had endured his own scary interactions with Elsa, including a parking lot debate some years ago.

"America flourished under the Christian fundamental ideology of its Founding Fathers," Saul had explained, looking up at Elsa that night. "It will never be the great country it once was without a return to a civic reliance on Biblical beliefs."

"Pastor Saul, the founding fathers might have been spiritual, but they clearly created a government designed to avoid promoting any one religion, including Christianity." Elsa was some twenty years younger than Saul but, unlike many locals, she was never slowed by Saul's slick, well-rehearsed arguments.

"I'm certain the constitution and our morality as a country believes in defending young kids," Elsa had responded to Saul's statements. "We need to help children who're being harassed and punished simply for being different. Surely your Jesus believes this!"

Saul frowned at the memory. Elsa, an openly queer woman, made a strong, intelligent case for her beliefs. She was firm in her tone, but Saul found her polite. He'd learned she was Harvard educated and rather interesting to talk to. However, like many Christians in Bekering and across the country, Saul felt beholden to the idea that God's top agenda items were passing laws against abortion and gay marriage. Saul, therefore, believed himself required to stand against the "gay agenda" as an act of obedience to his creator.

Watching Elsa across the lot, Saul again tugged nervously on his collar. Despite the fact that, in Bekering, the power and majority rested on Saul's side of these debates, Saul felt an internal wrestling match. No matter how impressive this Elsa might be, he was sure she was deceived from God's truth and Saul was the one who would stand on a stage with hundreds joining his crusade while Elsa would remain in the distance with only a handful, yellow police tape holding them at bay.

"Thou shalt not cross," Saul chuckled noting the tape before looking down at his well-shined, brown Oxford shoes. Saul licked his thumb and leaned down to work on a scuff on the toe of one shoe. He remembered Hal Beatty, the owner of the North Bekering Shopping Center, had advised Saul as to how they would keep the Love Coalition at bay, despite the permit they had secured to protest Saul's event.

"Earl will take care of it," said Hal with a smirk. He was speaking of Earl Gates, the Chief of the Bekering Police Department who, like Hal, was a member of Saul's BCC community. Earl would use that yellow tape to keep protesters far from the event stage.

"We call it the 'Thou Shalt Not Cross' tape," Chief Gates had joked.

Saul gave a satisfied nod, assured his shoes now met his expectations as he straightened himself again.

"I thought you weren't coming today, Pattz," he said, returning his eyes to Patty.

"I was out running errands and thought I'd stop by," she answered, taking Saul's right hand in her own. "I'm not going to stay, though." Saul's eyes glanced downward for only a moment but enough that his wife noticed his disappointment.

"I respect you and what you do with all of my heart, but you know I can't stand these events, Babe. Our people are too crazy." Her lips gently met his in a soft peck and Saul watched as his wife turned to leave the stage. Near the steps, she stopped and turned, cupping her hand to her mouth to give Saul a loud "stage whisper."

"And I can't stand Hal Beatty."

Patty smiled a knowing grin that momentarily confused Saul.

"How are you, Hal," Patty said a bit too loudly, pasting on a fake, tight-lipped smile as Hal gave way for her to descend. Saul grinned.

His wife had never developed his skill for stuffing true feelings in the name of propriety, a trait that made her more endearing and impressive to him. Saul watched her naturally well-shaped figure disappear down the steps. He marveled at beautiful she was, Even after all these years.

CHAPTER 2:
BEKERING POLITICS

"Nice day to give 'em hell, wouldn't you say, Pastor?" Saul's eyes shifted from Patty to Hal. He watched the sixty-ish land developer fight the losing battle to keep his light brown, comb-over hairdo together in the face of the same breeze that continued to frustrate Saul. Matthew McGinnis, the CEO of the Eastern Oregon Republican party, followed close behind.

Saul paused for a moment. Despite his long time connection with Hal, Saul was aware of the attributes in his friend that caused Patty's hesitation to be around him. Saul gathered his good graces, however, knowing he had better put his best face in front of these two influential men.

"Thanks for hosting us, Hal," Saul said as Hal as the two looked across the treeless landscape.

"Wouldn't have it anywhere else." Hal cackled as he grabbed Saul's hand in a forced yet handshake. Saul reached to give Matthew a shake as well, as Hal scanned his surroundings from the high stage like a king surveying his kingdom.

"Hard to believe this was fig orchards just two decades ago," Hal spoke with great pride. "To think the lefty-libs and the tree-huggers wanted to stop us from building this place." Saul watched as half of Hal's upper lip curled into a sneer.

"If they had their way, Bekering would still be a one-horse, hick town," Matthew joined in. He continued with a grand sweep of his hand.

"I love that we hold these events here now, isn't capitalism beautiful, boys?" Saul watched Matthew's politician-appropriate statement and nodded a feeble agreement. Inside he fought to hide a familiar discomfort that churned in his stomach.

Saul struggled with the "our side versus their side" view of the world held by men like Hal and Matthew. For these guys the other side was always bad, stupid, or evil for being in disagreement with "our side." Saul felt the contrast between such men and himself was Saul's belief in "godly righteousness" with standards based on biblical beliefs, particularly towards important issues like abortion, sexuality, and drug use. In Saul's assessment, this gave him a higher moral standing than someone after political victory or simple profit.

Sure, maybe people like Saul did conflate strong beliefs on issues such as taxes or patriotism with "biblical" principles despite no actual support for those stands in the New Testament, but those standards were, after all, part of the religious-conservative package and Saul was comfortable to walk in those values and still allow himself to feel less vitriolic than these two.

"Must be quiet downtown today," Hal said with a grin to Matthew before each laughed out loud. Before the completion of Hal's shopping complex, events such as today's rally had been held downtown.

"Always thought that place was a dump anyway," Hal continued. "Bunch of old buildings and homeless people." Saul stared into the distance and said nothing. Matthew, however, gleefully jumped in.

"Being up on this end of town makes me happy to live in Bekering," he chortled. Matthew sported a thick, Kennedy-like, full head of hair that didn't seem phased at all by today's breeze. Matthew had year-round tanned good looks and a charismatic personality, making him the poster-perfect political candidate. He'd lost an election for the Mayor's office years earlier, however, and had decided to take out his anger on his opponents through working behind the scenes, something he'd done with great success and with great financial reward. Very few people were elected to office in Bekering without Matthew's direct approval and support and with him getting to dip a hand into the fund raising till as compensation for his "consulting" expertise.

"Sure beats living with those socialists in Portland and Eugene, right Saul?"

Saul turned to see Matthew speaking through gritted teeth as if it was painful for him to even to speak the names of their state's major metropolitan areas. Saul's nervous intestines let out a distinct growl so loud, Saul feared the other two men must have heard it.

"Um, sure, Matthew," Saul responded quickly in hopes of avoiding any embarrassment. "I certainly love that our people care about important moral issues." Saul nodded towards the crowd now beginning to filter into the space in front of the stage.

"Today's a great opportunity to keep our people informed on the ungodly agenda of our state."

"Gotta keep the troops riled up, huh?" Hal snorted, jostling Saul with an elbow to the ribs.

"Yep, that's how we got our new mayor elected," Matthew chimed in, pointing towards Mayor Andy Strapp, who was shaking hands at the bottom of the stage steps. "Keep 'em scared and angry and they'll vote however you tell 'em to vote."

Saul flinched at the interpretation Hal and Matthew had given his comments, but, as usual, Saul felt any courage to disagree fade in the breeze.

Saul knew that Matthew, for the most part, was speaking truth. The fear of "the liberal agenda" was a powerful tool for galvanizing Bekering's conservative Christian community. Saul wasn't above tapping this fear for his own purposes from time to time.

Matthew had also voiced another truth: Bekering's separation from the western, more urban side of the state was more than geographical; it was philosophical, as well.

Bekering was the largest town on the sparsely populated eastern edge of Oregon. The city stood out as a conservative "red state" area in one of the nation's bluest of blue states. Over seventy percent of Bekering County residents had voted for the conservative candidate in the last presidential election while the state had gone overwhelmingly for the more liberal one.

"Why don't we go over our agenda, Matthew," urged Saul.

"You lead out and we'll follow, Pastor," Matthew replied dismissively without even bothering to look at Saul. "I'll get the mayor to stand up here and look good for everyone."

"Let's chat with the Mayor now, Matthew," Hal jumped in. "You know… on the new project."

Without a goodbye, Hal and Matthew quickly exited the stage.

Saul stared at the backs of the two men disappearing as the descended the stage steps then slowly allowed himself a grin and a head shake at the ungracious departure.

"They don't know any other way to live," he sighed to himself as he finally completed the task of buttoning his collar and sliding his tie into place.

Though discomforted with the angry, extreme political rhetoric of men like Hal and Matthew, Saul was strong in his religious principles. The Moral Majority of the 80's had its Pat Robertsons and Jerry Falwells. In Bekering, Saul was the voice of the ultra-conservative Evangelical Church. There was a culture war going on and Pastor Saul was the five-star general for God's conservative Christian army.

"Time to turn it on, Saul," he said to himself. The Channel 5 News truck had arrived and Michael Brookes, the political reporter from the Bekering Observer newspaper, was in the media pool on the risers behind the crowd. Saul took a deep breath and checked his watch. As he noted the start time for the event was just a few minutes away, Saul was completely unaware that his life would soon be turned upside down.

CHAPTER 3:
SEEING JOSEPH

The microphone was Saul's personal favorite, a silver Heil PR40 that was Saul's personal mic he used in various media work. It was stationed on a stand in the center of the stage near the front, perfectly positioned for Saul to gain the audience' attention. As Saul approached the mic, his eyes focused just over the top of it as he spotted a stir being created in the crowd. A young man was standing in front of an elderly woman, holding her two hands in his own. Saul thought the young man appeared to be praying with her and for reasons unbeknownst to Saul a crowd was gathering around the two.

"Who's this guy?" Saul thought, studying the young man who wore a bright yellow T-shirt with the imprint "God is NOT Mad at You." Saul's brow furrowed at the unusual statement. He moved to the stairwell and waved for his friend Abel Hackenworth, a rotund pastor from the Stanton Avenue Christian Church, who was standing in the front row near the stage.

"How are you, Pastor?" Greeted Pastor Hackenworth with his loud, baritone voice. Saul couldn't help but notice his fellow pastor's multicolored tie covering the straining buttons through which Hackenworth seemed about to burst on his white, stiff-collared shirt. Despite his somewhat unkempt appearance, Hackenworth commanded the respect of parishioner and fellow pastors alike. He displayed this authority with a large diamond ring on his right hand ring finger, diamond encrusted cuff links on each wrist and a large watch so gaudy it seemed to nearly blind Saul with its glint from the sun.

"Fine, just fine, Pastor," Saul answered. "I was wondering if you know that man." Saul pointed at the dark-haired, bearded man, just barely visible inside the group crowding around him. Hackenworth was in his seventies, one of the oldest pastors at one of the oldest churches in town.

"Ah, I've heard about him from a few of my people," the burly man answered as he scratched the sparse, curly black hair on the back of his head. "He does some sort of teaching around town."

"Who's he think he is, praying with people out here?" Saul guessed the dark complexioned young man to be in his early thirties with his youthful face encased by that dark curly hair on his head and beard.

"I'm told his name is Joseph," said Pastor Hackenworth.

"I'm going to have to find out his story," said Saul, nursing his hair through another gust of wind. Saul grew disquieted as he watched this "Joseph" being hugged by several nearby admirers.

"We must protect the sheep," Pastor Hackenworth bellowed, "I've seen these snake oil salesmen come through town before and bring all kinds of crazy, liberal ideas."

"Yeah," Saul mumbled in response, never taking his eyes from Joseph. "My son, Isaac, has connected with some pretty crazy ideas these days."

Saul tugged up his monogrammed sleeve to check his watch. The event was drawing near, and Saul wheeled about to climb the stage steps once again. Over his shoulder he took one last peek at Joseph and froze as the two locked eyes. Saul was surprised to see Joseph give a subtle nod and move away from the circle of people with whom he'd been chatting and praying. Joseph was moving towards him and Saul turned back towards the crowd in preparation to meet this stranger. Saul tried to play a conversation in his head but quickly dismissed the idea.

"What's your problem, Saul," he self-scolded, "no time to argue right now."

Saul's judgment, however, had been off. The young man was not walking towards Saul, but towards the open patch of parking lot pavement between the stage and The Love Coalition.

"What's he doing?" Wondered Saul, literally shaking himself as he realized their meeting was off. Saul's mouth fell open as he watched the man do something Saul found unthinkable. The mystery man walked to the yellow police tape and, upon reaching it, pulled it up to duck under and join the protesters. Suddenly, as if splashed with cold water, Saul's mind became clear and at ease.

"Why was I worried about this guy?" Saul silently cajoled himself. He laughed that moments ago he'd felt a strange surge of competitive jealousy seeing Joseph with his followers. But now Saul was certain those people wouldn't support Joseph. None would want to associate with a man who consorted with the likes of Elsa Kratt and her group.

"Saul, you need more sleep," he whispered with a grin. "You worry too much." He gave a slight nod to Pastor Hackenworth and ascended the steps. Once atop the stage, Saul strolled to the microphone, perfectly positioned in front of the news cameras.

"Thanks y'all for coming out on this beautiful day in Bekering," Saul chirped with his best TV news-clip grin. Saul was on his game for the program yet couldn't resist taking peeks towards the mysterious Joseph beyond the yellow tape. What was it about this outsider that caused Saul's inner peace to fade? Saul sensed there was something different about this stranger and he knew this was not be there last encounter. Bekering was Saul's town and some itinerant wasn't going to come in and rock the status quo. Saul would make sure of that.

CHAPTER 4:
AN UNEXPECTED GUEST

"Ted, I need to restructure our loan so we can get financing for the new children's wing."

Saul pleaded his case to his banker, Ted Freeman, as they walked from Saul's event to The North End Grill, located on the west side of the shopping center facing Beatty Avenue. Their conversation would frequently be interrupted by the need to avoid cars as they traversed the sidewalk-less development.

"Raising up godly children is the Lord's most important work. You know that, Ted."

"Yes, of course, Pastor Saul." Ted was a Vice President at Bekering Commercial Bank, the lending institution for BCC's building loan. "I'm ready to hear all about your proposal." Ted's shoulders slumped in resignation.

"That's why I love you, Ted," Saul lightly joked. Saul didn't see his pleading as manipulation, he knew Ted, a long-time member at BCC, loved helping the church. Saul merely needed to remind Ted of what would benefit their church community.

Ted was a bald man by choice, although likely choosing so after losing much of his hair naturally. In his late sixties, Ted wore hip, wire-framed glasses and finely tailored suits. Saul assumed Ted's look was an attempt to appear contemporary with his younger colleagues.

"Hello, Becky," Ted spoke up, addressing a professionally dressed woman approaching them from the parking lot adjacent to the North End Grill. "Pastor, this is Becky Townsend, our new Executive Vice President for business loans at the bank." Ted cleared his throat and Saul sensed Ted's nervousness in Becky's presence.

"Must be Ted's new boss," Saul thought. Saul had been around business people enough to know Becky's firm handshake, her short, professionally styled dirty blond hair, and her dark grey pantsuit were symbols of a woman well-practiced at portraying strength during business interactions with men.

"Nice to meet you, Pastor Saul," said Becky, making direct eye contact with Saul. "Ted tells me wonderful things about you."

"Well, I hope I can live up to billing," Saul chuckled. The attempt at humor sank like a balloon losing its helium as Becky stared, unmoved by Saul's campy response. "Nice to meet you, uh—Mrs. Townsend?"

"It's Miz," Becky quickly responded, "but please feel free to call me Becky."

Saul turned to glance at Ted but got nothing as Ted avoided eye contact. Saul knew his tactics with Ted would not fly with this amiable but calculating woman. Saul considered himself shrewd but tended to struggle in the presence of strong, attractive women. Saul worried his plan for church expansion might be foiled, unless he received help in his quest. And help was here, standing at the restaurant door.

"Come on in everyone," shouted Hal, waving the group towards the entrance. "I've had Mr. Abraham set us up at the front table."

"This is Becky Townsend, Ted's colleague at the bank," Saul gestured towards the woman with one hand and shook Hal's hand with the other.

"Uh… OK. I'll ask Abraham to set another place setting." Hal tried to keep a pleasant demeanor as Becky walked past him through the door. Hal gave an ugly look to Ted, displeased by the presence of this unannounced guest.

"Thanks Hal for getting us a table," Ted meekly spoke, trying to break the tension.

At the table, Saul took the opportunity to survey the room. He was well known for the local, political talk radio show he hosted and for pastoring a mega-church. Saul was never alone in a public setting.

"Hello," Saul said, waving to his friend Evan Brown, president of the Bekering City Council. Saul was about to turn his attention back to his table when he spotted Elsa, who must also have chosen this place for a post-rally lunch with associates. The Love Coalition leader gave Saul a wave as their eyes connected, but Saul shifted his gaze towards the front door, hoping neither

Hal nor Ted witnessed the interaction. Saul respected Elsa, but felt he must maintain an appropriate distance.

"I can't believe she waved at you," said Hal, indicating he had caught Elsa's acknowledgment. "Some nerve that... person." Saul placed his napkin in his lap and grabbed the menu, hoping this would end the conversation. It didn't

"I guess it's like they say," Hal continued, increasing his volume to be heard by the room, including Elsa, "'hate the sin but love the sinner.'" Saul noticed Becky's physical response to Hal's statement as she looked at Elsa and back at Hal. Her mouth was agape, like a game show host shocked by a contestant's answer. Saul was about to change the subject when someone beat him to it.

"Hello, Pastor Saul," said an exuberant voice over Saul's right shoulder. Saul turned to see a busboy cleaning the adjacent table.

"Hello," said Saul, not immediately recognizing the young man wearing the brown North End Grill apron over a yellow T-shirt and sporting a blue bandanna on his head.

"My name's Joseph," said the busboy, wiping his hand on a towel pulled from his apron pocket before offering a handshake. Saul stood and took the hand, looking closely at the friendly face in front of him. It was Joseph, the mysterious man from today's rally. The one praying with Saul's people.

"Oh, yes. Hello. I'm Saul."

"Of course, I know you, Pastor Saul," Joseph bellowed with a genuine smile, the same one Saul had noticed from a distance at the rally. "You're absolutely a man 'within whom there is no guile.'" Saul recognized the reference—a Bible story where a man spoke in jest about Jesus, then received the teasing compliment from Jesus of being a 'guile-less,' straightforward person.

"What makes you say that?" Saul responded a bit unnerved. He wasn't sure why this busboy took him off balance. There was some innocent goodness about him that made Saul feel his own internal dark spots would be exposed by the light in Joseph's brown eyes.

"Isn't it self-evident?" Joseph responded, looking around the table. Saul's cheek twitched in his effort to hide how destabilized he was by Joseph's unusual word play.

"Heaven likes you a lot," Joseph exclaimed as he threw his towel over his shoulder and pulled his bandanna from his head, freeing his black, curly locks. Saul's growing discomfort was a harsh contrast to Joseph's inviting manner. "But you still think you need to earn divine approval."

Saul flinched slightly at the off-putting statement, but felt unable to be offended as the tone and demeanor of this stranger made that difficult.

"You new in town?" Saul spit out, trying to regain control of the moment. Or at least control of himself.

"Not exactly, but I did come in just a few weeks ago."

"Really? What brought you?"

"Oh, felt drawn here, I guess you could say." Joseph paused, smiling comfortably at the somewhat puzzled group. Joseph tucked a curl behind his ear and pointed to the table where he had been cleaning. "Mr. Abraham was kind enough to give me this job cleaning, allowing the flexible schedule I need and giving me use of the back room for my real work."

"And what's your real work?" Saul asked with a barely hidden smirk, trying to act cool in front of his parishioners.

"I'm a storyteller," Joseph responded, straightening his posture as if describing the most important occupation available. "I'm a storyteller and a lover of people." Peering from the corner of his eye, Saul could see Hal's eyebrow shoot towards his hairline. Saul would also have found the statement odd were he not so struck by Joseph's complete sincerity.

"Interesting job," Saul said, looking into Joseph's eyes as if trying to see some indicator of some nefarious motive of this new acquaintance. But no such reveal was forthcoming.

"It certainly is, Pastor; it certainly is." Joseph shook his head and then replaced his bandana and turned apparently to resume his work.

"Uh, as you're new in town, let me invite you to visit us at the Bekering Christian Center on Sunday." Saul gave Joseph his business card made from heavy, expensive card stock with contact information and service times for the church, as well as the Bible verse John 3:7: "Ye must be born again..."

"I love that verse," said Joseph, putting the card into the pocket of his heavily distressed jeans, "and I might take you up on your invitation, Pastor Saul."

The table was silent, save for the punctuated clattering of dishes as a certain young man cleared and cleaned the table next to them. Saul had more questions for Joseph—about praying for the people, about his choice to hang with the protesters rather than the good churchgoers at the rally — but Saul hesitated. He didn't want to appear overly interested in this Joseph.

"Can I get your contact information?" Saul ventured to ask, leaning over. "So I can follow up on my invitation, Mr...?"

"Call me Joseph. And don't worry," Joseph called as he headed for the swinging kitchen doors, "you'll see me around."

CHAPTER 5:
POLITICALLY INCORRECT CONVERSATION

"The rate you have is truly the best we can do, Pastor," said Becky, firmly while pointing at the numbers on her small notepad. "In fact, the church was inappropriately given better terms than it should have received in the first place. This is not a profitable loan for the bank." Saul noticed Ted squirming a bit in his adjacent seat like a first grader caught looking at his neighbor's paper on a test.

"We can extend the term," said Ted, leaning forward to put Becky beyond his peripheral vision, "which would allow for better cash flow by reducing the church's monthly payments."

"But such a concession would require additional collateral, Pastor," Becky interrupted. "The church parsonage, perhaps." Saul held his breath, trying not to react, but Hal couldn't contain himself.

"You listen here Missus, er Mizz Townsend." Hal's cheeks reddened. "That's Pastor Saul's home you're talking about. We're not putting it up as collateral. We've never been treated this way before!"

"Now, Hal, let's not make this meeting acrimonious," Ted responded.

"Aw, this is bullshit, Ted."

Saul felt his breath tightening from the tension at the table. He leaned forward on his elbows, his pointer fingers forming a triangle on his lips as he tried to think of alternate solutions.

"Miss Towns—er, Becky. Surely there's a way for us to at least get the extension of our term without putting any more of the church's holdings at risk."

Becky eyed the two men and dabbed at the corner of her lip with a cloth napkin before placing it neatly in her lap. "There is one way." From the tone of her voice, Saul sensed this was a moment she'd come prepared for.

"Hal, you have land north of your shopping center we hear you want to have annexed for development." Saul's head snapped to his left in time to see Hal's persona change. Becky continued like a seasoned foreign spy leveraging a mark's deep, dark secret. "If we can get your assurance, in writing, to have first bid on that project's financing, I can ask the bank for a little flexibility with the church."

"That's farmland, right Hal?" Saul argued. "You promised the city council you would never develop that land."

Hal's cheeks blanched white as he looked down at the table. Saul knew Hal was a church going man, but equally knew Hal's morals could become flexible in his work.

"This is how the game is played," Hal had explained to Saul several times in the past.

"I'm not sure where you get your information, Ms. Townsend," Hal stammered, "but if I can take some of my commercial business to Bekering Commercial Bank in order to help the church, I'd be glad to have that discussion—discreetly in your office."

Becky leaned back in her chair and crossed her arms with apparent satisfaction. "Of course. I'll contact your office tomorrow to set up a time." Saul sat silently, lacking the courage to pursue the questions he had for Hal following Becky's revelation. Saul knew any further inquisition could risk the help Hal could now offer the church and Saul had learned the importance of pragmatism.

"All of this OK with you, Ted?" said Saul, working to include his friend.

"Yes…" Ted murmured absentmindedly while straightening the shirt cuffs under his jacket. He seemed to catch himself in time to be part of the discussion's conclusion. "Why yes. I think Becky can come up with some creative ideas for this project." Saul loved Ted, but it was clear Ted was not cutthroat like the other two people at the table who were smiling like two Cheshire cats holding on to a big secret from everyone else. The conversation moved from business to other regular luncheon fare.

Saul was surprised when Becky began to address heavier cultural issues, about which she voiced her opinions as vigorously as she had her business stances.

"I have the right to make choices for my own body and my own health," she opined. Saul finished his soup and pushed the bowl aside, ready to respond with his well-versed defense of the "unborn." He always felt a need to win this argument. This was more than a debate; Saul believed it was a battle for the righteous soul of America and that he was displaying his courage to stand for God.

"You absolutely have the right to make decisions for your own body, but in the case of abortion, you're deciding about someone else's body," Saul argued. His heart started pumping at a rapid rate. So much so that Saul could feel the pulse in his ears.

"But do we really know it's a baby? Science says it's simply a mass of cells."

"There you go," Saul thought, his face relaxing into an argument-winning smile. "She stepped right into my trap."

"If it's not a baby, why do we do in utero surgeries?" Saul responded, leaning forward in a posture more aggressive than intended. "Recently a hospital in Philadelphia was able to remove a fetus from the womb, perform surgery to correct a heart defect, and then return it to the womb to be born naturally five days later. Why would we go to all that trouble for a useless, disposable mass of cells?" Out of the corner of his eye, Saul noticed Ted shifting uncomfortably in his seat. Hal, on the other hand, smiled with his chin on his palm, ready for Saul to go for the victory.

"Our courts prosecute for double-homicides if a pregnant woman is murdered," Saul continued. "Isn't that a little crazy for something un-human?"

Becky looked down at the table and straightened her discarded fork beside her butter knife. For the first time in their brief relationship, Saul could see this skilled professional struggling with her carefully practiced demeanor. He pressed his advantage.

"In what other area of life do we stand for one human being to have the right to determine if another human being is valuable enough to live?" Saul sensed Becky was avoiding direct eye contact now and this encouraged him to press his point all the more. Saul rose to his apex, lost in the familiar cadence he used when speaking to his congregation.

"Why do you think abortion providers are against laws requiring women to have ultrasounds before abortions? Because they know if women could see the life they are snuffing out—with little fingers that are sucked and little toes played with—it would truly educate women and greatly reduce the number of abortions. This would cost abortion providers a lot of abortion-mill money!"

Saul signaled the end of his diatribe by lifting his cup to his lips and draining his post-lunch coffee. But, as the cup came back down, so did Saul's sense of triumph. Becky finally looked at him with tearful eyes and mascara edging down onto her cheeks. Saul went numb as several blackened tears slipped from her face and stained the white table cloth upon which they'd shared lunch.

"I'm—I'm sorry, Becky." Saul's voice fell, the air seeping out of his superiority. "Sometimes I get a little too aggressive in my opinions."

The need to win—so strong in him that Saul was always aware of its potential to do harm—was gone. Beneath it, Saul tasted the bitterness of regret.

Becky jumped from her chair, slung her purse strap over her shoulder and hurried past the swinging kitchen doors towards the hallway leading to the bathrooms, her hand covering her face. Saul could see that Becky, in her haste to avoid more public embarrassment, failed to see the man directly in her path. Before Saul could speak, she collided with Joseph.

CHAPTER 6:
A LIFE-CHANGING COLLISION

"God dammit!" Becky shouted as her nose collided with the shoulder of the bus boy leaning against the hallway wall. She was stunned and might have fallen had not Joseph grabbed her.

"It's OK," he said looking at her, eyes gentle, "and God doesn't damn you."

Becky stepped back and used her thumb and pointer finger to try and dry both eyes simultaneously while grabbing at her purse with the other. She struggled to breath as she worked to regain her decorum.

"Be that as it may," she answered, pulling a tissue from her purse to dab at the corner of her eye. "I'm sorry, I let a stupid conversation get to me."

"I heard." Becky's eyes grew wide with horror. "No, no. Don't be embarrassed," Joseph said. "I understand." Joseph took Becky's hand, and she watched his eyes turned glassy.

"You've had one, haven't you?" he asked gently.

"What?"

"An abortion, you've had one," Joseph repeated. Becky leaned back slightly, searching his face for clues as to this stranger's motivation for saying such a thing. All she saw was kindness. Becky felt strangely drawn to him and sensed this wasn't an accusation, but rather a non-judgmental fact.

"Who is this guy?" she thought. Whoever he was, Becky felt something overcome her desire to run from her very public display. Whether it was his reassuring voice or those twinkling, caring eyes, Becky felt she could reveal something no other human knew. She nodded as her eyes fell to the floor with a fresh wave of tears.

"Yes, I have," she said softly, "and if what Pastor Saul said is true, then I'm a murderer." Becky noticed the three men at her table were watching.

She bowed her head into the palm of her hand, a wave of vulnerability overcoming her.

"Oh my God," she said, wiping her eyes again. "Obviously, this has hit a button in me."

"Absolutely. A button you've kept hidden for years," Joseph responded sympathetically. "I'm so sorry you're feeling embarrassed—it's completely understandable—but I promise it's good this's coming out."

Becky looked around the room. "How can this be good?"

"I suspect the hard woman you project isn't exactly who you really are," he answered. Becky looked up, her face stern, ready to protest.

"Wait, don't get me wrong," Joseph interjected before she could speak, "you're brilliant. But it seems you think you have to be tough—and maybe that's just your way—to keep everyone at a distance." Becky tilted her head to the side and crossed her arms over her chest.

"You don't know anything about me," she finally was able to say.

"I know what Heaven has shown me," Joseph responded, his cheeks bunching up in a warm, inviting smile.

Becky knew BS and she knew gamesmanship. She stared at Joseph, searching for any selfish motives in this discussion. His brown eyes were piercing, and she suddenly felt as if Joseph had some mystical ability to stare into her soul. Becky always kept herself guarded and in control, but now she shifted uneasily.

"What? Like… God told you?"

"Some people call it intuition, or something like that. But Heaven is always ready to speak to us if we'll listen, and sometimes I hear or sense things from above."

"Why would… Heaven or God or anyone else up there tell you things about me?"

"So you know that you are known in the universe." Becky couldn't help but laugh.

"I don't think God cares about me. God and I haven't talked in a long time. Maybe you need to ring another voice up there." Joseph placed a hand on each of her arms and looked at her with a seriousness that made her joke die in her throat.

"Rebecca," Joseph said, his tone—and her full name—catching Becky's undivided attention. "The spirit of heaven told me you've not only had one abortion, but you've had two."

Becky felt the earth move under her feet and she reached for the wall to steady herself.

"I've never told anyone about that," she said. Shame rushed to her face, tightening her cheeks as tears began to stream down.

"Hey, there's no God in heaven that condemns you and neither do I," Joseph stated emphatically. "Providence brought us to this restaurant so you'd know you are worthy of love, no matter what secrets you've needed to keep."

Becky considered Joseph's words.

"But isn't it a sin?" She asked softly.

"Is it?" he asked. "Show me in the Bible where it says a desperate young person making the best decision they know how is a sin."

Becky found Joseph too good to be true, yet she couldn't deny he'd just told her things about her life he couldn't have known on his own. Joseph had shared her deepest secret with so much kindness, it had flipped on a light switch deep inside.

"I was scared—both times," she began in unsolicited confession. "The first time I had planned with my high school boyfriend, Bryan. Our families went to the same church." Suddenly, Becky saw Joseph look past her and felt a hand on her shoulder.

"Forgive me for intruding," said Elsa in a low voice. Becky looked up at the taller woman offering a napkin to replace Becky's saturated tissue. "I couldn't help but overhear and I know others can hear, as well. Perhaps it might be better if you all moved someplace a little more private?"

"Thanks, Elsa." Joseph gestured to his right. "Over here is the room where I do my storytelling. We can talk privately there."

Becky considered if she should go into that room. With the momentum of the discussion ended, maybe she had an escape route from the intimate sharing. But there remained a strange desire to know more about what Joseph was saying. Had she wrongly judged herself for this secret she alone had carried?

She decided to follow Joseph and Elsa into the musky room. It looked more like storage space than a place for story telling. Boxes of restaurant items were stacked all around. Joseph grabbed three folding chairs that had been leaning against the wall and they were seated with Joseph straight ahead of Becky and Elsa to her side.

"You were looking for someone to love you, weren't you, Becky?" Joseph asked, nudging Becky forward in her story.

"Yeah. I had a good family, but Bryan made me feel special. My dad..." her voice trailed off.

"He didn't show his love to you as well as you might have hoped," Joseph finished her thought. "So you looked for love in this boy."

Becky nodded again, her breath catching as she attempted maintain composure.

"Oh God, I was so stupid," she moaned. Becky knew she was completely out of character now, feeling emotions and questions she'd kept locked away. "I was sixteen freaking years old. I didn't know what the hell to do." The sobs came quickly and loudly as years of pent up pain flowed from her. Elsa leaned in and held her hand.

"I felt like what I was doing was wrong, but there I was at the clinic. It was surreal." Becky stared ahead deep in thought, searching for an expression of what she felt that day. "I'd been taught all my life I was going to hell if I had sex. But an abortion?" She paused again, edging a deep well of pain. She could barely get out what came next.

"I thought, in my heart, I was damned for what I was doing." She looked at Joseph, trying to judge his approval or disapproval. She was certain he was a religious man, and she expected her story would drive him to judge her, as had every other Christian she'd ever known. Seeing Joseph's unflinching look at her, however, prompted her to continue.

"I guess I decided I'd rather go to hell than tell my dad I'd had sex." Becky heard Elsa sniffle and saw sympathetic tears in the woman's eyes. Elsa wasn't running away either. Becky realized these people, odd as it was, seemed to care about her. Why had she waited to share with anyone?

"What kind of a God would hate a young girl for making such a decision?" Becky's skin prickled, her physical senses opening up as she churned with memories. "You're sitting in this clinic... I wanted my mom there with me. But I'm alone in the clinic waiting room, with a handful of girls who's had so much purity culture shame heaped on them we couldn't even look one another in the eye."

The three sat silent for a moment.

"I remember freaking yacht-rock playing in the waiting room speakers. Like, 'hey, just another fucking day!'" Becky had been holding back her usual language, assuming Joseph wouldn't appreciate her gutter-talk. But the painful memories unleashed her language and emotions like a flood.

"SHIT! I was sixteen, goddammit! How could I have a baby?" She sniffled. "I couldn't go to an R-rated movie without my mom, yet fucking Christianity told me I had to keep this a secret, even from her. So, there I was…"

"You did what you thought was best," Elsa empathized with a squeeze of Becky's hand.

"After it's over, they hand you some pamphlets and send you on your way. I went home and heard my mom in the kitchen so I ran to my room. I couldn't tell her." Becky realized Joseph was just listening, not saying a word. It was exactly what she needed. Her breath slowed a bit.

"My relationship with my mom was never the same," Becky sighed, wiping her nose. "Mom knew something was wrong, but I never told her."

Joseph let out a long exhale.

"A young girl shouldn't have to carry such pain alone, should she?"

"Hey, I sucked it up and went on with life," Becky's words will almost spat from her mouth. "Bryan wondered why I wouldn't let him to touch me anymore…"

Becky's tears had soaked the napkin through. Elsa got up and opened a box of paper towels nearby, handing a stack to Becky.

"The second time was with my asshole college boyfriend, Alex." It was all coming out, now, so Becky saw no reason to stop. "He told me he didn't believe the baby was his. I think it was but… he had reason to believe it might not be."

Becky noticed Elsa glance away likely to avoid any misunderstood reaction to Becky's admitted indiscretions. Joseph, on the other hand, continued to look directly at her, with the same caring face he'd worn the whole time.

"I thought the second abortion would be easier, but I went into a deep, dark place," she said. "Not only because I felt guilty for terminating the pregnancy, but now I felt something must be really wrong with me for feeling this badly about it."

"What do you mean?" asked Elsa. "Why'd you think there was something wrong with you?"

"I was so depressed—like postpartum. I mean, you're told it's like having a skin tag removed. What the hell was my problem, feeling it was something more? I mean that's what we're told by our church, right? By our parents? I've always wondered if I was the only woman who felt this way. Mourning for an abortion?"

"Life got to you, Becky, but now a heart healing is coming." Joseph smiled at her. "Tell us about your little girl."

Becky had observed Joseph's supernatural intuition in action already today, but it still surprised her. She pointed at the ceiling.

"Another message from…?" "Yes, from heaven. Your daughter is a gift to you."

This was still very strange for Becky. She looked at Elsa who shrugged as if to say she wasn't sure what was happening here either. Becky was surprised to find Joseph's insight into her life didn't make her as uncomfortable this time. In fact, it made her want to hear more of what he had to say.

"She's a gift even though she came from another stupid mistake?" Becky said with a shake of her head. "I couldn't believe I ended up pregnant a third time. This time, though, I sure as hell knew I was keeping the baby."

Becky started to continue her thought, then broke down again, burying her face in a paper towel.

"What is it? What's wrong?" asked Elsa, patting Becky's shoulder. Becky struggled to continue before collecting herself.

"When I saw the ultrasound of Esther, my daughter - She's six now…" she hesitated a moment. "When I saw the picture of Esther inside of me, I wondered if the other pregnancies…" The struggle inside Becky showed on her face.

"I've always believed in a woman's right to choose, but seeing that picture, well…?" Becky felt Elsa's hug again as she wiped her face.

"To survive, I had to put the notion away that I'd done something horrible, but Pastor Saul brought it all back today."

"Christians often don't know any better than to be condemning and self-righteous," Joseph responded, "but heaven holds nothing against you, Becky."

"You should feel proud," he continued. "You've made a life for yourself and your daughter, even though you were impacted by your shame and self-judgment more than you knew." Joseph touched her shoulder. Becky felt a powerful connection in that touch.

"Rebecca." The tone of his voice was now like a father, even though Becky was sure she was a bit Joseph's elder. She looked up from the paper towel. "I want you to know you're good. These secrets came to me for a good purpose. Even though you parents were not able to love you well, you are so valuable in the universe. You are connected to eternal love beyond measure."

A strange rush of self-acceptance made its way down Becky's spine. As her body responded to Joseph's words, her mind continued to argue.

"But I've done so many things wrong."

"Heaven knows why you did those things," Joseph assured her. "The Bible says sin is for those who know right things to do but don't do them. Nothing is held against those just finding natural human coping mechanisms to survive. Needing a loving touch, you reached for it in the only way you knew how. Finding yourself in a spot where you felt you couldn't be the mother a baby needed, you made the decision you felt was best. Assuming these things would hurt your mom and dad and maybe cause them to reject you? You kept a hard secret." Becky saw a soft smile form on Joseph's lips.

"There is no condemnation on you for doing what you did," he said. "You're completely good, Becky Townsend. Free from all guilt and all the secrets of your life."

Becky shook her head and looked at the floor. Could this be true? Could she really not have to be ashamed of all she'd done? Becky felt a lightness inside replacing the weight that had been there before. She'd always felt the need to impress people, but Joseph and Elsa seemed to be OK with her — secrets and all. At that thought, Becky couldn't stop herself from reaching out to hug a surprised Joseph.

"I don't know why I believe you, Joseph," she said, "but I do. Thank you, thank you, thank you."

"You're the reason I was brought here," Joseph laughed, returning the hug. "You're worth the journey and time, Becky." Becky felt Joseph disengage and look at his watch.

"Speaking of time, I better get back to my job or Mr. Abraham's not going to be happy."

"I went to church as a kid," said Becky thoughtfully as the three stood from their seats. "I heard about God all the time, but I never heard of anything like this."

"Me either," said Elsa.

"Sometimes in church we forget how amazing love really is." Joseph folded his chair and leaned it against the wall as the three moved from the backroom into the main dining area of the North End Grill.

"Becky, heaven wants you to know each day you were at the abortion clinic, angels were there with you." He smiled at her, "You felt alone and scared, but angels were dispatched to watch over you."

"Angels in an abortion clinic?" Becky exclaimed before the sound of Elsa's cleared throat interrupted her thought. Becky's new friend nodded her head towards the restaurant seating area causing Becky to realized she was close enough to be heard by the men still sitting at her table. She was too intrigued by the conversation, however, to end it.

"Really?" Becky lowered her voice. "I thought no angel would go within twenty miles of that place."

Nothing in Becky's upbringing gave her any understanding of such a thing.

"You know the Bible story of the death on the cross, right?" Joseph said, his excitement seemingly overcoming any worry others could hear. "Well, that story demonstrated that death is not an end, but a transition. Fear of death was defeated right there. So, we don't have to be afraid."

Becky had heard the Easter story hundreds of time in her life, but never had it been real or mattered to her personally. Relating it to her own life—applying it to her worst guilt—made Becky feel fresh air coming into her lungs; like exiting a hospital and being free of its antiseptic atmosphere. Maybe there is some version of a God in heaven, and maybe, like it said on Joseph's T-shirt, that god wasn't mad at her.

"Joseph, I don't know what to say." Becky stood up straight, separating herself from the hallway wall. "No one has ever talked to me about this part of my life. Why don't more Christians sound like you?"

Becky saw Joseph glance towards Saul at the table. He turned back, replacing his busboy apron as he said, "Let's say a person with a broken arm is going to have a hard time helping another person reset their broken arm.

Most Christians don't realize how free they can be to show love because they don't feel worthy of love themselves."

Joseph looked towards the kitchen and Becky peeked back at her table, locking eyes with Saul. She was surprised to see anger—his faced pulled into a tight grimace and his hands clenched together as he leaned on his elbows. She wondered if she could explain to those men what had occurred. She wasn't even sure she could make sense of it. This made her smile. She didn't feel the need to explain anything to them. She thought now she could just be herself.

"Ch Jes ," Becky said, thinking one last thought. "If I decided to go to church would you go with me?" She saw Joseph glance across the room at Saul.

"Well, I did receive an invitation to a church today," he said with a smile.

CHAPTER 7:
ISAAC'S QUEST

Isaac Thompson, the son of Pastor Saul, turned the ignition of his black Subaru and pulled out of the family driveway.

"Who's this guy we're going to see again?" Asked Tank, Isaac's friend and passenger. Charles "Tank" Cook was a fellow BCC teen with Isaac. The two of them had grown up together from the church nursery to playing hide and seek with the cute girls after service. Isaac was the taller of the two but Tank was much more the brute, thus the nickname.

"His name's Joseph," said Isaac. "Nobody knows much about him, but he puts on some sort of talk show at the North End Grill."

"A talk show?" Tank frowned.

"I hear he says some stuff but is kinda cool," Isaac replied. "Tina Bettz said the guy had all kind of weird stories."

"Like some of those podcasts you like on how much church sucks," chided Tank. Isaac pressed the accelerator to ease the car into traffic as Tank continued. "Not surprised you heard that from Tina. You'd NEVER miss a chance to talk to Tina Bettz."

"Oh, like you've never sneaked a look at Tina during youth group. And you know she checks you out, too."

"Shut up," said Tank, grabbing an empty water bottle from the door cup holder and tossing it playfully at his friend. Isaac wouldn't admit it out loud, but he suspected Tina was at least a little infatuated with him. Twenty-one years old, tall and slender with his mom's green eyes, Isaac received attention from a number of females. He had a "church bad boy" reputation, which seemed to make him all the more appealing to the BCC young ladies. Isaac, however, was focused on his life-journey, which didn't leave much time for more trivial pursuits.

Isaac was a seeker. He knew there was something big and new for him to grasp about the world, religion, and life in general. So, for now, the girls could wait.

"Dude, what's that?" Tank pointed at Isaac's arm where something hidden was exposed from under his bunched up sleeve. "Did you get a tat?" Isaac tugged his sleeve back into place, but the secret was out. Tank reached across Isaac's body to try and see.

"Dude, you're gonna make me crash," shouted Isaac with a push to his bulky friend.

"C'mon, show me," pleaded Tank. "What's it say?" Isaac finally gave in and used his right hand to slide back his sleeve as his left hand maintained the steering wheel. Isaac's left forearm bore script writing: "BELIEVE."

"No way!" Tank exclaimed in disbelief. "What's 'Father Saul' gonna say?"

"Father Saul doesn't know," said Isaac, using the pejorative nickname he'd invented for his dad in recent weeks. "He's disappointed enough in me already."

Isaac had never known a life where he wasn't identified by his father's visibility in Bekering. Isaac felt he'd been used as a prop throughout his childhood, from church plays to wearing political pins at events. As a young adult, he felt disenchanted, discovering there were others who didn't always agree with his father's staunch views.

"My dad would kill me if I got one of those," said Tank.

"No doubt!" Isaac mocked. "Officer Cook would be very unhappy with your rebellion." Isaac and Tank were products of hardline Bekering Christian Center families. Isaac's dad the pastor, Tank's a Bekering Police officer. Despite all the Sunday school classes and summer youth camps, each had their own way of spreading their wings. Isaac knew, however, that Tank's father was considerably more aggressive at reigning in Tank than was Saul. Father Saul simply seemed befuddled by Isaac's burgeoning nonconformity.

"So, this Joseph is different from the stuff we hear in church?" Asked Tank. "This might be the guy my dad said has just shown up in town. He said he's heard the guy smokes pot."

"Your dad thinks the last president was run by the Illuminati," Isaac popped back.

"He wasn't?" Tank half-joked, invoking an eye roll from Isaac. As much as Isaac desired to explore new ideas and beliefs, he knew it would be difficult for Tank to break away from his family's views, inculcated with harsh enforcement over a lifetime. Isaac surmised Tank was along to simply indulge his friend.

Isaac steered the car onto Beatty Avenue, heading towards the entrance of the North Bekering Shopping Center. The two rode in the silence that had settled in the car.

"Do you really believe all this stuff you listen to, Isaac?" asked Tank in a serious tone. The quietness must have given him a chance to ponder Isaac's quest. "Like, about God not sending hurricanes to punish people?"

"I'm not really sure... yet," said Isaac, using the time idling at a stoplight to roll his long hair into a man-bun. "I know God has to be different than the one we've heard about all our lives. There's got to be more to believing in God than praying for Republicans to be elected and the right Supreme Court Justice to be picked. There's gotta be."

"How do you know?"

"I just know," said Isaac, wiping some dust away from his car's dashboard. "But I need to prove it for myself."

"I think you're nuts. No, I know you are." Tank laughed. "Let's go check out this Joseph and then let's get some food. Oh, but we have to sneak in and out, to keep my dad from finding out."

"You're such a shrimp," Isaac said with a teasing shove as the car continued forward. Isaac's eyes stared ahead. What did he really believe? He assumed there was some sort of divine spirit but just not sure it was the evangelical God. Isaac only knew he was done following the God of Father Saul. Isaac reached for his phone to flip on some music.

"God is not a man, God is not an old man..." came the song lyrics from the phone through a USB connection with the car stereo, "...and God does not belong to Republicans."

"What is this?" asked Tank with a shriveled face.

"It's a singer named Gungar," answered Isaac. "He gets me."

"You better be careful, Dude," said Tank with a glare, "you're playing with some pretty weird stuff."

"...But God is Good, God is Good..." the song continued, "...and he loves everyone."

"Maybe 'weird,' is just no one has ever told us before." As he listened to the song, Isaac knew he would soon arrive at the next step on his search for truth. If this Joseph guy had any answers, then Isaac needed to know him.

CHAPTER 8:
TELLER OF A DIFFERENT STORY

"Guess you're not the only who wants to hear this guy," marveled Tank as he looked around the full room. The two young men had entered through the open emergency exit door into the back room of the North End Grill, the restaurant where Isaac's father had met with Hal and the bankers just hours before.

"Yeah, seems like it," Isaac mumbled as he made his own assessment of the group. Maybe thirty-five to forty people, most under the age of 30, were situated in a semi-circle around a small stage.

"Not a lot of older folks here," observed Tank.

"Yeah, don't think the old-school BCC crowd is quite ready for a guy like this," Isaac answered Tank without looking at him. His attention was directed towards the dark-haired man standing to the right of the stage with several young, college-aged people around him. Isaac correctly guessed this was Joseph and pressed forward, joining the group to eavesdrop.

"What did I think of the Defense of Marriage Rally?" Isaac heard Joseph respond to a questioner. "Let me ask you young people. What's the value of such an event?"

"To help inform people?" answered an uncertain young woman in the circle. "Start a discussion?" Isaac watched as Joseph responded to the young woman with a gentle smile.

"I saw a police tape confining The Love Coalition to a small space far from the event," Joseph shared. "It'd seem to me the Evangelical Republicans of Bekering didn't set up the event in order to have any discussion. What do you think?"

"I guess they just want to push their own viewpoint," said the young man to whom Joseph had pointed. Isaac quickly recognized Thad Perkins. Thad was a bit younger than Isaac, and from another prominent BCC family. Standing next to Thad was his friend, Peter North, whom Isaac met a couple times.

"Maybe they prefer preaching over discourse on important cultural issues?" Joseph answered with an arch of his eyebrow. Isaac found himself instantly liking Joseph. He sensed this process of asking questions and then allowing lingering silence was Joseph's challenge for the group to think and answer.

"A church they don't allow any discussion of tough issues," said Peter. "They just tell us what to do—or else!" Peter's face crinkled in an angry glare and he pointed menacingly at the crowd in mock impersonation of church leaders.

"So now you all know why Peter never comes to church," Thad responded with a resigned smile.

"Sorry, Thad," Peter answered, placing his hand gently on Thad's shoulder. "I'm just not republican enough to go to BCC." Isaac looked around the group of young people as Peter's statement drew a few nods of agreement.

"Perhaps a partnership with conservative politics was sewn into the history of the Evangelical church," Joseph answered before checking his watch. Isaac was fascinated with each response from this stranger. Joseph dealt with weighty issues in a way Isaac had never seen. No angry rhetoric or divisive ranting. And Joseph seemed rather… happy.

"Looks like it's time for us to begin," Joseph said to the small group. "Let's talk about that discussion." Isaac kept his eyes locked on Joseph who was stepping onto the small stage in the corner of the room. Wearing a jacket, T-shirt and blue jeans. Under that dark blue jean jacket Isaac could see a magenta T-shirt that said, "God likes your enemies. And He even likes you!"

"My friends and I were talking about the tendency of Evangelicals to want to win arguments and dwell on divisive issues," Joseph began as the group settled. Some were seated on folding chairs, others on the floor, and the rest stood several rows deep. Isaac moved to the back of the room and leaned against a stack of boxes, where his height gave him a good view of the stage. Tank, next to Isaac, had to lean side to side to see in between other bodies.

"Could this all have started way back in the sixteenth century with a guy named Martin Luther?" Isaac watch Joseph train of thought momentarily get lost as two more people entered the room and shuffled to find floor space.

Isaac guessed the room had originally been constructed for small events but had become a catch-all storage room. Pallets of toilet paper rolls, cleaning products and boxes of plastic gloves surrounded the perimeter and appeared to have been stacked high to make space for the event's seating area.

"In the 1600s," Joseph continued appearing to regather his focus, "Luther had a righteous battle against horrible things in the Catholic Church. What he built evolved into the division we see today." Isaac again noticed Joseph's easy style. No serious looks or threatening statements like most church speakers.

"It's like the story of 'The Blue People...'" Joseph paused, a small smile stretching across his face. In that moment, Isaac found himself leaning forward, becoming fully immersed in his first experience of one of Joseph's stories.

There was a people known as The Blue People, who, as you might have guessed, were all blue. One day, a man stood up and challenged the unjust, harsh leaders of a group known as the Royal Blues.

"I declare all people who are not Royal Blue will leave the Blue Kingdom and form the Non-Royal Blue Kingdom." Despite the protestations of the Royal Blues, the Non-Royal Blues broke away and this new kingdom was very pleasing to all Non-Royal Blues. That is, until the day when an Azure Blue person stepped up to speak.

"It seems we Azure Blues should have our own kingdom. We are different from other Non-Royal Blues."

"You can't break away," said the original leader of the Non-Royal Blues. "We're all Non-Royal Blues and none can break away."

The Non-Royal Blue leader understood the breakaway from the Royal Blues had been based upon significant abuse of leadership, and the Azure Blues' desire to break away was more about style than substance. He begged them not to do so.

"How can you say the Azures can't break away?" said the self-appointed leader of the Azure Blues. "You broke away from the Royal Blues because of differences, and we Azure Blues are different from the rest of the Non-Royal Blues. Who are you to tell us we can't break away?"

The Non-Royal Blue leader had always encouraged the Non-Royal Blues to celebrate their differences, but now the Azure Blues used them as an excuse to form their own kingdom. This opened an ominous door.

"We Turquoise Blues need to break away," said one group.

"The Cedar Blues feel we have differences from the Non-Royal Blues and must leave as well," said another.

Soon, the Ocean Blues, Sky Blues, and Midnight Blues left the Non-Royal Blues to form their own kingdoms, which dotted the countryside. It wasn't long, however, before division arose in these kingdoms, as well.

"We Light Turquoise Blues can no longer be part of the Turquoise Blue Kingdom, as we are very different," said a leader of the Light Turquoise Blues.

Other Blues looked at the Light Turquoise Blues and could scarcely tell a difference from the Turquoise Blues. To the Light Turquoise Blues, however, the differences had become insurmountable. So, the Light Turquoise Blues left the Turquoise Kingdom, which had left the Non-Royal Blues Kingdom, which had left the Blue Kingdom led by the Royal Blues.

Soon, the Paled Turquoise Blues left in disagreement with the Turquoise Blues, as did the #1 Turquoise Blues and the #2 Turquoise Blues. The same happened in all the other small kingdoms, and before long the one, righteous break away had led to thousands of divisions over completely inconsequential differences.

"So, what's the point of my story?" Joseph asked as he concluded.

"Don't spend too much time worrying about little things?" responded a young man in the far corner.

"Exactly!" Joseph said with a smile and a clap of his hands. Isaac could tell Joseph enjoyed this type of interaction. "If we aren't careful about where we put our focus, minor issues can become major points of division, and soon we forget why we're together in the first place." Joseph seemed to stop and measure the attention and apprehension of the group before he continued.

"Martin Luther's Protestant church left the Catholic Church for righteous reasons, just like the Non-Royal Blues in the story. But the word 'protestant' starts with 'protest.' Today the church is awfully proud of its heritage of protesting." Joseph took a drink from a water bottle.

"Did you know there are now more than ten thousand different denominations of Protestant churches in the world?" Joseph's fact brought some surprised looks to the group. "Some studies define as many as thirty-three thousand Protestant fractures throughout church history, dividing over everything from interpretation of the Bible to the color of the carpet."

Laughter wafted through the group.

"How do churches divide over the Bible?" asked Thad, now sitting with Peter on the floor in front of center stage. "Doesn't it say what it says?"

"Does it?" Joseph asked. Isaac looked around and saw the group unable to answer.

After an awkward moment of silence, Joseph said, "Let's try this: Protestants divided into the 'Fundamentalists' and 'Modernists.'" Joseph demonstrated this by moving from one side of the stage to the other. "What's the difference?"

Isaac could tell Joseph was comfortable letting the silence linger in order to try and elicit response from the group. Joseph looked at the floor and put his hands on his knees, allowing time for the deafening silence to overpower someone.

"How they interpret the Bible?" Isaac finally blurted out, unable to take the silence one more second.

"Yes!" Joseph responded with another clap and smile as he straightened. "The Fundamentalists, over here, were very focused on a literal, fundamental interpretation of the Bible. As this young man put it, 'it says what it says,' and that's the end of discussion." Joseph moved to the other side of the stage.

"Over here were the Modernists. Did the Fundamentalists like the Modernists?"

"No," some of the young people responded.

"No they didn't," Joseph agreed dramatically as he walked back to the other side of the stage. "The Fundamentalists stood over here judging those Modernists to be as bad as the Catholics. Do you know why?" Isaac followed Joseph's eyes around the room and saw they landed on him.

"They thought the Modernists were too soft on sin," Isaac answered.

"That's a helluva answer," Joseph said, his mouth forming in a big smile, "you're our grand prize winner today! What's your name?"

"Isaac."

"Isaac, do you know why the Modernists saw the Bible differently than the Fundamentalists?" Isaac looked at the floor for a moment. He was hesitant to answer in front of the group but summoned up the courage to do so.

"I guess because they knew the Bible was written back in the old days and not in our culture," Isaac answered in a soft voice that showed his uncertainty. "They took what the Bible said and tried to understand what it meant for today's culture?"

"Wow, the rest of you need to hang with Isaac!" bellowed Joseph. "In simple terms I might say the Modernists believed the Bible wasn't written by Americans for Americans." The group laughed.

"You have to understand what the people of the time were hearing and then translate to something similar today. Because many American Christians have never been taught this — they completely miss the true meaning of what the Bible is saying. They love God, they've just missed his message."

Isaac smiled. He was filled with information about the Bible, but Joseph's message caused Isaac to feel something deep in his core, not unlike a roller coaster ride where your stomach has excitement and terror in anticipation of the next curve. Joseph was challenging the old precepts Isaac had always known, which both thrilled and worried the young pastor's son.

"So, now we have this divide in the Protestant church between Fundamentalists and Modernists. A group of Fundamentalists became very focused on converting non-believers through evangelism and, thus, the Evangelical wing of the Fundamental Christian Church was born." Joseph paused, the room silent in rapt attention.

"So, take a group of Fundamentalists Christians, very staunch in their views, believing God had called them to convert everyone around them, with a history steeped in protest and division, and perhaps we can see how it easily evolved into the politically active church of today. Add in big political victories like the Moral Majority of the '80's and we see the results." Joseph's wide eyes narrowed and his smile faded, "A group of really ticked off people who have a heritage of division that makes them believe they're supposed to despise the other side and enjoy being despised. It unfortunately seems to just be part of their nature. That desire to be right totally overcomes any belief that 'God so loves the world.'"

"But God doesn't love sinners!" Tank blurted out, causing Isaac to jump with surprise.

"Great thought," Joseph responded, his hand touching his chin in thought. "Didn't God command us to love our enemies?"

"God blew up cities full of sinners," Tank shot back. Isaac could see Tank's face was serious and his brow set hard across his forehead. As much as Isaac was enjoying his beliefs being challenged by Joseph's message, he could tell Tank wasn't.

"I hear you," said Joseph, turning fully towards Tank. "Tell me, who would God not love and want to punish?"

"Murderers, for one," Tank snapped. "OK, good answer," said Joseph, who then took his eyes off Tank and looked around the room. "Who else?"

"The guys who plotted 9/11," another young man answered.

"Now we're gettin' real," said Joseph. "Anyone else?"

"Danville High School!" said a younger, high school-aged boy in a letterman's jacket. Isaac didn't recognize the boy but chuckled along with the rest of the crowd at the idea of God hating North Bekering High's sports rival.

"Very good," Joseph answered with a big laugh before his face again turned serious. "Imagine if the people of Danville weren't only your sports rivals, but they'd actually been at war with your town and killed your relatives. Would you want God to punish them?" Isaac was glued to every word, totally unaware of the clink of utensils against plates and the chatter of guests in the working restaurant on the other side of the wall.

"In the Bible, this guy Jonah was ticked when God demanded he preach to the rival town of Nineveh," Joseph shared. "Jonah felt he had the right to be angry at the people who'd terrorized his family?" Joseph stopped and turned back to face Tank.

"Did God blow up that city full of sinners?" Isaac turned and saw Tank's eyes burning at Joseph.

"No," Tank responded through tight lips, "but only because they repented."

"But, Jonah was pissed even about that, wasn't he?" Joseph responded. Isaac could see the straight line of Joseph's mouth as the speaker pressed towards the heart of today's discussion.

"Jonah told God he'd rather die than see God have mercy on his enemies," Joseph said, staring straight at Tank. "God said to Jonah, 'how's that feeling workin' out for ya?'" The air seemed to shimmer with silence as the room looked between the two men. Joseph's voice grew soft. "What's your name?"

"Tank," Isaac's friend responded curtly.

"Ch[...] better be careful with someone named 'Tank.'" Tank didn't crack a sm[...] the group chuckled around him.

"T[a]nk, [s]eems God didn't want Jonah to hate his enemies," Joseph contin[u]ed, [p]alms open, seeming to invite Tank into discussion. "Do you know [why?] [Ta]nk again shrugged his shoulders and crossed his arms. Joseph seemed to [se]e that his discussions was not working with Tank, so his eyes moved to a[noth]er part of the group.

"B[e]ing [ang]ry at people for not believing as you is like catching a burglar in your ho[use], [s]napping handcuffs between the two of you, and then sitting in jail with [the] two of you attached as you try to make sure he gets justice." Joseph paus[ed] [w]ith a grin and scanned the room.

"D[o yo]u [see] the problem? You might get justice that way, but now neither of you are [al]right?" Isaac saw heads nodding even as Tank released a huff.

"T[r]ust[ing] [ju]stice to the love from heaven frees us to be people of hope, not an[g]e[r]. S[o n]o. The goodness of heaven doesn't want to blow up cities of 'sinners,'" J[osep]h said, curling his fingers into air quotes. "There is a universal care for p[eople] in the cosmos and we are commanded to care, too." Isaac unknowingly [r]ubbed his sensitive, newly tattooed arm as he listened to Joseph's co[nclus]ion.

"M[aybe] [Go]d didn't blow up Nineveh but he sure did destroy Sodom," Tank s[a]id i[n the t]one Isaac recognized as Tank's argument voice.

"Y[ou kn]o[w] your Old Testament stories, Tank, good for you," Joseph said, his eyes st[il]l [lo]cked on Isaac's friend. "In the New Testament, when two disciple[s a]s[ked] Jesus for fire to come down from heaven and destroy a city that ha[d rej]e[cte]d him, what did Jesus say?" Tank shrugged his shoulders.

"Is[aa]c, [do] you know?" Joseph asked, his eyes shifting to connect with Is[aac].

"He sai[d he] didn't come to destroy people but came to save them," Isaac answer[e]d so[mew]hat meekly, hoping Tank didn't feel betrayed by his answer.

"T[h]at's [righ]t," Joseph responded. "He said the disciples had partnered with a spiri[t th]at was not from heaven in making such a request." Joseph's cadenc[e w]a[s pi]cking up speed. "The God of the Hebrew scripture felt the same a[bou]t [Jon]ah. He was pissed that Jonah wanted heaven to kill a hundred and tw[enty-tho]usand residents of Nineveh,"—The group buzzed at the use of gruff la[ng]u[age] — "just as the same god would not like our fundamentalist,

Evangelical beliefs to give us permission to hate others today. It's partnering with a spirit that is NOT from heaven!"

Isaac had heard the Bible story of Jonah a thousand times, but never like this. He could feel his heart beating. He'd always believed the story of the Bible was about love from heaven, not destruction and punishment. Now someone was telling him that feeling was true.

"Nineveh was about the same size as Bekering, located where modern day Mosul sits—ISIS's base. Do you think the biblical God wanted to blow up Mosul or do you think that god loved the people there?"

"You think God loves even crazy religious people who cut off people's heads?" Tank shouted.

"It seems you don't think so?" Joseph responded, leaning forward on the stage in Tank's direction. "Do you think worthiness to be loved is about people's behavior? Or their inherent value as part of creation? Tank, the love of heaven is even for you, no matter what you do."

"This is bullcrap, man," Tank said, turning to Isaac. "Let's get out of here." Isaac glared at his friend and gave an emphatic shake of his head. Tank sighed as Isaac continued to listen to Joseph.

"That doesn't mean we have to approve of bad things people do, like cutting off heads or letting our religion to give us permission to demonize people around us if they have differing beliefs, race or nationality," Joseph said, answering his own question, "but, thankfully for all of us, we deserve love no matter what."

"I'm outta here," Tank said to Isaac as he stared at Joseph with a scowl. "You with me?"

"No, man," Isaac responded with a shake of his head. "Chill, Tank."

"You keep getting twisted with this stuff. I'm going to enjoy my day."

"But, I'm your ride."

"Not anymore," Tank answered. Tank walked out without a look back and disappeared through the door. Isaac wondered if his friendship was disappearing as well.

With a shake of his head, Isaac turned back to the room, only now noticing everyone was watching him. They'd all witnessed Tank's departure. Isaac stooped a little, hoping they'd again focus on Joseph.

"When we say today that God hates sinners, or even that famous 'love the sinner not the sin' hypocrisy," Joseph said, relaxing from his confrontation with Tank, "that god says to us as was said to Jonah: 'how's that workin' out for ya?'"

The meeting soon ended and Isaac saw Joseph heading straight for him.

"Sorry about your friend," Joseph said, shaking Isaac's hand. "My heart breaks for Christians trapped in this mindset. I know your friend's heart is sincere—but he's sincerely wrong."

"It's all good," Isaac responded, "I'm still trying to figure it all out myself."

"This is different stuff than what your dad shares," said Tina Bettz, who had come to join Isaac and Joseph in the discussion.

"Who's your dad?" Joseph asked.

"He's Pastor Saul's kid!" Tina shouted before Isaac could answer.

"Pastor Saul is your dad?" Joseph laughed. "No wonder you know so much about Fundamentalists." Tension rose in the back of Isaac's neck as he wondered what Joseph might say. "I met Pastor Saul. I like him." Isaac felt himself able to breath. Already, he cared about Joseph's approval.

"Listen, your dad isn't wrong in his desire. Good laws matter for heaven as much as any fervent Christian on earth. But laws don't change hearts. The Bible says if hearts are softened and transformed with love, then righteous government and behavior will follow. That's the true Gospel."

"Joseph, do you believe God isn't Republican?" asked Tina, bringing laughter to the handful of others who still remained from the meeting. Tina flushed and Isaac guessed she wasn't completely joking.

"The fact you ask makes me sad, Miss," Joseph answered, his head tilting to the side. "No, God's not Republican." Joseph leaned forward and put a hand to his mouth.

"In fact, God's not even American." The group laughed.

"Isaac, we all need someone to give us permission to think differently than we've always known," Joseph said, turning to him like a mentor delivering advice to a prized student. "I give you permission to do so."

That statement shook Isaac. Joseph seemed to know what was happening inside of him. Could it really be true? Could Isaac believe differently than he always had? Differently than his father?

CHAPTER 9:
SAUL AND HIS SERMON

The following Sunday, Saul sat at his office desk deep in thought. This was normally his favorite time of the week, surrounded by the mahogany of his plush office, relaxing in his high-backed desk chair. Today, however, Saul lacked his usual pre-service excitement.

"...Hi, Mary! Hello, Al..."

Saul could hear the chatter of voices in the parking lot below his third story window. BCC held Sunday services at eight-thirty, ten, and eleven-thirty. Soon, Saul would walk out and take his seat on the stage, enjoy the end of the music and deliver the message for the third time today. This service would have more than one thousand people, always the largest of the three services. Pastoring a mega-church was Saul's dream. It afforded a generous salary and high prestige, but Saul found the job unsatisfactory today.

He gave a big sigh and unbuttoned the top button on his shirt.

"Wow, you're not the Saul I normally see in this office," said Patty popping through the doorway. Saul jerked upright, startled from his thoughts. "What's wrong? You've been off all week." Saul hesitated before letting out a breath and giving into the fact that he couldn't fool his wife.

"I'm still bugged with this episode of Becky Townsend and Joseph. And Isaac's been hanging around that guy."

"Oh, Isaac's a young man, Saul," Patty said with a touch on his shoulder. Saul felt like a child being scolded. "Let him search out his own path."

Saul gazed again out his window at his people coming into the third service.

"I try and teach these people how to be godly," he said, "a person like Joseph makes the job more difficult." Saul had always struggled with his inability to see change in the people in his church. Seeing Becky's transformation at the restaurant made him wonder what magic Joseph had. The mysterious stranger wasn't holding to true scripture as Saul did, yet people loved Joseph for it. Saul burned inside, thinking the situation unfair.

"You said she was happy," Patty countered. "Isn't that a good thing?"

"Joseph's words are dangerous, honey." Saul watched his wife move to perch on the corner of his desk, brushing the bottom of her blue flower print dress underneath her.

"Nobody can simply wipe away hundreds of years of church teaching because it makes someone 'happy,'" Saul insisted. "Wouldn't we all like to teach a Bible all rosy and lovey-dovey?"

"Actually, a little lovey-dovey might not be such a bad thing," she responded with a tilt of her head and wry grin. Patty rose and kissed Saul on the cheek. "No matter what, I'll be in the front row as always."

Saul smiled at his wife's kindness as she exited the room. He knew church had ceased being a joy for her years ago, yet here she was.

Saul's mind raced. Maybe Patty was right and Becky's transformation that day was worth investigating. Yet he knew Joseph's teaching was not truth. At least not the truth Saul had been taught. Angels in an abortion clinic? Sin was sin and God demanded that sinners repent.

Saul own conversion had taken him from sinner to saint—it was hardly lovey or dovey.

"The old hymn says, 'would you be free from your burden of sin,'" Saul remembered the old preacher had taught on that hot Ohio night. It was during Saul's second year at Ohio State. "We need power to be free from sin, don't we?"

"Yes, Pastor!" the church responded.

"God cannot even look upon sinners, as he could not look upon his own son who bore the world's sin on the cross." Saul hadn't gone to church looking for Jesus. Instead, his eyes were on Patricia Neal. Everyone knew Patty wouldn't date guys who didn't go to church.

"Do you want to be free from your sinful life?" the preacher shouted. "The fires of hell are at the door. Tonight could be your last chance!" Saul's heart pounded in his chest, convicted of his life and afraid of going to hell, his legs leaped forward when invited to the altar before his mind knew what was happening.

Saul never wanted to be a pastor, as the meager life of his uncle, who pastored a small church in Eastern Ohio, seemed like a poor second choice to Saul's desire to be a professional golfer or sports broadcaster. Condemned of his sin, however, Saul felt he owed it to God to follow his uncle's footsteps.

"Bam!" A car door slamming in the parking lot brought Saul back to the present. He stared out the window remembering how he'd quit school after his "born again" experience. He married Patty and headed to pastoral seminary. Upon graduation, the denomination sent them to Oregon, which seemed like the other side of the world. Now it was home and Saul was the leader of BCC, with an obligation to speak the truth to his people as he had learned it. That's what Saul was going to do today.

"...God wants to call us out of deception," Saul preached, the microphone on his cheek blasting his words to the large audience. It was called a Countryman microphone, but it was more like a badge of honor to Saul.

"I saw this week how the world can pull us in if we're not careful to love the sinner yet hate the sin."

The "Amens" and "Preach Its" echoed around the hall, as was the tradition in this style of church. While churches like BCC had toned down on some of the more exuberant elements of their service to become more "seeker-friendly," BCC's people still loved to shout their support to Pastor Saul.

"I saw a man subverting the truth this week." Saul paused and pursed his lips to dramatically show his disapproval. "This man twisted scripture about sin to fit his own desires and he's been sharing his twisted messages with our young people. Well, hear me, friends, I would be derelict in my duty if I didn't bring you truth, as your pastor."

More "Amens," the people's enthusiasm palpable.

"The word 'pastor' means 'shepherd,' and I'm to lead you into green pastures." When Saul preached sermons like these he tended to turn on his Midwestern accent more than normal and get a roll in his voice and a bounce in his knees as he dramatically brought his word to a climax.

"Because, you know, the devil can come with great words and twist the Bible. These words can lead you to hang with the sinners rather than your brothers and sisters in Christ. I have seen it with my own eyes, this week here in Bekering."

"Ch___ ___y ___he cries rang out and grimaces filled the faces of the crowd. Saul di__n't ___t to blatantly call Joseph out, but he was trying to make the referen__e a__ __nt.

"I __w a __n, who claimed to be a Christian, giving approval to abortion rather ha__ ___ding for the hard truth for which you and I fight."

"A__nen!"

"T__e B___ says in Second Timothy Chapter 3 there will be men in these last da__s..." ___or Saul paused for emphasis and looked over the crowd, "...men w__o l___ __leasure more than they love God..."

"Y__s, s__ __each the truth, Pastor!"

"...and t__ __scripture told us these men would prey upon the weak..." Saul dramatical__ __vered his voice. "But like it says in Timothy, you have listened to my __ac__ __ and you're not going to be reeled in by any deceiver..."

"Y__S! __ __T'S RIGHT!"

"...__nd __ won't be overcome by any agenda of the devil. You won't endors__ __ __ortionists or the mother who aborts her own baby for conver__ien__

"__H__ __!"

"...__ ___ God has given us the truth and the truth has set us free—AMEN?" __ ___aised his hands in the air as an organ blast punctuated his last statem__nt. __ __repared for a powerful prayer to wrap up when his eye caught movem__nt i__ __e balcony. It was Becky Townsend, the banker about whom he'd be__n __ ___hing. She was heading up the steps to the exit.

"N__!" __ __hought. "I had no idea she'd be here."

Sa__l's __ __hifted to Becky's empty seat. To the left sat the protagonist of Saul's ___ness __ Joseph had come to church and had brought Becky. Saul's familia__ in__ __l struggle rose up once again. He was proud to share truth, but he was __ __tified Becky had heard his diatribe. Saul didn't mind a good argum__nt __ __s Patty had pointed out at the marriage rally, he didn't like to be disl__ked

Sa__l st___ __frozen as Joseph's eyes met his. A thousand thoughts flooded Saul's h__ad. __ __w angry Joseph must be and how Becky must have been hurt by his ch__ra__ __ization of her. It struck Saul, however, that Joseph really didn't look a__gry, __ Saul might have expected. He looked more—sad. As if he directe__ pi__ __wards Saul rather than anger.

Saul shook free of those thoughts. Breaking his gaze with Joseph, he proceeded to finish his message with prayer. After all, Saul knew he'd been called to speak the truth no matter the consequences. The service finished with a flourish and soon hundreds of people would be shaking Saul's hand and thanking him for what he shared. Saul would have to worry about Joseph and Becky another day.

CHAPTER 10:
MIGRANTS, MUSLIMS AND MIRACLES

"OK, I'll share a story..." Saul was walking out of BCC after the service and heard a voice speaking around the corner.

"This is the story of the Migrant Farm Worker and the Muslim..." It was Joseph's voice and it caused Saul to freeze. Saul's normal Sunday routine was to shake hands with people, then meet Patty and another church family for lunch. Today, however, Patty had a planning meeting for an upcoming women's event requiring her to stay late at the church. Saul had walked his normal path towards the staff parking lot through the BCC Coffee Shop alone, resolving to have a quiet lunch at home. Now, Saul shifted his plan to stop and peek around the corner.

"Three men jumped the farm worker..." said Joseph to a group of about twenty young people in the shop's main seating area. Some sat backwards in their chairs, others on the floor, and one young man even sprawled on the coffee shop couch. All were listening intently, including the staff. In the middle of the front row, Saul spotted Isaac taking in every word.

...They mugged the migrant farm worker, beating him about the head. Once down, they broke his ribs with a bat, ripped off his clothes, and stole all he had. The bandits had planned this attack on payday to benefit from the cashed paycheck the farm worker was sure to be carrying. Farm workers generally had no legal identification to open a bank account and were in great danger since they were forced to carry cash. The bandits left the worker on the side of the road and took off with no regard to whether he would live or die.

Soon, a limo happened by carrying one of the local elected officials as well as a political party leader. The occupants of the limo saw the beaten man and discussed the situation as they pulled aside.

"I wonder if it's safe to help," said the elected official.

"He looks like an illegal. This might not look good in the press," said the party official. "We better drive on." They left the beaten man behind. Next, one of the town's prominent business owners came by with his wife and saw the man. They were headed to an important charity event and were hesitant to help.

"We're in our nice clothes," said the wife.

"Let's call 9-1-1," said the husband. Finding it to be an area of low mobile service, they decided to drive on and alert someone at the charity event.

"You're telling 'The Good Samaritan Story,'" Saul heard Isaac interrupt.

"Yes, Isaac," Joseph laughed, "but I want you to understand the full context of the story. The impact gets lost in our cultural translation. We miss how radical it was in those days to call a Samaritan 'good.'"

Joseph continued.

A religious leader of a big church was headed to a political rally and came by...

"He's talking about me," thought Saul from his hiding place.

...Seeing the man on the side of the road, the religious leader felt convicted to stop.

"Probably a drug deal gone wrong," the religious leader surmised.

"We all have to pay for the consequences of our sin," The religious leader said a prayer for the man and passed on by.

Finally, a young Muslim happened upon the scene. The young man's family was not well liked in the local community, as the residents feared Islamic people.

"Go home, terrorist," the boy had been told at the supermarket last week. Those moments were painful for the proud young man, but his parents had operated a small farm for many years and tried their best to integrate into the town. The humiliation of his treatment burned into the young man and, unable to retaliate, he grew ever angrier.

Today, this young Muslim came upon the broken man and stopped his Jeep.

"The ambulance will not make it in time to save you," the young man said in his heavy, middle-eastern accent. "I'm going to have to take you home." The worker tried to thank the young Muslim, but the young man insisted he save his strength.

At the Muslim home, the family tended to the worker by stopping his bleeding and caring for his wounds. They kept him stabilized until an ambulance finally arrived. The farm worker was amazed at the selfless act of the Muslim family while others had simply passed by.

"So, now," Joseph asked his young audience, "are you understanding my story?"

Around the corner, Saul felt he understood the story precisely. Saul assumed the characters in the story—an elected official, a party leader, a business leader, and a religious leader—represented Saul and his friends. Saul crossed his arms firmly as he seethed in anger.

"Kind of a 'can't judge a book by its cover' kinda story?" a high school-aged kid in the group guessed.

"Good idea," said Joseph, "but it's talking about mercy, as well. Do you think heaven wants us to give mercy to people we think might not deserve mercy?"

"I think my dad would say 'no,'" Isaac laughed, joined by the snickers of the group. Saul winced in his hiding place.

"Sometimes we're too busy or too judgmental to help others," Joseph responded. "But I believe mercy is powerful, wherever it's given and by whomever it's given."

"We learn in school not to look down on people because of their race or financial status or sexual preferences." Saul heard the voice of a female. He couldn't know, from his vantage point, that it was Tina Bettz, the daughter of Vern and Tabitha Bettz. "It seems weird to me that we don't learn that at church. I feel like my parents look down on people that are different."

"Miss Bettz," Joseph continued, revealing the identity of the young lady to Saul. "I bet your parents are really good people and are only reacting to what they see and are taught in the echo chamber of this church community. They grew up in a country that valued prosperity but sometimes failed to value minority races and ideas of equality."

As Joseph paused, Saul peaked around the corner again. Joseph had pulled up a chair and straddled it backwards in the center of the room, putting Joseph's line of sight directly towards Saul's hiding place. Saul quickly ducked back into hiding.

"Don't you think heaven wants everyone to prosper?" Joseph continued. "Blessing came to those fighting for the rights of other races in our country.

If those who claim to follow Jesus won't do the right thing, the goodness of heaven will descend on those who do."

Saul heard the silence of Joseph's pause. Joseph seemed to be taking his time to deliver this message. "Do you think environmentalists and animal rights people are connected to divine love?" Joseph asked. Saul could hear a rustle in the group.

"Our pastor says those people worship created stuff, not God," said a young man's voice.

"I think the Bible couldn't be more clear that earthly dominion given to humans carries with it an expectation of stewardship," Joseph stated, answering his own question. "There's even a proverb about an upright person regarding the needs of their beast. Your parents believed there was a god itching to blow up the earth, which allowed them to devalue creation, so heaven blessed crazy 'tree-hugger' people who did care about it, even if they loved the created more than the creator."

"Weren't our parents and grandparents, like, the hippies who protested war and did drugs in the sixties and seventies?" said another young lady. Saul heard a pause.

"How do I explain this?" Seeming to gather his thoughts, Joseph continued.

"An orphan at a nice foster home will still try to sneak extra food into his pockets because he's never sure if good things available today will be available tomorrow." Saul could hear the smile in Joseph's voice.

"No matter how many times the foster parent tells the child there'll be more food in the morning, the orphan will have to experience a new way of thinking before he can live in a new way."

"Your parents' generation adopted an orphan mindset. They feared if anyone else was blessed, there wouldn't be blessing left for them. They bought into the idea they had to fight and scrape for what was theirs, rather than trust kindness to carry a reward of kindness in return."

Saul peeked when he heard Joseph's chair scrape the floor. Joseph had moved to his left and looked out over another part of the group, giving Saul a chance to spy on this person who had dominated his thoughts this week. Saul could see Joseph in his jeans and jean jacket and a pink T-shirt that said, "Love is not a four-letter word."

"It see[ms a]s minority groups or more liberal groups seemed to receive divine [he]lp. [Ou]r parents felt something was being taken from them. Having benefit[ed fr]o[m] the systems in our culture for a great deal of history, they imagin[ed] t[hem]selves to be victims of these heaven-sent changes in culture."

"V[eri]l[y, o]h my word..." Saul steamed in his hiding place. He wondered if he sh[ou]ld [ste]p around the corner and end this meeting. Saul struggled for breath, his [...u]se growing with every word.

"T[o s]te[m th]e tide of this victimization, your parents' generation turned to a conse[r]v[at]i[ve id]eology," said Joseph. "Conservative talk radio and cable news reache[d pe]a[k p]opularity as these outlets fed a generation's desire to be suppo[rted in th]eir outrage. So, your parents struggle to display hope and love becaus[e they've] been led in fear and anger for so long. To think differently for this en[trenched] generation is as difficult as, say, uh—an elephant trying to becom[e a ca]n[ar]y." Saul heard the young people laugh at the political analogy.

"Jo[seph, I lo]ve how you teach about God," said Tina. Saul could now see the you[ng wom]an who had grown up in his church. "You make the Bible real. Like, f[or to]d[ay's] world."

"Y[e]ah, [you] make us actually want to hear about it, not fall asleep like in church," j[oine]d in a young man Saul recognized as Thad Perkins. The laughs grew, [m]irro[ring] Saul's expanding hatred for Joseph.

"F[or to]o [lon]g, we've been taught to simply accept the prevailing thought withou[t bei]n[g] curious as to other ideas," Joseph shared. "Sorting through differe[nt op]i[nio]ns allows us to truly identify if what we believe is in line with heaven [rat]h[er t]han blindly following dogma fed to us." The group began to chatter i[n ag]r[ee]ment. Saul was less impressed.

"T[h]is m[an i]s teaching nonsense!" he mentally groused, clenching his fists at his s[i]de. [An]d in my own coffee shop!" Saul hit a breaking point and had to step f[orw]a[rd] and stop this.

"H[i, Pa]s[tor] Saul." A voice from behind brought a flash of embarrassment as the [v]oic[e cau]sed every eye in the shop to turn towards Saul. It was Becky Towns[e]nd'[s voi]ce. She'd just come into the shop and revealed Saul's hiding place a[n]d l[eft him as] a desperately trapped man.

CHAPTER 11:
SAUL CAUGHT SPYING

Saul felt all eyes burning into him and his usual feeling of shame locked on to him, as well. It was a feeling he'd done something wrong. It welled up in his chest like pressure from drinking a caffeinated beverage too quickly. Not in a million years would Saul have guessed Joseph would bring Becky to BCC. Had he known, he wouldn't have referenced her in his sermon.

"Ms. Townsend, please let me apologize," he said, reaching his hands out to shake hers as his ears turned red. "I had truth to share with my people today, but I didn't mean to force you to leave." Confusion seemed to cross Becky's face as her eyes shifted in search of comprehension. Finally, her features settled and she looked up at Saul. This woman, who was so hardened when he'd met her earlier this week, now gave a gracious smile.

"Oh, Pastor Saul, I didn't leave because of anything you said," Becky responded, "I wanted my friend Ruby to meet Joseph, so I left as you were wrapping up." Becky gestured to the young lady standing next to her, but Saul's eyes looked right through her. He'd expected a brusk response to his sermon. As at the restaurant, Saul could see the change in Becky.

"Ruby, this is Pastor Saul," Becky said, breaking the silence as Saul finally recovered to say hello.

"And this—is Joseph," Becky pulled Ruby by the shoulder of her orange sweater and moved inside the main room of the coffee shop.

"Come meet this guy," she said. "He told me things about my life he couldn't have known." The two women walked away from Saul and he noticed Ruby's limp. She wore a black knee brace covering her right leg from mid-thigh to mid-shin. As Ruby approached Joseph, he gave her his big smile before glancing at Saul with a quick nod. Saul shifted nervously, aware Joseph must know of Saul's spying. He felt exposed as he watched the two women interact with Joseph.

"Are you psychic?" Ruby asked.

"No," Joseph laughed. "A psychic has their own path to see and hear things. I hear from the spirit of heaven." Saul leaned back against the wall and crossed his arms as Joseph spoke to Ruby in a low voice only Ruby and Becky could hear. Soon, Ruby's eyes were watering, and she was giving Joseph a hug.

"For Pete's sake," Saul thought as his face contorted. "This guy's a busboy." Saul's jealousy made him feel petty, but he hated that Joseph seemed free to love people while Saul had to carry the weight of leading a church and a political movement.

"He wouldn't last a day in my shoes," Saul thought, unaware an angry snarl had snuck onto his face. He happened to catch Isaac's eye in the front of the group. The snarl faded and his chest groaned as he saw Isaac's usual look of displeasure.

Isaac was as beloved as any firstborn son, but was born into a family living in pain. Isaac wasn't the family's first pregnancy. The Thompson's first baby had been stillborn, meaning Isaac's healthy birth was hailed as a miracle.

Early in Isaac's infancy, Patty had walked into the boy's bedroom and found his lips were turning blue. Patty called Saul on the way to the emergency room.

"You have to help," she said, her voice filled with terror. "I can't lose another son."

Unsure what to do, Saul immediately had called their neighbor, Christian Anderson. Christian was then a new pastor who led a church much different from BCC. Saul considered Christian's church low on the socio-economic scale and to be one of those "crazy" churches.

"Pastor Anderson, you believe in praying for healing," Saul had said to his neighbor. "We need you to pray right now." Saul probably would never admit to it, but if they'd lived next to a voodoo doctor, Saul would have called him, too. Pastor Anderson and his wife arrived quickly to the hospital and prayed beside Isaac's antiseptic hospital basin. Even as they were still speaking, the color returned to the baby's face and Isaac was still alive today. While Isaac's birth and healing were miracles in the household, the pain of the first loss had never gone away, especially for Patty. Now, as Saul continued to look at the floor, his eyes glistened at the memory of Patty's face as she struggled through those difficult motherhood experiences.

"Why would God save one child and not the other?" Patty had asked. Saul truly had no answer. Patty coped by throwing herself into life as a doting mother, and Saul had used his work to accomplish the same goal. Isaac's birth didn't completely salve Patty's wounds of loss from the first child. Not long after the miscarriage, Patty began drinking occasionally, Saul assumed to help ease the pain, and she seemed to need that help more often these days.

"Hey, what are you doing here?" Patty's voice rang out behind Saul as she came through the shop entrance. "I thought you'd have gone." She hugged Saul as she spotted Isaac and waved to him across the room.

"What's going on here?"

"I was watching our young people get a lesson from this Joseph character," Saul snapped, his tearful memories and his tears quickly evaporating.

"Oh, so this is the Joseph you've been talking about," said Patty, looking past Saul to see the man who had drawn so much of her husband's distaste. A wry smile formed on her face. "He looks harmless."

"He's a wolf in sheep's clothing," Saul grumbled. Patty touched Saul's arm and pointed in the direction of Joseph and Ruby. Saul watched with his wife as Joseph engaged the group of young people still strewn about the main room of the BCC Coffee Shop.

"Who wants to join me to pray for something cool?" Joseph asked the group. Saul was stunned to see Isaac's hand shoot in the air as he leaped to his feet.

"Come on up," Joseph said, wheeling his arm in a way to beckon Isaac towards the front. Isaac, Tina Bettz, and several others walked forward to stand with Joseph, Becky, and Ruby. They stood in front of the service counter where the staff was working to close the shop for the day.

"So, the Bible tells us the power of Jesus' story doesn't only make us guilt free," Joseph explained, "but it also gives us energy and power to carry each other's burdens." Joseph stood by Ruby as he addressed the group.

"We don't believe that stuff here," said one of the boys in the circle that Saul estimated to thirteen.

"Yeah, nothing cool ever happens here in our church," said a young lady sitting down the row from the boy. Saul flinched.

"If you're never taught of your connection to divine love and power, then you have no faith to believe," Joseph answered. "Our churches no longer see healing because they've never seen healing. It's like chickens that can fly but don't because they've never seen another chicken fly in the coop."

"Let's see if some chickens can fly today," Joseph laughed.

Patty took Saul by the arm and encouraged him to walk closer with her. They sat at a table to the left side of the group. Saul noticed several young people cast a wary eye towards him before quickly avoiding his glare.

"Ruby, I see the knee brace you're using. Can I ask for healing to come from heaven?" Joseph asked, raising his voice for the entire group to hear. Joseph stood flanked by Isaac, Tina, and the others.

Ruby looked at Becky with a bit of hesitance. Becky gave a quick nod of assurance.

"Ligament damage playing soccer," Ruby said with a nod. "I'm having surgery next week."

"Ruby," said Joseph, sliding down to one knee, "I'm so sorry that happened to you. Maybe we could avoid that surgery." Ruby answered with a nervous laugh. Saul couldn't help but think of Pastor Christian Anderson in the hospital, holding Isaac's lifeless body. Saul hadn't believed then, and he was struggling to believe now. Joseph's courage to pray was either praiseworthy or foolish. Saul felt his heart wrestling between the two choices.

"Could this really happen?" Patty whispered to Saul, taking his hand.

"Maybe I should stop this to keep Ruby from disappointment," he whispered back. "I don't want our kids to lose faith in God."

"You'll do no such thing," said Patty. Saul had witnessed Patty's struggles in life. Now he could see the anticipation on her face. It was clear she was hoping to see something miraculous happen.

"I'm going to lightly touch your knee over the knee brace. I don't want to hurt you." Joseph waited until Ruby indicated it was OK. He called Isaac and the others to kneel around him.

"Ruby, you are loved by heaven a lot," Joseph prayed in a way Saul had never heard before. "And we love her too and share our love to make it on earth as it is in heaven where nobody needs knee surgery."

"Weird prayer," whispered Saul.

"Hush, Saul," said Patty with a stage whisper and a squeeze of his hand.

"Do you feel anything, Ruby?" Joseph asked. All eyes in the room were fixed on Ruby, including Saul's. Ruby gazed into the distance as if taking inventory of her knee.

"I—I well, kinda." She walked a couple steps.

"In the past we were taught we have to beg for healing to come," Joseph explained. "We missed the power that walking alongside one another in pain can do. Ruby, can you take off the knee brace?"

Ruby reached down and the sound of Velcro tearing open filled the room.

"So cool that Ruby's feeling something," Joseph prayed, reaching his hands towards Ruby's jeans-covered knee. Saul could see even the coffee shop staff had halted their work to watch.

"Come on," he heard Patty whisper.

"Isaac, you're on," said Joseph. It took a moment for Isaac to react to what Saul thought must be difficult words to register.

"I've never prayed for anyone to be healed," Isaac said with a quivering voice. Patty's grip on Saul's hand tightened.

"There's no magic, Isaac," Joseph said with his trademark chuckle, "and I don't want anyone to think this is some magic of mine. Just connect your heart to heaven and to Ruby's and find someplace for you both to believe it can happen and let's see."

Isaac's face displayed uncertainty. Saul watched Isaac ask permission and place his hands on Ruby's knee.

"I, uh, don't really know what to say, but I sure would like to see Ruby's knee feel better." Isaac's head quickly snapped around and looked at Joseph.

"What is it, Isaac?"

"I—I think I felt something move!" Isaac said, his eyes growing wide.

"I felt it too," said Ruby, "like something moved back into place."

"That's so weird," stammered Isaac.

"Nah, that's so cool." Joseph shot back. "How does your knee feel, Ruby?" All watched as Ruby leaned forward, putting slight pressure on the knee. Then she did it again, as if stretching her calf muscle and stressing her knee even more. The moment was interrupted by Ruby's high-pitched exclamation.

"Oh my God!"

Saul knew well what the Bible taught about prayer and healing, only he didn't believe it on such a practical level as Joseph had displayed. Saul had prayed for hundreds of sick people, never really believing it would fix the problem. All Saul knew was to pray for comfort and ask God to help the doctor. He was fully unprepared for the scene unfolding before his eyes.

"Ch my god!" Ruby screamed again as she jumped to her left and lurched in a circle right on the soccer field. This was followed by a couple of cutting moves, pushing off on each leg sharply. Ruby began clapping and screaming and running around in front of the checkout counter. The BCC Coffee Shop appeared to have witnessed its first miracle.

"What happened?" asked Becky in seeming amazement while her friend bounced around the room.

"I don't know," Ruby exclaimed in the same high pitched voice. "He touched my knee and I… like, felt some heat and then I had no pain! Look, I can move." Ruby showed off a few more soccer moves as Joseph laughed. Isaac, on the other hand, was still down on one knee. Patty looked hopefully at Saul.

"What?" he said to his wife. She stared silently, her eyes wide until Ruby's moves led her face-to-face with Saul and Patty at their table.

"Pastor Saul, thank you," she said, giving the stunned man a big hug. "He told me things about my life and he prayed and my—my knee doesn't hurt anymore." The young woman was literally yelling in Saul's face as she pointed at Joseph.

"I could only limp on this when I came in—now look at me!" Saul sat dumbfounded as Ruby held her knee brace in her hand and continued to move around the room. He saw tears running down Patty's face.

"Maybe it's true," she said as she began to rummage through her purse and brought out a tissue. She wiped her eyes and kissed Saul on the cheek. "I'm with you, honey, whatever you need to do. But right now, I need to believe there's something divine that can help like this." Saul didn't speak as Patty told him she was going home. Patty might be touched by what the two of them had witnessed, but Saul hardened his heart and felt disdain for Joseph. He leaned back into his chair and crossed his arms, glaring at Joseph.

"Ch, thank you, Isaac," Saul heard Ruby exclaim. Isaac nodded and rose from his kneeling position. His height forced Ruby to stand on tiptoes as she reached to hug the stunned young man in a grateful embrace.

"Wasn't that amazing?" said a young man of college age. He looked up and noticed Saul staring at him, then quickly and silently hurried from the room. Saul watched some of the other young people cast pensive looks his way. Soon, only Saul, Joseph, and Isaac remained, as even the staff exited with Saul's assurance he would lock up.

"Joseph, whatever it is you have, I want it," Saul heard Isaac say as Saul approached. Isaac's face seemed to glow with his big, toothy smile, a smile Saul hadn't seen in a long time.

"This is not about what's in me, Isaac," Joseph said, putting his hand on Isaac's shoulder. "This is about you and the connection to heaven you've never known before. Live knowing you are seated in heavenly realms and see what amazing things can happen." Isaac thought to answer, but let his eyes drop to the floor as his father walked up.

"Your son is pretty cool, Saul," said Joseph, pointing a thumb at Isaac.

"Wow, I—I guess so," Saul responded awkwardly.

"You look troubled, Pastor Saul," he said with a gentle laugh. It struck Saul that this demeanor was what drew people to the bearded man. "There was a girl here in pain and our prayers brought God's power and took the pain away. So good, right?"

"Yes, of course, it is," Saul nervously chuckled. He couldn't help but let his curiosity leak. "What do you do to make people enjoy interacting with you as they do?"

"I love them," Joseph quickly answered, "with the love of heaven." Joseph gave Saul a pat on the shoulder as he headed for the door.

"Joseph," Saul called out, causing Joseph to stop his exit, even as his hand rested on the chrome exit bar on the door. "Why do you say, 'spirit of heaven' when you talk about God?" This caused Joseph's smile to dissolve into a serious look.

"With all due respect, Pastor, so many people have been hurt by the God portrayed by your religious sect," Joseph said softly. "Patriarchal authoritarianism was all people knew when the Bible was being written. And I truly believe God is more than some vengeful guy on a throne somewhere with two eyes, two ears and a nose. So why not make 'God' accessible to those hurt by their church by adjusting our language." Saul was perplexed.

"What if instead of being 'in the hands of an angry God'," Joseph said looking at the clock on the wall, "we are able to have true connection with the powerful love and goodness of heaven? It's all a human guess at mystical secrets."

"I'll stick with calling him 'God,' if it's all the same to you," said Saul.

"Fair enough. But my hope is for everyone to know there is no god who's mad at them," Joseph said with a wink. "Heaven is not even mad at you, Pastor Saul."

Saul's heart began to pump, and his ears reddened slightly as he fought to maintain control. Why did this guy get to him?

"By the way, Isaac," Joseph said, "your dad is more than you know." Joseph stepped onto the sidewalk, then leaned back in through the door. "And he's more than he knows, too."

Isaac followed Joseph out the door, grunting a goodbye to his father. Saul frowned as he pulled out his keys, locked up the coffee shop and moved through the side door to the staff parking lot. Saul's mind recounted furiously the moments of the day, his heart was steeled all the more as he drove home. Patty might want to believe in this Joseph, but Saul knew his task was to clean up Joseph's messiness and set everything in Bekering right again.

CHAPTER 12:
A PASTOR AND THE MAYOR

Springtime in Bekering was beautiful as winter lost its grip on the town. Located east of the intersection of U.S. Route 95 and State Highway 78, the Bekering Valley enjoyed a climate much different from the coastal areas of the state. Tucked between the Owyhee Mountain range and the Owyhee River on the east and Steen's Mountain on the Western ridge, the Valley had an endless amount of hunting and fishing to the north and south. This time of year, Bekering residents turned their thoughts to the outdoor life that drew many to the area.

Mayor Andy Strapp had driven into town on Route 95 and took the Volland Avenue exit just before Route 95 veered south towards California. Upon entering Bekering proper, Andy guided his tan Jeep Wagoneer onto Beatty drive, a road known to the locals as 'The Loop.' The Loop was thanks to Hal Beatty, who lobbied to avoid a costly railroad crossing at Volland and instead make a big semi-circle around the city before connecting to the crossing at Beatty and E Street. At the corner of this intersection, the Bekering Christian Center rose from the Valley floor.

The three large, golden crosses of BCC's parking lot greeted the mayor, and the colossal set of fountains with a spinning copper globe hung in the middle of the water. The building was covered by an ornate V-shaped roof hanging over crystal windows feeding sunshine into the church foyer.

Saul was drinking in the view from his third story office in the Beatty Administration Building on the BCC campus, resting his feet on his desk with his phone to his ear.

"Yes, Pastor, he was telling our young people all kinds of crazy things," said Saul, chatting with Pastor Abel Hackenworth. Saul pictured the large, elder pastor on the other end of the phone, likely seated at his office desk as well, his jacket off and shirt escaping his belt line.

"I heard there was perchance some sort of miracle healing?" Pastor Hackenworth inquired quietly to avoid being overheard by his staff.

"He prayed for a girl and she said she felt better," Saul answered with a shrug. "We ought not get carried away with some idea of miracles. We need to be more concerned about the false teaching he's bringing to our young people."

"Absolutely," answered Pastor Hackenworth. "It behooves us to devise an advisory for people to not be swayed by this man."

"I wholeheartedly agree, Pastor," said Saul as he wrestled against mimicking Pastor Hackenworth's Colonel Sanders speech pattern. Pastor Hackenworth spoke with a cadence of a spirited preacher, his vowels dragged out and an occasional extra "uh" sound at the end of sentences to emphasize his point. "The Bahble tells us-uh; to avoid a 'Charla-tan' such as this-uh," Pastor Hackenworth said, almost singing. "From whereabouts did this-uh mysterious man come?"

"I—well, I guess I don't really know." Saul stopped mid-speech, realizing he'd never asked. Joseph had simply told Saul he'd been drawn back to town. "I don't know, Pastor, but I'll have someone find out." The conversation was interrupted by the sound of Saul's assistant, speaking through the speaker system in his office phone.

"Mayor Strapp has arrived, he's in the reception area," the voice said.

"Pastor, I have to go," said Saul, his feet coming off his desk and hitting the floor.

"Welcome, Andy," Saul greeted his friend informally as he opened his large oak office door.

"Always a pleasure, Pastor Saul," the mayor responded, his southern drawl denoting his upbringing in a poor, rural area on the outskirts of Bekering. "People always treat me nicer here than at some of those city council meetings." The two men shared a laugh as Saul motioned Andy to the tan leather couch by the coffee table in Saul's cavernous office.

"Would you like some coffee, Mayor," said Christy, Saul's assistant. "Ma'am how about a good ol' glass of water," Andy answered, "and in any old glass. Nothing fancy for me."

Saul felt dwarfed by the hulking leader. Andy had a chiseled face and god-like wavy, blonde hair Saul thought was probably a little too long in the back for a man of Andy's position. Saul often felt for Andy, a young man constantly being pulled on by everyone, from party leaders to Bekering citizens. Andy owed his election to Bekering's conservative, evangelical community. They were a group of people who took great pride in their ability to see people from their own ranks elected, and also expected a lot from those afforded their loyalty.

"How're you doing, Andy?" asked Saul as Christy handed the mayor a glass of water and exited the office.

"Things are pretty crazy, Pastor," said Andy as he leaned forward on the couch. "I thought people'd appreciate me trying to help them. But these days everyone is mad as a possum caught in a hen house net."

"You know I'm always praying for you," Saul responded, tapping his foot to dislodge the tension he felt rolling off Andy. For a guy like Andy, who lived for the cheering crowd, this life was difficult to bear.

"Matthew McGinnis tells me not to worry about complainers," Andy answered. "He says keep punching the issues our people care about and I'll get to the state legislature, but..." Andy seemed to look through Saul more than at him.

"But you feel you actually want to help people," Saul completed the thought.

Saul knew Andy was sincere, although fairly new to the Christian faith. Andy held prayer meetings and Bible studies right in the Mayor's office, much to the consternation of the town's liberal wing. The prayer meetings were attended by Saul and some of the other elite members of BCC, as well as council members, city management staff, and others.

"Separation of church and state!" screamed the opponents, but Saul and his people enjoyed being in power and having a government lean towards Christian cultural causes. The prayer meetings were known as a place to gain influence with city officials. The opponents called it the "pray to play" method of getting projects green lit by the city. Those who might espouse wrong positions on social issues such as gay marriage or abortion were not welcome.

"Helping people is what got me into this," Andy confirmed, "that means serving the people, not taking care of Matthew and the party."

Andy ran his big right hand through his thick mane and leaned back.

"But the really important issues we care about are party issues," responded Saul.

"Does our party not care about potholes? And putting together a good city plan and budget that cares for people in all parts of the city?" Andy countered as he sat forward to grab his water glass. "Does God not care about those issues, Pastor?"

Saul stopped and folded his hands onto his knee.

"Andy, abortion and what our kids are learning in school, those are close to God's heart."

"But what about the poor folks? Seems to me Jesus cared about them," Andy pleaded. "Matthew jumps all over me anytime I want to do something for poor people—like the new bus system."

Saul remembered the meeting of the Evangelical Republicans of Bekering, which had taken place in the BCC Fellowship Hall.

"I want to inform all of you of our battle against another city spending bill," Matthew had told the group, bringing a groan throughout the room. "City bill 22 is supposed to upgrade public transportation in Bekering with this new-fangled bus. I think it will take money out of our pockets." Matthew had emphasized his conspiracy theory—the bus was part of the City's new zoning plan which, he argued, was aimed at making it impossible for builders to profit in Bekering.

"This could even open a Pandora's Box of liberal ideas to stop all growth in our town and to even take away our cars," Matthew had said with a loud fist pound on the lectern.

"Yeah, Matthew got a little crazy, didn't he," Saul said to Andy with a head shake and a laugh. Andy agreed but didn't laugh. "Matthew did make some good points about taxes. We need to keep our government small and focused on its primary job."

"Moving people around town is part of the job of city government. We haven't upgraded our public transit system in decades," Andy spoke in his slow country twang. "Heck, all Matthew does is holler 'taxes' and all his followers fall into line." Saul hadn't seen this side of Andy. He'd only known Andy to do as told by Matthew and the conservative leaders. "Not everyone in Bekering has a car," Andy said, waving his hand holding the glass, causing water to fly over the rim onto the carpet.

"My family used the bus to come into town when I was a kid." Andy dabbed at the spill on the carpet and drank the remaining water in the glass. "I'm awfully sorry to rile up in front of you, Pastor, but it's getting to me."

Andy's voice softened.

"You know a state official said to me last week, 'You Bekering people never let ignorance get in the way of having a strong opinion.' Matt gets all his folks riled up and lose all sense of reason. He'll use them to put the screws to me."

Saul wondered if Andy regretted running for office. Or regretted doing so as a Republican.

"What steams my hide is Matthew is perpetuating Bekering's history of keeping the poor in poor neighborhoods," Andy stated, "and to keep people who look different out of the rich white neighborhoods, as well."

"Now wait, Andy," argued Saul. "Let's not play the race card here, this is about money."

"Are you sure, Saul?" Andy sizzled, his eyes burning. "Matthew said he's worried the busses would bring 'those people' to Hal's shopping center. Exactly who are 'those people' to Matthew? And why is he worried about them coming?"

Saul stopped for a moment, letting Andy's statement sink in, but only for a moment.

"Andy, Hal and Matthew are good, Christian men," Saul responded as he stood and put his hands in his pockets. "We need the party to be strong for fighting God's battles in the courtrooms and at the ballot box. You need Matthew and the party to help your career. Think about the good you could do for the Lord in state government."

"I hear ya, Saul. I have to toe the party line." Saul was surprised to see Andy's eyes soften and fill with tears. "You know, Saul, I'm one of 'those people' Matthew is talking about." Andy studied the wall as he paused.

"Forgive me for sayin', Pastor. Matthew and Hal might be Christian men, but I'm not so sure they're good." Andy slapped his hands on his knees and stood from his and allowed Saul to lead him towards the door.

"Like I said, I'll be praying for you," Saul said weakly.

Saul knew "I'll pray for you" was really just a platitude Christians said when they had nothing else to offer. Saul didn't have the time or energy to deal with Andy's concerns, Saul had his own responsibility to the Christians of Bekering and to God's work in the city. He wasn't going to let his group fracture over some city busses and Andy's soft heart.

CHAPTER 13:
MEMORIES PACKED AWAY

The small engine built to roll back the soft top of Saul's BMW churned to life. Saul was headed from BCC to a radio interview and was happy for the fresh air. He punched up a Christian music playlist from his phone app and whistled along in an effort to free his mind. His plan failed, however, and the helplessness he felt for Andy mentally dragged Saul to some painful places. His humming stopped as the car drove on.

Saul found himself remembering a day many years ago when he, as a young boy, climbed into the old '67 Buick. Young Saul instantly knew something was wrong inside the family car.

"Hey, Sport!" said Saul's dad. Saul normally rode the bus home from school, but today his mom and dad were here to pick him up.

Ralph Thompson was Saul's hero. He worked as a manager in the local food production plant and, to Saul, his dad was the king of the world. Saul loved to go to his dad's plant, put on the hard hat, and walk around with him. Everyone respected his dad, calling him 'Mr. Thompson.' On this day, Saul's dad was unexpectedly there to meet his eight-year-old son at the sidewalk of Central Elementary School in Youngstown.

"What're you doing here?" Saul asked from the back seat.

"Oh, I'm happy to see my boy," Ralph said with a smile as he reached back to pat Saul on the knee. Saul slid into the middle of the back seat and looked at his mother. Dad could hide his pain, Mom couldn't.

"Mom, what's wrong?" He watched his mother wipe away moisture under her eyes.

"Nothing, honey." Saul stared at the back of the bench seat in front of him as the car pulled away from the school. It was an overcast Ohio day, and the sky seemed to reflect the car's atmosphere.

Home at the kitchen table, Saul's mother finally shared the news.

"Daddy lost his job," she said as she served Saul a sandwich. "We wanted to make sure and help you to not worry." Saul watch his father shift nervously in his chair as the trademark smile disappeared. For the first time ever, Saul spotted fear on his father's face.

"There are other jobs," Ralph said, giving Saul a wink and reaching to cover his wife's folded hands comfortingly.

Ralph was wrong.

Soon the household tightened their spending on food and entertainment. Then came the move from their house into an apartment. Soon after, a move to a new town, then four more new towns. Saul's young life never really knew rest again as his father searched for ways to provide for his family.

Often, during that time in his life, Saul knelt by his bed to pray.

"God, please send my family a miracle," he'd prayed. Saul's mom and dad weren't religious, but his uncle said God would answer sincere prayer. Saul thought his prayers sincere, yet his dad sank further into depression and into the vices that can go along with it.

"Don't you care, God?" Saul had prayed nightly, his body draped over his bed. No comfort came. Saul's father grew ever more disconnected and ever more violent. Ralph Thompson died at the young age of 63.

"Mostly of a broken heart," Saul would tell people. Saul worked hard, made good grades, and ultimately paid his way through college with scholarships. But he never fully recovered from that day in the backseat.

Saul's mind emerged back to the present as he continued to drive. Although Saul had pledged to never let his father's plight happen to him, the haunting of his father's plight to Saul back to another scene from his past.

"The Bible doesn't say, 'God helps those who help themselves,'" Saul's favorite seminary professor had once told him. "You're quoting Poor Richard's Almanac. The Bible commands us nearly two thousand times to seek justice for the poor, foreigner, the marginalized and the widow — which means those held back from access to the economic system. It's the one true test of our love for God throughout all of scripture."

"But the Bible does say, 'the man unwilling to work shall not eat,'" Saul responded. At the time, Saul dismissed the conversation as university political correctness. He was never going to be on the short end of helping God to help him.

Saul rubbed his face in the rearview mirror as if the act would rub away thoughts that had been packed away for decades. Saul had always been determined to leave them stowed in the recesses of his mind. He'd done well navigating life through all kinds of tricky situations, and Saul wasn't going to lose control now. Arriving at his destination, Saul stuffed the past in the past and planned to move forward with his day.

CHAPTER 14:
A RADIO SHOW AND A STRAW MAN

The vinyl backdrop on the outdoor dining patio of the North End Grill was big, maybe seven feet high and the same size wide, held up by a frame made of painted PVC pipe. It had a black background with bold orange and yellow colors in a mosaic behind the headshot photo of the radio host and the words "KBEK LIVE!" in large white letters, outlined in orange in the upper left corner.

"You've never seen my face so big, huh?" Dirk Rogers said to Saul, pointing at the gaudy promotion. Saul laughed as he ordered an iced tea from the waitress. Saul sat on a barstool situated behind the radio remote desk, set up on the northernmost wall of the patio. The desk had a red, metal desktop with silver metal, three-legged stands on each side holding the tabletop in place. On the front of the desk was a silver metal grill with the words "KBEK, We Have Bekering Talking" on the front. All these metal parts were manufactured to easily be assembled, disassembled, and carried from the remote location back to the radio station.

Dirk sat down onto the barstool next to Saul's. He was the host of the wildly popular eponymous talk radio show, the same time every weekday on KBEK AM.

"This is the setup," said Saul.

"Station finally spent some money to help me look professional on remotes," Dirk said with a crooked smile, adding, "cheap bastards."

KBEK was Bekering's local, conservative news talk radio station, the most listened to in eastern Oregon. "You'd think the company was flat broke to hear management talk. Keep driving up my sales quotas and cutting my commission percentage."

80

"You're the big draw on this thing, they ought to keep you happy, shouldn't they?" Saul asked. Dirk shrugged, his face pinched in a grimace.

"Guess they figure they could run twenty-four hours of national conservative blabber and save my salary. I tell ya, Saul, I've been in this business for over 30 years and since corporations have taken over, it's no fun anymore."

"Well, I'll bet Hal is paying a pretty penny to have you broadcasting out here today," Saul said looking around. "You've drawn a good crowd."

"He sure the hell is," Dirk answered, a devious smile sneaking onto his face. "This Greek boy needs to pay for his two divorces. Let's do this."

Saul knew Dirk had been forced by an old radio boss to use an on-air pseudonym as a young, rock station DJ, and the name Dirk Rogers had stuck. Dirk had given up his name for a radio career. Now he'd given up his long hair and hippie beliefs to serve as champion for the buttoned-up, well-to-do, conservative-minded audience.

"Show me a young man who's a conservative and I'll show you a man with no heart," Dirk liked to quote. "But show me an old man who's a liberal and I'll show you a man with no brain." This was how Dirk explained his dramatic transformation in his later years.

Saul and Dirk slipped on their black headphones for the show. Attached to one ear of each pair was a microphone with a black felt covering that extended in front of each man's mouth by a metal arm.

"Should a person be able to choose which bathroom they use?" Dirk chimed as the show's engineer back at the station slowly faded out the Dirk Rogers Show theme song. "Are our children in danger of men walking into the bathroom with young girls? When did we get this crazy? Talking about it today is our guest commentator, Saul Thompson."

Saul enjoyed his regular guest spots on Dirk's show. It gave Saul the powerful feeling he made a difference for God by shaping the opinion of people outside the walls of his church. The two dove into the topic of a proposed state law to allow people who identified as transgender to have their choice of public bathrooms. Each shared their shock and horror at the proposed law before Dirk invited listeners to call in with their opinions after a short commercial break.

"This is a real red-meat topic," Dirk said, smiling at Saul as each removed their headset for three minutes of commercials. "The type of thing that gets people really ticked off."

"It should get them upset, our legislators have lost their minds," Saul answered, his voice climbing high in his register as it tended to do when expressing strong concern. Saul recognized he was focused on issues and Dirk tended to be more concerned about the volume of callers a topic generated. Soon the break ended, and the engineer counted down the show's return through Dirk's headset.

"Our first caller is Al," said Dirk, his voice echoing through the back patio. "Go ahead, Al."

"Thanks, Dirk, love the show," said the caller. Al could be heard by the live audience at the restaurant through the speakers standing on poles on either side of Dirk's desk, and through Dirk's and Saul's headphones. "What if some guy puts on a dress with the plan to walk into the women's restroom and my wife and daughter are in there? I wouldn't feel very safe letting my family go to a public restroom if this law passes."

"Isn't that the truth, Al," Saul said into his microphone. "This law is literally putting our children in the firing line of pedophiles. The guy you're talking about could stand in the women's restroom and leer at the women and girls coming in."

"Yeah, crazy isn't it," echoed Dirk. He smiled at Saul, but quickly changed his expression as he noted Saul's seriousness. "Let's see... Elsa is the next caller. Elsa, go ahead." Saul immediately recognized the caller to be Elsa Kratt of The Love Coalition. She was a regular caller to this program, almost always bringing a dissenting opinion to the discussion.

"Boo," shouted a fan of the show sitting on the patio, recognizing Elsa's identity as well.

"Yeah, thanks for taking my call," Elsa's voice came through Saul's headset. "I think you guys are missing the point of the law and are creating straw men to scare people."

"OK," said Dirk. Saul could see from Dirk's crooked grin. The radio host was sensing something juicy for his audience. "Set us straight, Elsa."

"If anyone stands in a bathroom and leers at people, as the last caller suggested, that's already against the law. No matter what gender a person or in which bathroom." Elsa's voice was measured and calm. "Also, I think most people would say they're already cautious when they send their children to public restrooms, as pedophiles statistically are far more likely to be male in a men's restroom than a trans person in the opposite gendered restroom."

"Well, Elsa, I think you're the one setting up a straw man," Saul responded. "It's common sense men should use a men's restroom and women should use the women's. This law is ruling against basic common sense and the creation of humanity."

"Pastor Saul, the law is about dignity," said Elsa. Saul tugged at his collar as he listened. "Why should a transitioning person have to face the humiliation of going into a men's restroom wearing female attire? By the way, there are already transgendered and transitioning people using the other restroom and you're not even aware of it."

"We get your point, Elsa," Dirk jumped in, continuing to milk this moment, "but what would you say to a mother worried about her daughter having to face a man in the women's restroom?"

"Dirk, we already have moments where a dad has to take a young daughter into the men's restroom or a mom taking a son into hers," said Elsa. "The parent just covers the child's eyes and goes on in."

Dirk and Saul looked at each other, neither immediately jumping in with a response. Dirk nodded his head at Saul, encouraging Saul to answer. Saul looked back, eyes widening. He was unsure what to say.

"Hello?" Elsa was heard through the speakers. "Am I still on?" Elsa's question brought a smattering of nervous laughter through the patio crowd. Finally, Dirk jumped in.

"Yes, Elsa, you're still on. Go ahead." Dirk shrugged his shoulders at Saul.

"If Caitlyn Jenner walked into Pastor Saul's church in an elegant dress, would he make her use the men's restroom?" Elsa continued, using the famous trans celebrity to emphasize her point. "Wouldn't that make everyone even more uncomfortable?"

Saul looked around as Elsa's question caused a murmur in the patio.

"And if Caitlyn used the women's restroom, would the little girls in there really be in danger?" The two hosts stared each other down. Dirk eyes showed he was adamant that Saul respond.

"Uh, Elsa," Saul finally jumped in, the silence becoming awkward, "we have to error on the side of caution when it comes to our children. You liberals say you care about people, but aren't willing to protect the youngest, most vulnerable people there are."

"I doubt Caitlyn will be coming to the Bekering Christian Center anytime soon," Dirk jumped in, not allowing Elsa a chance to respond. "Thanks for the call, Elsa." Dirk looked at the computer screen in front of him for the name of the next caller. The computer was connected to the station where the show producer would take the calls, put them on hold, and then send the name of the caller to Dirk.

"Agnes, you're next," Dirk spoke into the microphone. "Hi, Agnes."

"Oh, what a horrible woman. I'm glad you put that liberal in her place, Pastor Saul," said an elderly woman. Her voice was low and gravelly, and she punctuated each word in an angry tone. "Liberals like her are always against common sense. We all know God created only two genders, there's no third choice."

"Amen, Agnes," said Saul, giving a big smile to the live audience. "How many of you here think men in a dress should be allowed in a girl's restroom?" Boos rang out from the crowd.

"Yep, Dirk was right—red meat," Saul conceded as Dirk interacted with the next caller. Saul surveyed the patio and froze when he saw Joseph to the right of the KBEK display desk, cleaning a vacated patio table. Saul quickly shifted to look away from the mysterious man and pretended not to see when Joseph gave a smile and a wave.

"What do you think, Saul?" asked Dirk. Saul hadn't heard the question and paused like a deer caught in the headlights.

"Uh, well, Dirk it's obvious to me how serious people are in wanting to fundamentally change our culture." Saul had no idea what the question was but Dirk seemed to like the answer. Saul poked the table with his finger for emphasis. "If good people don't stand up right away, we will lose the Judeo-Christian heritage of our country."

"I'll keep fighting the good fight, and so will this audience. Call your representative today, everyone," said Dirk, wrapping up the segment. "Don't forget to come see us at the North End Grill until two. If you come in the next hour, you can have the KBEK special of the day—a juicy T-bone steak. Wow, is my mouth watering..."

Saul was always impressed with Dirk's ability to turn from the angst of the day to offering specials on everything from cars to backyard furniture to fine dining. There was no one better in Bekering at compelling people to purchase products he endorsed.

As commercials and the top-of-the-hour newsbreak filled the airwaves, Dirk and Saul removed their headsets and addressed the live crowd.

"Anyone here have a question for Pastor Saul?"

"I do," said Joseph as he loaded the last of the dishes and flatware from the table into his plastic black box used to bus tables. Joseph pulled the top of his apron over his head, letting it hang at his waist as he wiped his brow. His black T-shirt displayed the logo of the movie "Straight Outta Compton." The logo had been altered to say, "Straight Outta Heaven."

"It seems you feel life was much better in America's past," Joseph stated in his calm voice, with a smile so genuine it put everyone at ease. Everyone but Saul. "Isn't it true, though, in America's past a man could freely abuse his wife and people wouldn't get involved? Wouldn't a black person have had to use a different bathroom than a white person? Are you sure fighting for the country as it was decades ago is the best goal?"

"Well, there were bad things, but they were certainly simpler times," Saul answered, adjusting his tie. "I'd say it was a more family oriented time in this country." Saul watched as Joseph slowly nodded his head and his measured gaze dropped, as if looking at Saul would cause him to respond in a less-than-gentle manner.

"Would you say life was more simple in those days for the wife whose husband abused her while her neighbors and family said, 'it's none of our business?'" Joseph finally said in a soft voice as his eyes zeroed back in on Saul. "Or the young, effeminate boy who was teased and beaten by other boys on the playground for being 'different'?" Saul wanted to look away. Joseph's eyes were gentle but had a knowing behind them that made Saul squirm deep inside.

"Well, uh, those things might have been true at times..." Saul finally broke their stare and looked at Dirk. Saul grinned to hide his discomfort but with such a sideways awkwardness that it was easy to identify his struggle to respond. Saul finally straightened in his seat and summoned a matter-of-fact voice. "Joseph, we were a godlier nation then." Saul watched the heads flip back and forth between him and Joseph like it was a tennis match. All eyes were now on Joseph, anxiously awaiting his next volley.

"Godlie…" The smile faded from Joseph's face. He seemed incredulous at Saul's response.

"There's … l now that didn't exist fifty years ago," Saul increased his volume to … d more assertive. "If good people are afraid to see it, or stand up against i… il will win."

A simp… ile returned to Joseph's lips, neutralizing Saul's aggression.

"You're … vonderful proctologist of the world, Saul." The audience laughed at … ph's statement, causing Saul to feel a bit of irritation as he looked at … rmerly friendly faces now enjoying his opponent seemingly gaining the … er hand in their discussion.

"What … heck does that mean?"

"Two … were discussing the human body," Joseph responded, casually seating him… on the edge of the table he'd been cleaning. His eased posture reminded S… of watching Joseph share his Good Samaritan story with the young peop… the BCC Coffee Shop.

"One … said how disgusting the human body was, full of things that cause diseas… he other said the human body was beautiful, with amazing structure o… uld study for hours. Do you know the difference in the two men, Pastor … l?"

"I'm sur… ou're going to tell me," Saul snapped despite his attempt to hide his irr… orkings from those viewing the exchange.

"One … was a proctologist, the other a painter."

"Oh, I g… t," a woman said to her friend at a nearby table, echoing the sounds arou… the patio. Saul understood it, too, and his smile faded.

"So, I'm … proctologist, you say?"

"You loo… t the worst of the world and say, 'we have to stop this,'" Joseph explained. "… ow heaven to let love and goodness flow through me and I get to see t e go… in the world and say, 'how do we get more of this?' In a search for evil we … make ourselves blind to evidence of good."

With t at, … he busboy picked up his box and held it against his hip as he gave the t l… one last cleaning wipe with the towel pulled from his back pocket.

"What … ou see as 'good,' Joseph?" Saul said, now displaying his ugly displeasure. … l heard Dirk whisper in his microphone for the engineer to add a few c… ercials to the break. Dirk apparently wanted to hear what was coming nex…

"Did you know there is less illiteracy in the world today than ever in human history?" Joseph stated as he stopped and turned back towards Saul. "There's less death from childhood illnesses worldwide because vaccines are more accessible than ever. There're more people living at middle class economic levels worldwide while extreme hunger and extreme could be extinguished from our planet our lifetime — if authoritarians didn't stand in the way."

Joseph leaned towards Saul from ten feet away.

"Pastor Saul, don't you think those things would please your God as much as a group of people putting on ties and nice dresses and going to church on Sunday?" Saul leaned back against his barstool and sighed.

"Yes, of course those are good things," he said, the loud, aggressive tone now deflated from the conversation. "I think there's plenty bad going on in the world today…"

"Oh, there's no question of that, Pastor Saul," Joseph interrupted, now speaking stronger, faster. "There's a whole population right here in Bekering literally dying for some help and Father is ready for the people in His churches to open their eyes and see those people. We'll have to step out of ideological and political boxes, though. Otherwise we give ourselves the excuse to not care."

Dirk gave a light whistle sounding like a bomb dropping and said, "Boom" at the end of Joseph's rant. Dirk replaced his headset and turned up the volume on the speakers to continue his show.

Saul's eyes burned. He jumped up from behind the desk and approached the reason behind his fury.

"Joseph, you know the Bible says, 'the poor will always be with us.'" Saul suddenly felt empowered again, drawing from his tool belt of regular cultural arguments. "This is a good town of good people. Everywhere I go, I tell people we're a small town with wonderful people…"

"You live in a small town, Pastor Saul!" Joseph shot back, his smile gone and his busboy box making a loud crashing sound as he dropped it on the table in front of him. "There are one hundred and twenty-thousand people in Bekering, Pastor. Heaven would like for you to care about all of them, not only those in your circle and those who share your beliefs. And certainly not only those who live and work on the north end."

Saul's advance was stopped dead in his tracks by Joseph's aggressive retort, and in that instant, the war of words was over. The two stood motionless for a moment before Joseph finally bent down to pick up a fork that had rattled onto the floor during his outburst.

"Joseph," Saul spoke up in one last, feeble effort to save face. "Don't be naive. Some of us have to fight the evil in the world." Joseph reversed himself slowly, holding his load of dirty dishes and flatware to his side, the same serious look on his face.

"Saul, if a child falls into a canal, who's the better person: the one teaching everyone how wrong it is to play around a canal? Or the person who pulls the poor child from the water?" Joseph pointed at Saul. "Don't let your need to be right take away the heart you have for loving people."

Joseph walked into the kitchen, leaving behind the stunned, silent crowd. Saul felt the need to break the tension.

"Well, you can never accuse us of being boring," he said with a feeble smile. Several people nodded and some went back to their food to avoid looking at Saul's embarrassment. Saul waved to Dirk and headed towards the patio exit, nearly running down Mayor Strapp who'd just entered for his radio interview.

"You alright, Pastor?" Andy asked, grabbing Saul by the elbows to make sure he didn't lose his balance.

"Yeah, of course," Saul mumbled, quickly brushing past the stunned mayor. Saul hit the silver bar that opened the exit door on the patio fence, ironically noting the mechanism's name: "panic bar." It served such a purpose now. Saul needed to escape as quickly as possible.

"Who is Joseph to call me out?" he thought as he leaned against the outside wall and yanked to loosen the knot on his tie. Saul, again, felt deeply offended by Joseph. It was time to hatch a plan to turn the tables on this stranger.

CHAPTER 15:
THE RADIO HOST

"Thanks to all of you for listening in to this edition of the Dirk Rogers Show." Dirk pressed the button shutting off the microphones on the red Comrex Remote Broadcast Unit which sat on the desk in front of him. He thanked Mayor Strapp for joining him as Andy stepped aside to take a call and shake a few hands around the room.

The radio station was airing the "KBEK Top of the Hour News and Information" break as Dirk began the process of unplugging the mics and headphones to pack up and take his remote back to the station. Dirk noticed the busboy, Joseph, coming his way.

"Mr. Rogers, I presume," Joseph said with a chuckle as he held out his hand across the desk. Dirk observed Joseph was no longer wearing his apron and had changed into a clean T-shirt. It was light blue and said, "Heaven Loves You and There's Nothing You Can Do About It!"

"Call me Dirk," the radio host said, noting the man's firm handshake. "After hearing what you with Pastor Saul, maybe I should have you on my show."

Dirk noticed Joseph's hesitation.

"What? You don't like my show?" Dirk questioned as he rolled up a headset cord and gently set the headset in its storage case.

"Oh, I think you're absolutely fantastic at what you do," said Joseph, his smile returning. "What an amazing gift you have." Joseph stopped for a moment and Dirk sensed he was choosing his words carefully.

"I know you believe you're doing your best, but I'm not sure it's in alignment with heaven."

"What? You think God is unhappy with me?" Dirk asked with a befuddled tone as he pointed skyward. "Why would God not like my show? Does he even care?"

"Oh, what you do reverberates through heaven. The divine spirit cares a lot," Joseph insisted. "The media is always going to play a major role in the mindset of a community."

Dirk stopped in his process of packing his equipment and viewed the dark-haired man. Dirk loved to create good conflict for entertainment. He was not nearly as open to honest discussion around his personal and professional life. He thought of telling Joseph to preach his message somewhere else.

"When you come to your job every day, how do you decide which topics to discuss?" Joseph asked.

"We talk about 'the most important issues of the day,'" Dirk responded in his best radio voice, sharing the station's motto heard in recorded liners.

"Really?" Joseph's tone struck Dirk as a reporter trying to coax the real story from an interviewee. "There's no story in the world today more important than the bathroom story you discussed with Pastor Saul?"

"Well… " Dirk's response hung in the air for a moment. "I'm sure there might be something more important, but…"

"But you choose reactionary topics, right?" Joseph answered his own question. "Your job requires people to emote, so they'll call or come down here. I understand—you have a job to do."

"It's not so simple," Dirk wrestled back. "I want to talk about what people are talking about."

"You need a reaction, and what better way to get people to call than to make them angry and feeling victimized. True?"

"Well, that's not really fair." Dirk was set for a fight but found Joseph completely disarming. The man seemed so sure of who he was. Somehow, it made Joseph less threatening. Dirk went back to winding up a microphone cord.

"Dirk, in the world there are 'thermometers' and there are 'thermostats,'" Joseph shared. "Do you know the difference?"

"I guess a thermometer checks the temperature?"

"And the thermostat changes it," Joseph exclaimed. "You, Antonin Alexandrou, were created to be a thermostat." Dirk's head popped up like he'd just been startled by the loud pop of a firecracker. He squinted as he processed what he'd heard.

"How'd you know my real name?" Dirk asked, his forehead crinkled with curiosity. "Did you find that online?"

"I hear things from heaven sometimes so people can know they're known," Joseph answered, his words drifting through Dirk's ears but didn't land in a way Dirk could understand.

"I'm divinely inspired to know you're a defender of men, and that's amazing." Dirk had frozen in his efforts to stow away his gear and stared blankly at Joseph. He became aware Andy Strapp had come back to table.

"Now, that's weird," Dirk said, turning to Andy.

"What's weird?" Mayor Strapp asked. Dirk felt a shiver run up his spine.

"I looked up the genealogy of my name a few years ago. It came from two words: 'Alexin' which means 'to defend' and 'Andros' which means 'men' or 'humanity.' My name means 'defender of men,' and that's what this guy just said." Dirk nodded towards Joseph and dropped the cable he was holding into a plastic storage box on the floor.

"You're kiddin'," said Andy.

"I always thought my name's meaning was cool but knew other people would find it campy, so I've never told anyone." Dirk could feel something stirring in his heart. Suddenly, this man standing in front of him was more than a simple busboy.

"In the Bible, names were tied to a person's identity and purpose," Joseph said gently. "Your name, Antonin, speaks to your life's purpose and your role here in your radio job." Dirk wasn't one to cry. He joked his way through every emotional experience of life. But now he felt an almost unstoppable wave of emotion.

"That's crazy. How can I be a defender of men?"

"By refusing to be a peddler of fear and anger on the radio," Joseph's look turned serious. "You have power in your voice to impact Bekering with darkness or light. I believe looking for real truth on difference-making issues will fulfill your purpose of defending the people of Bekering."

Dirk hesitated to answer. Deep in thought, his finger touched his lips. Dirk always thought himself a talented showman. But he'd wondered if he could be more than just entertainment.

"I--uh," he stammered. "I guess I honestly do feel like some cheap, daytime TV host sometimes, but the company demands I get ratings."

"Why don't you try something different and see what happens?" Joseph said, continuing to hold Dirk in his direct gaze. "Try it and see if doing the right thing, even in the face of uncertainty, doesn't bring some reward. At very least, you'll sleep better at night." Dirk looked Joseph over, amused, then turned to Andy.

"This guy is unbelievable," said Dirk. Andy shrugged his shoulders and smiled as if he was as intrigued, yet as clueless as Dirk as to what was happening.

Dirk's mind shuttled back to his early days in radio, when he was a young man with passion. A protestor against the status quo. This mystery man was reminding him of a stowed away inner-longing to be the young hippie who cared deeply about important things happening around him.

"Who are you?" Dirk asked, his voice quivering along with his bottom lip. Joseph smiled gently.

"Someone brought by providence to clean tables on this patio today, so I could share our purpose with you." Joseph tipped his head and headed back into the restaurant.

"I--uh," Dirk looked away as tears spilled from his eyes. His cheeks reddened as he looked again at Andy. "Sorry, Andy. It's not often I get like this." Dirk felt relieved as Andy smiled and gave him a pat on the back with his big hand.

"Some kinda' guy, huh?" Andy said.

In his career, Dirk had met every type of celebrity and important person. From famous singers and dancers to Presidents of the United States, Dirk had seen them all. But he had to admit, he'd never met anyone like Joseph.

CHAPTER 16:
FISHING FOR ANSWERS

Isaac and Joseph exited Isaac's Subaru and extracted the fishing gear from the car's hatchback.

"Now this is heaven on earth," said Joseph as he tossed his baited hook into the small pond just outside the Bekering city limits, a popular spot for local anglers. Joseph's bait, hook, and line landed in the water with a quiet splop as he relaxed in his folding fishing chair with a built-in rod holder. It was clear to Isaac this wasn't Joseph's first time fishing.

"Get your hook in the water, we have to show these others out here how to fish!" Joseph smiled, clearly happy to have Isaac alongside, which made Isaac feel more at ease, even as he struggled to bait his hook.

"So?" Joseph said, finally reaching for Isaac's line to demonstrate proper baiting technique.

"So, what?" Isaac asked as he finally got his line in the water and imitated the way Joseph turned the reel on his fishing rod several times to keep any nearby fish enticed.

"I'm sitting here. Ask your questions." Isaac relaxed as the breeze blew through his long mane. Joseph seemed to know Isaac had come with an agenda.

"How can the things you say be true?" Isaac finally blurted out. "Almost everyone I know disagrees with you." Joseph smiled and pulled a cooling towel from his backpack and laid it across the back of his neck.

"Throughout history, how often has the mob been right?" Joseph responded as he fed his line into the water. "Just because a people group have all bought into the same echo chamber narrative, it doesn't make that narrative true."

Joseph suddenly yanked his pole upward.

"Oh dang, I had that thing!" Joseph brought his line in for the next cast as he continued to share with his younger friend. "Perhaps shutting out the noise from your life for a bit might help you tune in to heavenly wisdom and know what is good and right."

"Doesn't the Bible tell us what is good and right?" Isaac asked. Joseph rubbed his chin for a moment in thought.

"You love your mother, right, Isaac?" Isaac gave a slow, confused nod.

"What if there was a book written about your mom's whole life?" Joseph used his left hand, which was not holding the pole, to mime the act of turning pages in a book. "Here's a chapter on her childhood. Here's another chapter on her favorite times as your mother and another on the dishes she most likes to cook. Her whole life is in this book."

Joseph held the imaginary book aloft, the smile fading from his face.

"What if you read this book, but never talked to your mom?" Isaac fidgeted, running his hand back and forth across his lips. "You wouldn't really know your mom's heart or character. The book would give you great topics for discussion, but you can really only know your mom through actual relationship with heaven and with other people." Isaac watched Joseph's pole bend gently for a moment as a fish tested the bait on the other end.

"You know there was a guy named Saul in the Bible who knew more about scripture than anyone," said Joseph. "yet, he really didn't know the true character of divine love. So, he came to the very wrong conclusion that the vengeful God he'd grown up with would certainly want him to kill Christians. You can be very strong in your Bible reading and very weak in your Bible understanding."

"My Dad's name is Saul," Isaac laughed.

"Mmmm Hmmm," Joseph responded simply, his gaze flicking out of the corner of his eyes and mouth twisting in a wry smile.

"The way to know what is good and right, according to the Bible," Joseph said in a quick shift back to his line of thought, "is to avoid being conformed to your community narrative and to be transformed by the never ending renewing of your mind."

"Isaac, I'm trying to help you think for yourself," said Joseph with another cast of his line. "I'm not the one to tell you that your dad is wrong. I'm encouraging you to partner with heaven to find the answers already inside you."

"I don't know what's inside me," Isaac exclaimed, jumping to his feet and tossing his pole to the ground. He watched some kids playing in the water across the pond as he jammed his hands in his pockets deeply feeling his frustration.

"Oh, but you do. Right now you're trying out the bait, like that fish," Joseph smiled, pointing at his bobbing line. "At some point you have to risk taking a bite and trusting the love and goodness of heaven to help you walk it out."

Joseph gave his pole another slight tug.

"Take racism, for example," Joseph started again. "Kids aren't racist. We're all born with a love for all people. But once taught that people of other skin town are somehow not 'us,' then it takes a lot of humility and work to unlearn those exclusive mindsets. Religious people are the worst at it because they believe God gives them permission to be racist, misogynistic, and nationalistic. Those unhealthy ways of self preservation become difficult to unwind. And in that mindset, the fear people have of other people becomes a powerful tool for manipulation in politics, conspiracy theories — you name it."

Suddenly, Joseph put his finger to his lips, requesting momentary silence. But the kids made a big splash and broke out in laughter.

"Oh, dang it," Joseph exclaimed, "those kids scared away my fish." He frowned hard and reeled in the line. "I promise you I will catch something today!"

The two men continued to cast their lines and reel them in, still awaiting the first catch. Isaac continued to ponder their conversation and decided to take it to a more literal level.

"What about gay marriage?" he asked.

"What does your heart say?" Joseph answered the question with a question.

"I guess I think gay people who'd like to marry... are just people. Maybe it's not so horrible." Isaac paused. He sat on the ground. Not having a chair like Joseph's, he leaned back placing his free hand behind him to ease the stress on his back. He looked again at Joseph. "Isn't it good to pass laws to keep people from sinning?"

"Ok, let me finish this with a story," said Joseph, taking a peek at his watch.

There was a young college student who'd started his first semester living a bit of a wild life. His studies suffered as he enjoyed his first time away from home.

As the semester progressed, the student realized his grades were poor and he became worried he wasn't going to pass a particular class. A failing grade would mean he'd lose his scholarship and no longer be able to attend college. The young man tried to do better, but when it became obvious he wasn't going to make up his deficit, he simply gave up and stopped attending the class.

With only a few weeks left in the semester, the student decided he'd go to the professor of that class with a made up story in hopes the professor would take pity on him.

As the young man shared his fake story, it was clear the professor wasn't buying it. The young student was losing hope and stopped. The professor gave him a sympathetic look and began to speak.

"You're a good student, even if you don't display it at times," the professor began. "I want you to pass my class. I'm going to promise you an 'A' at the end of this semester." The student looked at the professor in shock, and then his head dropped.

"But I don't deserve that grade," said the student.

"I know you haven't earned that grade, but earning and deserving are two different things." The student looked at the professor with amazement and gratitude.

"I believe in you," the kind professor added, "and I believe if I do this for you, you will become the student I know you to be."

For the rest of the semester the grateful student never missed that professor's class and did, in fact, go on to become a very good student, graduating with honors.

Isaac saw Joseph studying his face.

"So, it was the professor's grace that brought out the best in the student," Isaac answered Joseph's unasked question, "not making him follow rules?"

"Exactly," said Joseph, casting out his line once again.

"But the student didn't deserve the A." Isaac cast his own line back into the water. "Isn't it unfair to the other students who did the work and attended the class all semester?"

"The professor is the only true judge of the appropriate grade for each student," Joseph answered, locking eyes with Isaac. "The other student's grades aren't impacted at all by the grace the professor gave to this student. But the student in the story had his entire life changed by this one act of mercy." Joseph looked out across the darkening red sky.

"Imagine how big heaven's love is for humanity. People may not always earn divine love and goodness, but they always deserve it because each one of us is inherently valuable in the universe."

"When we know this, we can share divine love and grace with others," Joseph added, "and one act of love and grace can change people far more than any rule or law ever could." Isaac nodded in understanding.

"You know, I've always thought it would be good if the Christian community stopped fighting legal battles over gay marriage and LGBTQ+ issues," Isaac shared. "Would the queer community be able to hear more of what we have to share about God if we stopped our fight and reached out in love, acceptance and understanding?" Suddenly Isaac's pole bent harshly.

"Hey, I got something!" Isaac exclaimed, tugging on his fishing pole. Joseph jumped to his feet excitedly shouting orders to Isaac. Isaac tugged and reeled and followed instructions from his more experienced friend, and soon Isaac landed the biggest fish of his life.

"Well, well, look who made the catch of the day!" Joseph laughed, hugging his friend as Isaac held the fish aloft. The two snapped pictures of the fish and released it back into the pond before they packed up and headed for home.

"You're quiet," Joseph prodded as they drove in silence. Isaac looked at him with a grim smile and pulled up his shirt sleeve to show Joseph his tattoo.

"I got this to encourage myself to risk exactly as you say," Isaac said with a deep sigh. "But to do that, I have to leave a lot of old stuff behind."

"Like Neo in the Matrix movies," chuckled Joseph. "It's uncomfortable to realize the truth you've always known isn't the whole truth. Do you wish you could settle back into the bliss of ignorance?"

"Guess that's what I'm trying to figure out," Isaac replied as the car arrived back in the only hometown Isaac had ever known.

CHAPTER 17:
A GALA EVENT

Saul and Patty stepped from their car and were immediately greeted by a bevy of friends and acquaintances. Patty returned the greetings but pulled back to Saul him as Matthew McGinnis approached.

"Hey, Saul," said Matthew, with a punch on Saul's shoulder, "you clean up good."

Patty had dusted off the tuxedo Saul generally wore only for this and other rare occasions. He did look good, Patty thought. She knew, however, Matthew's compliment was more of his usual backhanded humor towards her husband.

Patty picked a piece of lint off Saul's shoulder before receiving a gratuitous hug from an overly friendly Sandy, Matthew's wife.

"You look absolutely ravishing, Patty," said Sandy as she mashed their faces together.

Saul had complimented Patty on her appearance as they were preparing to leave the house, and Patty had to admit she did feel quite pretty in her black silk dress and the modest jewelry purchased at Bennigan's Jewelry, where they received a clergy discount. Patty knew Saul's income from leading of a mega-church and his radio fame brought in enough to afford better, but Patty had learned to keep the visuals of their circumstances muted in front of the offerings givers of BCC. In a world where the Bible said God looked at inward appearance, Patty found it very ironic the outward meant so much to their church people.

"Matthew, it's good to see you," Saul said, patting the party leader on the arm.

"Wouldn't miss the biggest party of the year!" Matthew chortled. He began to greet others in the crowd. Patty angled her face to Saul and bulged her eyes to show this was a process she suffered through rather than enjoyed. He gave a knowing smile.

"Thanks for your sacrifice, Pattz."

Patty's attention moved to the front of the museum. It was colorfully decorated and brightly lit with huge canned lights. Those lights could be seen from a great distance in every direction. Matthew was right about the event. The Bekering Historical Museum and Art Gallery Annual Fundraiser was the one event each year that drew almost everyone.

Patty and Saul knew the drill: the wealthy and influential would come and make their black-tie appearance, would be recognized for their donations (most lower than was let on, Patty surmised), and then would leave at an appropriate time. The less well-heeled would come dressed in business casual, ready to enjoy a great party. It would be a night of dancing and frivolity in the atmosphere of art and history in this underfunded, yet well-preserved, historical venue. From the best Christians to the worst sinners, it was a night to be out on the town.

"Oh God, here he comes," said Patty as they entered the museum and Hal Beatty approached with a Scotch in his left hand.

"Nice penguin suit, Pastor," Hal said, his face a bit too close to Saul's. Patty watched Saul nod to Hal's wife, Betty, who was dressed to impress.

"Nice fur," said Saul pointing to Betty's stole.

"Kopenhagen fur, most expensive on the market," said Hal, leaning in for a stage whisper. "Thing set me back seven hundred and fifty bucks."

"Wow," Saul exclaimed. Patty saw him steal a knowing look at her. "What a blessing from God."

"Or a blessing from Beatty Development," Hal said in a mocking tone, speaking out of the corner of his mouth. "Betty, take Patty for a libation. The men need to talk business." Hal took a swig of Scotch and motioned towards the bar with his glass as a sign to his wife. Patty sighed through the pasted-on smile she wore.

"Come on, Betty Beatty," Patty joked at her friend's unfortunate married name, "let's leave the smart men to do their thing."

"Get me a Coke to go with yours, please, hon," said Saul. Patty knew this was Saul's way of suggesting she go non-alcoholic tonight.

Patty felt patronized by her husband and disregarded by Hal, despite being well acquainted with the gender discrimination still celebrated in

Christian circles. She was an Ohio State honors graduate with a business degree and was every bit as brilliant as Hal. She simply had chosen motherhood and serving as a pastor's wife over the corporate world.

"Wine spritzer for me," said Betty to the bartender as the two women squeezed to the bar. "And for you, Patty dear?"

"Coke, please." Patty met Betty's fake smile with one of her own. The two women chit-chatted for only a few moments before Betty whisked off to mingle with other friends, leaving Patty at the bar alone.

"Why don't you put a little rum in it, as well," she said handing her glass to the bartender, "and keep that between you and me."

Patty wasn't wired to be a pastor's wife. Her mother was a fiercely independent woman who had coached Patty to never need a man to make her way in life. Patty's father was an Easter-and-Christmas Catholic, which would have been Patty's religious story had she not been dragged by a friend to a life-changing high school youth camp.

The people at the camp talked about God as if he was real, not some statue figurine, and Patty became enamored with the idea of knowing God in a more real way. Today, this was still the longing of Patty's heart, even as she'd become disenchanted with so much in the Evangelical church.

It was true Patty would only date young men who attended her college Methodist church, and that's where she met Saul, who swept her off her feet with his good looks, great hair, and attractive swagger. When Saul decided to go into pastoral ministry, Patty put her career goals aside and became his supportive wife.

"What a mistake," she said to herself, looking at the bottom of her empty glass. Sliding it towards the bartender she asked for a refill.

Patty had pain from the loss of a child, but just as painful was the loss of the husband she had known and loved so much. Saul's heart for God had been changed by his constant exposure to the Evangelical life. His efforts to build and grow his church and his constant delving into politics hardened Saul and made him constantly disappointed and angry. Oh, he still loved her well enough, she simply didn't like the man she saw now as much as the one she had married. Patty always hoped the first Saul would reappear someday.

"Hey, Mom, you look great," said Isaac, approaching Patty with Joseph beside him. She thought her son so handsome wearing his hair long tonight and dressed in a tan dress shirt and brown khaki pants. Isaac leaned in and gave her a kiss on the cheek.

"I hope you have mints tonight," he whispered in her ear. Patty covered her mouth.

"It's only one little rum and Coke, Isaac," she whispered as she grabbed her purse. Finding a breath mint, she discreetly placed it in her mouth.

"Mom, I don't know if you've met Joseph," said Isaac with a smile.

"No, but I did see you at the BCC Coffee Shop last Sunday," she answered as Joseph shook her hand. Patty noted his attire of blue jeans and a white T-shirt paired with the black bow tie. The shirt said, "The Religious Right is Religiously Wrong!" Patty realized she'd tilted her head and closed one eye as she checked out his less-than-formal wear for the evening. Becoming aware of this, she straightened up, nearly teetering backwards from such a sharp adjustment of her posture.

"I've heard a lot about you," she said as Joseph continued to hold her hand to help her maintain balance on the bar stool. "You surely attract people's attention."

"You have a really awesome son. I'm very impressed with him," said Joseph, nodding his head towards Isaac. "And a really great husband, too."

Patty stared at him for a moment. She was stunned again at how non-threatening he appeared to be.

"Well, my husband speaks well of you, too," she lied, unable to stifle a slight laugh.

"I'm sure he does." Joseph joined in her laugh, giving a slight bow. Soon, Isaac excused himself while Joseph stayed back to order a beer.

"You're not afraid to drink beer in front of this crowd?" Patty asked, giving a wave of her glass towards the room.

"The Bible doesn't prohibit alcohol, just says to do so in moderation," he smiled. Patty looked down and placed her glass on the bar. Joseph may be as ordinary as she had assessed, but the way he looked at her was definitely not.

"What?" she finally asked under his gaze.

"I believe the amazing things Isaac will do in his life are going to make up for all you've lost," he said simply as he pulled his wallet from his pocket and paid for his drink. Patty's eyes grew glassy, as if tears had been waiting beneath the surface. Joseph hoisted his oversized mug of beer and took a drink. Foam clung to his mustache, making Patty laugh through her burgeoning tears.

Joseph wiped his mouth with a gentle smile.

"You've endured some difficult things as a mother and a wife," he said. Patty nodded and picked up her drink for a sip before turning towards the bar and looking into the mirror behind the bottles and kegs.

"And there was one lost." Joseph put his mug down and leaned forward on his seat to meet her eyes in the mirror. Tears escaped her lower eyelids.

"Patty, there's awareness in the heavens of how hard it's been. The time for healing is coming." Patty dabbed her eyes, again checking herself in the bartender's mirror.

"I can't do this here," she said, "not now."

"I understand." Joseph picked up his drink with a grin. "I'm so hopeful what your household is to go through will bring out the best in all of you. Your sacrifices will be worth it."

Patty patted Joseph's hand as he saluted her with his beer before walking back across the room. The ice clinked in her glass as she struggled to bring it to her lips and take a long sip.

"I need one more," Patty said to the bartender. She wheeled on her barstool and faced the room. Joseph definitely had a gift for pinpointing people's needs. If he could tell her where she needed to be healed, perhaps he would know how such healing might occur.

"More help than I can get at my church," Patty said out loud as she drained her refreshed drink. She looked through the bottom of her glass in time to see her husband's disapproving look.

CHAPTER 18:
BEKERING, WE HAVE A PROBLEM

Saul might have disapproved of Patty's behavior, but he knew that paled in comparison to the disapproval she had for the circle of men with him. Saul knew she hated the pull these people had on him, and their impact on both their lives.

"Andy, we're not going to have a problem, are we?" Hal asked the mayor while giving Saul a nudge to stop him from staring across the room and bring him back to the conversation. The group included the mayor, Ted Freeman, and Matthew McGinnis.

"I'm saying we need a little more thought on this, fellas" Andy responded. Andy's posture exposed his inner discomfort. He was almost leaning away from Hal, his face etched with awkward discomfort that didn't befit a man of his physical stature.

"Sounds like we may have a problem, don't you think, Matt" Hal motioned towards Matthew before tilting his head back and emptying his glass.

"Andy knows how this works, don't you, Andy?" Matthew responded. "We all pray together every week for the city. You got elected to stand up against liberals who want to stop our city's progress."

"You guys can pray, my New City project is real action." Hal extended his index finger from the empty glass in his hand and lightly poked Andy in the chest. "If you're not on board with the annexation, Andy, we're gonna have an issue." Andy instinctively batted away Hal's hand like a martial arts master and took a step towards the older man.

"Gentlemen, stop this," Saul jumped in. "We're all brothers here." Saul spotted the waiter and handed him his empty Coke glass and hoped ordering refills could de-escalate the conversation. It didn't.

"A man who messes with my business is not my brother," Hal said, his yellowing teeth displayed in a sneer. Hal took another swig and glared at Andy, seemingly ready to advance again until Matthew pushed Hal aside.

"Andy will do what we need him to do," Matthew insisted in a low voice aimed at Hal. "Relax, don't do this here in public."

"Guys, it might not be up to me," Andy answered standing behind the two men and holding his hands up. "The council's not going to pass it anyway."

"You let me handle the city council," Hal flipped around and shot back, Matthew was still holding him in restraint. "You can override them. So get ready to do what we elected you to do."

"Hal, that's enough," Matthew scolded.

Saul got involved this time as Andy stepped forward aggressively towards Hal. Saul's strength didn't match the hulking mayor, so he was relieved his mere presence caused Andy to pause his advance. Saul took Andy by the shoulder and guided him away from Hal.

"Hal's had too much to drink," Saul whispered.

"This is gettin' to me, Saul," Andy lamented. "I don't know how much more I can take of these fellas thinking they own me."

"Andy, you don't want this fight," Saul retorted. "Not with Matthew and Hal, at least not here in public." With a reluctant nod, Andy acquiesced and headed toward the bar.

"Guys, this is a party," Saul said turning back to the group and holding up his hand to acknowledge the grand venue. "Can't we enjoy the moment?"

A shrill of feedback came over the speakers on the temporary stage constructed in the large marble foyer. Elsa Kratt stepped to the microphone to kick off the evening's program. Her short hair had been professionally styled and she wore a business suit befitting her role as MC for the evening.

"Ch Gee, his woman," Saul heard Hal mumble beside him.

"Welcome everyone to this very special night," said Elsa with a wave of her hands. Saul pulled Hal towards him as the circle of men fanned out. Matthew leaned in to hear the conversation.

"Hal, I didn't want to do this in front of Andy. You told the city council that this New City land was to be a farm."

Saul remembered Hal's statement during the battle for approval of the North Bekering Shopping Center development. Hal assured the council the land he owned north of the shopping center development was to serve as a farm, despite the opposition's insistence Hal intended to sprawl the city even farther to the north. Hal had convinced the council with a heart-tugging tale about fulfilling his father's life-long dream.

"Whose side are you on, Pastor?" said Hal, his mouth barely moving as he gritted his teeth. Saul grimaced as he felt his chest tighten and his breathing grow shallow. He didn't like being bullied by Hal and Matthew any more than Andy. "If Andy gets loose in his support, the damn Observer's gonna be all over this."

"I hate that damn newspaper," said Matthew, crossing his arms. "Michael Brookes is the king of fake news."

"Brookes can be pesky, guys, but he has integrity," Saul answered, keeping his voice low.

"Anybody else you want to defend, Pastor?" snapped Hal. "Maybe Isis or North Korea? Matthew, you need to make Andy understand the importance of sticking together. And let him know there's consequences if he doesn't."

Hal was unflinching and clearly unwilling to answer Saul's question about the farm. Saul looked again to check on Patty at the bar and remembered she had told him ten years ago Hal was lying about the farmland.

"Hal has great morals right up to the point where it might cost him three dollars and fifty cents," she'd told Saul. Saul smiled at the memory. He realized how smart his wife really was and how uncomfortable he was in being entangled in Hal's ongoing actions.

"I have an idea," said Matthew, "let's grab the mayor on Sunday at church and bring Evan Brown in and talk this through."

"Good idea. We'll pull them into your office, Saul," Hal agreed. "And I'll get Council Member Duarte to come, too."

"Evan Brown? The council president?" Saul questioned, his voice rising almost an octave. "Guys, that's illegal."

"...Our Gold Sponsor for tonight," Elsa announced, the program proceeding on the stage, "Mr. and Mrs. Hal Beatty."

Saul and Matthew stopped their discussion to clap politely as Hal met Betty in front of the stage and the two went up to receive their clear, acrylic plaque of honor from "that woman." Elsa reached to shake Hal's hand only to see him give her a wave as he walked away. Saul and Matthew smiled as Hal rejoined them. He immediately jumped back into the conversation.

"Saul, you need to remember what's important here," Hal said, leaning in close enough for Saul to smell the liquor on his breath. "This project means a lot of money to me and my company. When it goes through, it will mean a big donation for the new kid's building you want." Saul knew he should be offended at Hal's attempt to buy him off, but he'd given a pass to Hal so many times before. What could he do now?

"But no meeting in my office, guys," Saul responded, trying to take a stand. "I don't want the church to be involved with anything illegal."

"C'mon Saul, this is big boy politics here," Matthew said. As Saul looked at Matthew's cheesy political grin, he was struck at Matthew's ability to think of this as a big game. "This isn't the race for junior high class president."

Saul forced himself to take a breath. The FBI had run a sting operation in town a few years back and Hal was one of several developers arrested after being recorded offering bribes to public officials for votes. Hal had avoided prison only by a legal technicality worked by his highly paid attorneys. The city followed the incident by passing a law prohibiting contact between a city official and any representative of a company with business on an upcoming city council meeting agenda.

"You have to break a few eggs to make an omelet," said Matthew. "The other side is fighting a war; we have to fight one, too."

"Lose our soul, but gain the world, huh, Matthew?" Saul answered back in a weaker voice than he'd hoped. A darkness Saul had never seen crossed Hal's face. A chill ran up Saul's spine like a cold wind had blown through. Saul was sure Hal was about to threaten him had the moment not been interrupted by the dimming museum lights. Saul frowned as he considered the "consequences" to which Hal had referred if Saul or Andy were ever to do the right thing and stand up to these men.

CHAPTER 19:
BEKERING'S PAST AND FUTURE

"Over eighty years ago, Adam Elder saw the need for Bekering's history to be preserved and he set out to be its preserver," Elsa read from her script, motioning towards a screen temporarily attached to the wall behind her. The screen came alive with a video about the museum's original benefactor. "Please let me introduce you to a great man, Adam Elder."

Patty sidled up behind Saul and wrapped her arm around his waist and laid her chin on his shoulder. Saul could smell the rum on her breath but kept his thoughts to himself as they watched the video together. The music rose from the museum speakers and the screen filled with black and white photos sharing this story of Bekering's history.

"...Mr. Elder tragically lost his wife and daughter when their cruise ship went down in the Pacific Ocean," stated the deep bass of the video's recorded voice. Saul watched with interest as the video zoomed in on a picture of Elder's face. This was a piece of history unfamiliar to him. "With no survivors in his lineage, Elder poured his money into Bekering's charitable causes, building the city's first convention center, baseball stadium, and of course, its museum, later enlarged to add an art gallery."

Saul couldn't help but think Adam Elder looked like Gomez Addams from the television show "The Addams Family."

"Here's a man who was visionary," Elsa shared at video's end. "He put his money into an endowment fund still benefiting a generation of people Mr. Elder would never meet." Elsa ended the program for the night and moved into the crowd where people were mixing. She ended up face-to-face with Hal.

"Thank you for your generosity to help make this wonderful night possible, Mr. Beatty," Elsa said, again offering her hand to Hal. Hal looked down at her hand for a moment before finally reaching and returning the handshake.

"Um, yes. Thank you for the honor," Hal said with a lightly hidden scowl. Hal's morals might have been malleable when it came to finance, but on social issues, he was unwavering. "Honestly, though, Ms. Kratt, I could think of many other things for Mr. Elder to do with his money than a museum."

Saul cringed. He saw Hal wobble a bit as he continued to shake Elsa's hand. Elsa looked to Saul as if he could help her assess Hal's statement as serious or light-hearted. She offered Hal a pleasant smile before moving on to shake hands with Patty. Hal, however, wasn't finished.

"What the town really needed was a dam and a good highway." Hal laughed. Saul watched Elsa stop in her tracks. She seemed torn by the thought she should let it go as simply a drunk man's rambling. And a benefactor at that.

"What a waste of money," Hal said even louder, making sure those close by could hear, "and we're still wasting it even tonight."

If Elsa had thought to walk away, Hal's prodding took away that option.

"Are you really standing here in this museum telling me Adam Elder should have spent his money drying up our river rather than preserving our history?"

"Oh, don't get all steamed, Missus, er, Mizz Kratt." Hal nudged Saul on the arm. "I mean, you make it sound like something evil, but you don't understand the economics of a city."

"Sir, I'm a Harvard graduate," Elsa responded with an exasperated gasp. "Oh, forget it." She hesitated before once again moving on from Hal. Saul could see Hal's smug grin of a man feeling victorious.

"That's right, Ms. Kratt, let's keep our perspective," Hal said, grinning to those nearby. "I mean, we're talking about people's hard-earned money here."

"Without your dad's money and heaven's blessing you'd have nothing." The taunt came from behind Hal, who looked over his shoulder to see Joseph jumping into the conversation.

"What the hell do you have to say about it?" Hal spat at Joseph, his speech slurring a bit. Hal seemed to realize he'd cursed in front of people and lowered his voice and tone. "I have nothing to say to you."

Joseph grabbed Hal's arm and wouldn't let him walk away. Saul had become familiar with Joseph's easy smile, but now that face was stern and cold.

"You've been given a gift from past generation so you can pass them on to future ones," Joseph said through gritted teeth. "Because of your selfishness, you'll be forgotten soon after you depart this earth."

Several people gasped as the group of listeners grew. Saul looked around and saw the silent shock on their faces. Nobody spoke to Hal Beatty like this.

"You claim to be self made when it was your father's seed money that gave you a head start of those you claim to be lazy and on the take from government assistance," Joseph droned, not even blinking in this stare down. "You think you're doing well with your money, but actually you're completely blind as to how heaven measures success."

"Heaven? You mean God, right?" Hal growled. "What'dya think you are, some kind of mystic, peace-pipe smoker?"

"Some of don't need mood altering substances to be connected to any god or others people," Joseph answered, pointing at the drink in Hal's hand. This caused another buzz in the crowd.

"You..." Saul watched as Joseph pointed at the older man and then dropped his hand to his side and turned to look in the opposite direction from Hal. It was an act of exasperation that told Saul Joseph had a particular angst towards people like Hal.

"You call the spirit of heaven 'God' because you want a figurehead far off somewhere that you can manipulate through dogma and bad Bible interpretation," Joseph was speaking more loudly and in short, staccato bursts. "You use your god as weapon but make sure he never interferes in your business."

Joseph turned his torso squarely towards the well-dressed developer.

"People who truly love God want to share that love with others.'" Hal's eyebrows shot upwards as he processed what he'd just heard. His face showed the response of a bully struggling with the reality that someone was standing up to him.

"I've been a Christian longer than you've been alive," Hal answered somewhat meekly. "Y-You should be careful who you judge." This caused Joseph's countenance to lighten a bit.

"I'm not your judge," Joseph answered with a slight grin, "heaven is, and we can all see that heaven declares you a 'Hezekiah.'" While Joseph's tone had softened, Saul could see his eyes were locked onto Hal, who seemed to be looking around for support. Joseph's expression was that of an interrogator playing 'good cop' in an effort to get a confession from a perpetrator.

"Heza-what-uh?" responded Hal.

"A long-term Christian like you doesn't know the story of Hezekiah?" Joseph mocked the older man. "Hezekiah was a king who deserved to be punished, but God said he would punish future generations for his sins rather than punish Hezekiah." Saul looked around. The crowd encircling them had grown to around fifty people.

"Hezekiah was supposed to benefit future generations. Your generation is doing likewise."

Hal gave a whimpering scoff, turning his head, seeming to search for any sympathy he had.

"Tell me our national debt being laid upon your children's children," Joseph continued. "Your generation seems very content to give that debt to future generations, rather than an inheritance."

"How'd that make me a Hezekiah," Hal shot back.

"You're a manifestation the sin of a selfish generation," Joseph responded, again pointing his finger menacingly at Hal. He moved in closer, his smile fading. "You care only about your short-term gain without a thought to the impact you're having on future Bekering generations."

Joseph and Hal stood silent for a moment until Joseph finally broke his gaze and looked around the room. This reprieve from Joseph's icy stare gave Hal a moment to try and collect some dignity.

"I'm not going to stand here and be insulted anymore," Hal snarled as he tugged on the bottom of his suit coat to straighten it. "Let's get out of here and get some dinner, Saul."

Saul guessed and found Patty right behind him. He saw her smiling, clearly enjoying Hal getting publicly called out. Saul took her by the arm, helping to steady his tipsy wife as they joined a group of people moving toward the exit doors. Slowed by the two-door bottleneck, Saul was in the room long enough to hear Joseph's final declaration.

"The Bible says to lay up treasures in heaven, not on earth," Joseph shouted. "You were given an amazing country of roads and schools and bridges and railroads, yet this generation has built virtually nothing to benefit their children and still run up a massive debt and have done little to care for the earth or the infrastructure. These actions will not be forgotten in eternity."

Hal spun on his heels, nearly knocking Saul over.

"You keep talking, Junior!" Hal spotted Elsa to his right. "Good day to you, Ms. Kratt. There'll not be another check written to this place."

Hal brusquely grabbed Saul by the bicep, pulling him towards the door and away from Patty.

"What're we gonna do about that son of a... about that guy," Hal asked, pointing his thumb over his shoulder.

"Some pastors and I have been discussing a plan," Saul answered, relieved to finally have a conversation where his goals were aligned with Hal's.

"I'll get my men investigating him right away," Hal snorted. "We're gonna make him pay."

CHAPTER 20:
THE OTHER SIDE OF THE RELIGIOUS WAR

Elsa walked into the event room at the back of the museum. She had changed from formal attire to her more relaxed, normal dress of a white V-neck T-shirt and faded blue jeans with the knees cut open. The Mighty Mississippis, a jazz band that regularly headlined at The Leaky Drink, was now playing for the post-party entertainment. The Leaky Drink was Elsa's favorite Downtown Bekering Jazz Club. In fact, The Leaky Drink was the only jazz club in Bekering and truly the only place for live music, other than the city's churches on Sunday morning. Elsa entered the room snapping her fingers with the music.

She noticed Joseph sitting alone, nursing a beer. He looked up at her and waved her over.

"I think I owe you an apology for my earlier outburst," said Joseph as he stood to greet her.

"Oh, no apology necessary," she responded. "It was SO worth it to see the shock on Hal Beatty's face." She gave a huge smile as she sat in the chair opposite him and let out a heavy breath. She was relieved the hard part of the evening was over and the blue bloods had gone home.

"Then again, my days on the museum board may be over," she laughed.

"Well, the least I can do is buy you a drink," Joseph responded with a laugh of his own. Elsa had a husky build and had always been a head taller than most her age. This often made her the butt of painful jokes on the elementary school playground. Her early life was very difficult due to discomfort of understanding she was different and the shame she felt knowing her family church disapproved of the physical and emotional attractions she just couldn't shake. Now grown up she enjoyed more freedom, but those childhood moments still left their mark.

"You've made quite an impact here in Bekering," Joseph said in a voice loud enough to be heard over the music.

"When I went to college, I vowed I'd never be back," she shared as she ordered a Vodka drink from the waiter. Elsa guarded access to her personal life. She rarely told of how, at Harvard, discovering herself and discovering others like her had literally saved her life — just in the nick of time.

A summer visit back home quickly reminded Becky of how different Bekering was from Cambridge, Mass. That difference drew her back. She didn't want other Bekering kids considered "different" to barely survive their hometown.

"This town has a way of calling you back." She looked thoughtfully across the beautiful museum event room, with ornate high ceilings and sculpted walls. The kind of room modern culture could never seem to replicate. "I guess I want to see it redeemed somehow."

Elsa eyed the man across the table. Her family had generally avoided the church and Christians over the past few years. The fact that Joseph would even sit alone with Elsa made her more intrigued to have a conversation with him.

"Here's a crazy idea," Joseph responded, his lip curling playfully. "Let's dance." Elsa laughed nervously.

"You serious?" she said, surprised to find herself a bit bashful. "What the hell. I knew I took those swing dance classes last summer for some reason."

"I've been known to do a Boogie-Woogie or an East Coast Swing myself," Joseph shot back.

The two joined several other couples in front of the stage. Elsa was shocked at Joseph's expertise and sheer joy in dancing. He was clearly a man who enjoyed life, not like other church people she knew.

"I'm sorry for your church experience." Joseph shouted so she could hear as they danced together. Elsa saw the sincerity in his eyes and in the upturn of his cheeks. It was the same, soft, sympathetic look Elsa had witnessed as he spoke to Becky at the North End Grill. "The Bible never teaches its followers to be this judgmental."

"That's a message our wonderful, local Christian community needs to hear," Elsa shouted back as Joseph took her hand and spun her around. The two laughed and clapped as the song came to an end.

"You have a lot to say about the Christians here in Bekering," Joseph huffed, trying to catch his breath from the movement on the dance floor. "Do you think your community is in need of a little heart-check, too?" Elsa thought those twinkling eyes were piercing as she prepared to answer, yet he still seemed as gentle as could be.

"What are you trying to say?" she answered. He smiled as the next song kicked in and they began to dance again.

"What your side of all these political arguments is failing to realize is you're sometimes similar to the other side," he leaned in and spoke towards Elsa's ear to be heard. "We all like to win and be powerful."

"Like the Religious Right?" Elsa answered back in a loud voice, her brow creasing in puzzlement as they continued to swing with the music. As they joined hands and came together for a moment, she added, "They're judgmental and exclusive. We try to love everyone!"

"Do you love them," Joseph challenged, stepping back and clapping with the beat. Elsa stopped dancing and looked at Joseph, incredulous.

"The 'Churchies' are so set in their ways," she argued. "You can't talk reasonably with someone who gets their rules from... from, God!"

"Have you ever tried?" Joseph took hold of her hands to entice her to continue the dance, but Elsa stood firm in frustration. Joseph finally stopped moving, as well.

"I'm not saying you have to endorse their actions or even forgive them. But I do always say, Elsa, religion kills the dead and the survivors." Joseph motioned her to the table and grabbed his mug and emptied it as they sat back down. "You're in a war against one another and either side has the chance to call itself religiously right... er... correct. Your side can be religiously fervent, too. It's impossible for two sides to have healthy interaction when you're in a winner-take-all battle."

"We're not fighting a war. They are," she said, pounding her finger into the table. "We're fighting for people's right to live their lives."

"But doesn't your side have some power now, too?" Joseph quickly answered back. "Haven't you won your battles in the courts and in culture? The question is will your side handle power any better than they have, or be as religious and zealous about your beliefs as they are." Elsa looked at him, tight-lipped.

"Let me explain with a story," he said.

There was a man who owned a very large farm, and he passed away. His two workers, who'd operated the farm for years, were called to hear the reading of his will.

"The farm is to be divided and each of you are receiving a parcel," said the trustee of the will. The two men were very excited at the generosity of the old man and gave each other a hug and a pat on the back. Each was ready to build his own farm after working as employees for so long.

As the parcels were laid out, it was realized the younger man had a received the great majority of the farm while the older worker had received only a small remnant. This caused the older worker to be very jealous and upset. The younger worker held a party and celebrated his good fortune with his friends. He didn't invite the older worker.

One day, the trustee showed up at the farmland and called the two men together.

"There's been a mistake," he said, "the parcels were accidentally switched." The larger portion belonged to the older worker, the trustee stated, while the younger man would have the smaller one.

Well, this obviously did not sit well with the younger worker, but the older one took full advantage. He enjoyed superior farming profits and even began to undercut the price of the younger man to drive him out of business.

The situation became dire for the younger worker and he began to react inappropriately. He started a fire in the older worker's fields, destroying a big portion of the older man's crops. Then he destroyed the older man's water pumps, causing several other fields to dry up.

Knowing it was the younger man who caused these problems, the older worker called the police to prosecute and obtained a writ of order from the court to stop the younger man from harvesting any crops until all this disorder was sorted out. Soon, both farms had ceased production and the deceased farmer's beautiful land was falling into disrepair.

Upon hearing about the situation, the trustee again called the men together, this time before the court. He had a proposal. The trustee told the judge he knew the old man loved each of his workers equally and it must have been some mistake by the surveyor that caused the parcels to be divided unever[...] trustee suggested a re-survey of the land so the boundaries could [...] with equal portions for each worker.

The ju[...] agreed to the plan and to drop all matters before the court, on one co[...] The two men had to work together for one year to make sure both fa[...] equally successful and rebuilt for the future.

Jos[...]y ended, and he leaned back in his chair.

"C[...]ry," Elsa laughed and took another drink as Joseph watched.

"I get th[...] point you're trying to make," she finally answered his stare. She was a l[...]yed as she put down her drink. "You're trying to say people with p[...]wer could save a lot of grief by reaching out to those with less power.

"A[...] don't," Joseph jumped in, "those with less power are going to react a[...] and it's going to be bad for everyone. The Bible does say, 'blessed a[...] peacemakers.'"

"C[...] must not read the Bible then because they are definitely not 'peacemakers[...]

"C[...] have marginalized themselves in culture because they truly believe the[...]ighting for truth," Joseph stated. "They don't realize the God of their Bib[...] early prefers those who fight for people, but if your side lives by the [...] self-righteousness, you too will fall by it."

"That's [...]shit, Joseph!" she exclaimed, slamming her drink so ferociously on the table [...]t half of the liquid spilled over the top, down her hand, and onto the [...] wood.

"W[...] w me, here," Joseph responded, holding his hands up in mock surrender. "[...] not the enemy." Elsa nodded as she began to wipe up her mess with a [...]pkin.

"The [...]onmentalist, for example," he began to explain, turning his empty mu[...] a circle absentmindedly. "They have a history of a righteous cause. Chr[...]s ignore climate change because of their theology and political beliefs, ever[...]ugh those beliefs differed with the commands of the Bible. So, heaven [...]ed the environmentalists and their cause, even though many might not [...] have a spiritual belief. Someone needed to care for the planet and receive [...]lessing available to those who did."

"H[...]" Elsa mumbled, unsure of where Joseph was going with this. Both s[...] or a moment as the waiter brought each another drink and used a wet [...]l to clean up Elsa's mess.

"OK, that's clean," Joseph said nodding towards the table. "Now let me see if I can clean up my point." Elsa couldn't help but smile. She found this man fascinating and somehow... safe. She wanted to know what was coming next, even as she anticipated her disagreement.

"As the balance of power began to tip in the favor of the environmentalists," Joseph continued, "they could no longer be satisfied with trying to win sensible arguments. It became a zero-sum game. That's the nature of religious division in human beings." Joseph paused to sip his refilled mug.

"Development and building always became the enemy. There could be no reasonable discussion. Every lizard, bird, and you-name-it became a weapon. If we're all honest with each other, it quite often isn't about saving the lizards for the environmentalist today as much as it is about maintaining power and punishing any opponents."

Elsa stared at him and he seemed to pause for a moment, gauging her response before he continued.

"I could say the same for unions and other groups. Your side isn't immune to being the self-righteous religious ones. Intolerant of anyone who disagrees with your position." He leaned forward to punctuate the end of his explanation.

"I'm calling 'bullshit' again on this, Joseph." Elsa shifted sideways in her chair as the music suddenly stopped and she looked around to see who might have overheard her language. After a long moment of silence, she adjusted back towards him.

"That's BS," she said with greater control.

"If it's BS, then why would people on your side want to destroy a family's cake business for not serving a cake at a same-sex wedding?"

"They refused a cake because the customers were gay!" Tears welled up in Elsa's eyes. "All they wanted was a cake for their special day and the religious bastards wouldn't do it because of their stupid religion. That's always their excuse for their bigoted behavior."

"I understand, I would have told them to just make the cake and love the couple," said Joseph, now looking directly at Elsa with a serious stare.

"Elsa, you wouldn't make a Kosher Jewish restaurateur serve non-kosher food. Or an African-American caterer to serve at a White Supremacist event. Would you?" Elsa looked up as the band announced it was taking a break and Elsa looked back to see Joseph studying her again. "Religion says, 'we have to punish these cake makers to pay for the sins of a generation.' Like the farmers in the story, that only works as long as you hold the power. And it sets up the other side to feel victimized with no hope but to try and steal the power back by any means necessary."

Joseph stopped and Elsa watched him pick up his mug as if to take another drink, but he set the mug down before it reached his lips.

"I know they've hurt you, Elsa Emile," Joseph said, looking at her with the same fatherly look he had shown Becky. Elsa couldn't stop herself from closing her eyes and taking a big breath.

"What just happened?" he asked.

"You said my middle name. That name has always made me feel special. Not many other things in my childhood did." As Elsa shared, her eyes stared far away, at a memory seen only by her. "My mother chose that name for me."

"Heaven loves that name, too," Joseph said. "Your name speaks of the mercy you have for others and your pastor's heart for them."

"Pastor? Me?" Elsa snickered at the thought.

"'Pastor' means 'shepherd,'" Joseph explained. "A pastor is someone who gathers and tends to the needs of others. I've watched you. You are a great pastor to your people. But some of that pastoring heart comes out of your own pain." Elsa sat back in her chair for a moment and looked down at her drink. She decided, again, Joseph was someone with whom she could share.

"Listen, I'm a big girl. I've always been able to take it." Elsa tried to look at Joseph but then looked again at the table.

"It's..." Elsa struggled. "It's crazy to have sweet, elderly women come up to me and tell me I'm going to hell." Elsa felt a tear escape the corner of her eye and quickly dabbed at it with the wet napkin in her hand. Finally, her face grew stern as she leaned forward with her hands against the table and looked Joseph in the eye.

"Saul Thompson? Hal Beatty?" she exclaimed. "Who the hell are they to tell me what I am and what everyone should believe? Pious sons of bitches is what they are." Elsa looked up at Joseph as the tears began to overflow the bottoms of her eyes. Her stomach churned. Continuing on would mean she would not be able to constrain her emotions. Finally, she breathed another deep sigh.

"I don't know why this is messing me up," she said, trying to smile at him while fighting back tears. "You have a way of doing this to people, don't you?"

"Heaven wants you to be free from the pain," he answered gently.

"Right - those God-people tell me God hates me!"

"Do you believe God hates you?" The question knocked Elsa from her train of thought. "If he doesn't hate you then it doesn't matter what they think."

"I really don't know. I... well, does he? You seem to be connected to something... up there."

"You can have that connection, too," Joseph shared. "The greek word 'sozo,' which is translated as 'saved' or 'healed' in the Bible, really means to be completely reconciled to heaven — knowing ones true value in the eyes of the divine. Today can be a day of solo for you — of really knowing your beautiful and powerful identity."

"But..." Elsa averted her eyes to look again at the ceiling. As she studied its patterns, she soon noticed Joseph had been silent for some time as she sorted through her thoughts. "The Church says my identity is an abomination?"

Just then, the band reintroduced themselves and started playing again. Joseph leaned in closely.

"And again I say it doesn't matter what they think, it matters what you think," Joseph smiled from his forward leaning posture and gave her a look of great anticipation. "And you can ask heaven for spiritual wisdom to know the truth of your identity. Do you want to hear that wisdom from heaven?"

"What? Now?" Elsa looked around the room with an amused, half-smile. She almost expected a camera from some silly reality show to pop out from hiding. "I can't talk to... God with jazz music playing."

"Of course you can," Joseph laughed, nodding and pointing towards the band. "I happen to know heaven loves jazz. Particularly this band." Joseph's humor gave Elsa the chance to laugh even as she clasped her eyelids closed to continue her battle against the tears trying to fight their way from her eyes.

"You make this stuff all sound so real," she said, dabbing a napkin under one eye and then the other. She sat her napkin on the table and studied the face of her new friend. "How does it happen, I pray or something? Or maybe a seance?"

"Now you're making fun of me," he responded wrinkling his smiling face.

"Sorry." Elsa thought how nice to be able to joke in this moment.

"Just let your thoughts soar and ask whatever you want to know," Joseph encouraged her. "You don't even need to say, 'thee' or 'thou.'"

Both sat silent for a moment. Elsa wasn't sure what to do.

"Try this: ask your heart. 'Was I alone on the playground when kids called me bad names?'"

Elsa felt the surreal nature of the moment. She understood mindfulness, but this was something much more concrete than just feeling a sense of peace. She closed her eyes for just a moment.

"What'd you hear?" Joseph interrupted. Elsa was about to protest when she felt a shiver run down her spine.

"Weird," she stammered. "Somehow, in some dimension of the universe, I feel this amazing, pure love."

Joseph smiled a warmth-producing smile which encouraged Elsa to go on.

"I also had a high school teacher come to mind," Elsa said, shaking her head and breaking a bit of a smile as she stared down at the table. "Strange, the picture popped into my head from nowhere. That teacher, Mr. Tally, I haven't thought of him in years. He was so kind. He told me I was a great person and inspired me to dream big." Now the tears came in force and she tried in vain to halt their advance with her saturated paper napkin.

"I don't know if I'd have survived without encouragement like that," she cried fully now. Joseph handed her the napkin from under his mug and she covered her face.

"Do you think a connection to heaven brought this memory to you?" Joseph asked. Elsa nodded without uncovering her eyes. "That's how it works, then."

Elsa was pondering what had just occurred when she heard laughter from people chatting at the next table. The private woman realized how public this display of emotion was.

"I better go freshen up," she said, rising from her chair. "I don't want to look like crap the rest of the night."

"A new life journey has begun for you," Joseph said, looking up at her from his seat. "Let me encourage you to connect to others on the same journey. I can connect you to Pastor Christian Anderson, I promise you he's safe." Elsa breathed in again to collect herself and smiled at Joseph.

"We'll see."

"Oh, one more thing," Joseph suddenly shouted out, grabbing Elsa's hand as she started to pass by his seat. "Be kind to Pastor Saul."

Joseph released her hand and scratched his black beard.

"I know he hasn't always been kind to you, but he really is a man with good in him. He's gonna need friends."

"You're gonna need friends, Joseph," she said with a serious look.

"Heaven never promised me Bekering'd be easy. I made that bargain," he said with a light grimace "I worry, though, Saul's about to be hit in ways he never bargained for."

CHAPTER 21:
THE STRESS OF BEING MAYOR

"Guys, like I've told you, this proposal may not go through." Andy Strapp spoke into his black Bluetooth even as he lay prone on the weight bench machine preparing to hoist a rather impressive amount of weight. Andy was sure the men on the other end of the conference call could hear clanking weight, elliptical machines, and loud music at the North Bekering Fitness Center but he wasn't worried about it. On stressful days, this gym often became Andy's work space.

"Andy, I can't stress enough how important your proper handling of this will mean to our future," said Matthew McGinnis on the other end of the call. Matthew had instigated the conference call with Andy and Hal. "We need your support to push the council members forward. They're getting a little skittish."

Andy shook his head and rolled his eyes knowing the men on the phone couldn't see him. This was just another in a long series of conversations Andy had to endure on Hal's pet project.

During their last conversation, at Bible study, Andy remembered staring at the large map of Bekering on his office wall. The map already showed the patchwork of a city with decades of poor planning. After his election, Andy had dived into learning about good planning practices for a city and was eager to try and implement those ideas in Bekering. Good planning was not valued in Bekering's history, and this was a big cause of the city's issues today.

"Your project is miles beyond the... oh, what's that term they used?" said Andy, scratching his sweaty head. "Beyond the sphere of influence. It's outside the city's sphere of influence, Matt."

"The shopping center was, too," Hal jumped in, "and look at how that's turned out for the city. Those boundaries are nothing but paper put together by bureaucrats. They don't mean anything in the real world." Andy knew Hal regularly touted his developments as benefitting the city. Andy was somewhat sure everyone on the phone, however, knew better. Only two months ago, Andy brought in a national authority on the subject of city planning and had invited the council members and various leaders, including the two men on the phone right now, to receive expert insight.

"Development, like you have in Bekering, is a Ponzi scheme," said the consultant. "You can only pay the cost of one development by taking the sales tax from the next development. Should the sales cycle ever slows down, your city will be on the verge of bankruptcy, as you were in the last housing bust." Andy had looked around the room and viewed the sullen and angry expressions from his Bible study friends.

"In my research on Bekering," the expert continued, "the property taxes from new housing developments don't cover the long-term costs of the services the city has to provide to take care of them," the expert stated, "like water, sewer, police, and fire. And the city is on the hook for those costs in perpetuity." Andy had hoped truly expert insight would overcome any ideological bias and push the group towards good solutions. So far, that hadn't been the outcome.

"The shopping center is a real beautiful thing, Hal," Andy tried to flatter his antagonistic acquaintance as he sat up on the bench, "but you and I both know a lot of people have beef with it, as well. Continuing to grow north is a knockout blow for downtown. We'll be tapping out like a beaten MMA fighter."

"I get sick of hearing about the dang downtown," spouted Hal. "I mean who really cares? Let the old dog die and let's move on."

Andy's powerful legs spread wide on either side of the bench as he grabbed the collar of his grey Bekering High School T-shirt and wiped sweat from his eyes. As the shirt descended, Andy noticed a familiar face working out on the squat machine across the way. It was that Joseph he had met at the North End Grill radio remote. As he pondered the surprise of seeing Joseph, a voice in his ear drew his attention back to the phone call.

"Andy, you there?" shouted Matthew. "We need to make sure we're on the same page." Andy gave another look to Joseph and then lay back on the bench as he caved on the phone.

"Alright, I'll do what I can with the folks on the council," he said and tapped the plastic earpiece to end the call. As he was about to position his hands to resume his workout, he looked up to see Joseph walking his way.

"Tough call?"

"Yeah, too many of 'em in this job," the mayor responded. Andy sized up the man standing in front of him in sweats and a T-shirt which said, "God's Gym" on the chest, and underneath "Be Strong and Courageous – 2 Chron. 32:7."

"Looks like you know your way around a gym, partner," said Andy.

"Yeah, it's important to keep a healthy mind, spirit, and body," Joseph answered with his usual smile. "In fact, I was hoping to do some free weights work. I could use someone to spot for me, if you wouldn't mind."

"Lead on," Andy said, returning the smile, "I could use the workout to clear my mind."

The pair ended up in a back corner area with steel frames for holding large amounts of weight, designated for strengthening legs and back muscles. Joseph groaned loudly as he squatted beneath the bar holding three plates on each side of his shoulders. His face turned a bright red as he shouted and rose to a victorious standing position.

"Darn impressive," said Andy as he helped lift the bar into its resting place, allowing Joseph to escape. "Not bad for a newbie."

"I could say the same thing about you," Joseph said breathlessly, his chest heaving as he leaned against the metal frame of the workout area. "You seem to be in the process of wanting to do some big things in your new role."

"Are you gonna tell me my life story, like ya did Dirk?" He laughed. Andy knew humor was his go-to emotion when fighting off nervousness. Maybe it was the exchange he'd witnessed with Dirk, or maybe it was simply Joseph's presence. Something about Joseph was making Andy jittery.

"No, it doesn't work like that," Joseph laughed. "I want to encourage you." Andy took a breath, trying to relax his shoulders.

"Whatcha got?" asked Andy as he took a seat on a weight bench and grabbed his water bottle from the floor.

Joseph paused for a moment and seemed to look at the big clock on the wall opposite of there the two were standing. Then Andy saw Joseph's face change from a look of searching for a thought to an assurance he knew what he wanted to share.

"What heaven has for you is that Matthew may be talking to you about preparing for your next elected office," Joseph began, "but heaven is pleased with the job you have now." Andy nodded politely. He was amazed at how casual Joseph appeared, even as he shared things he claimed to hear from another world.

Andy was a Christian, but he'd never experienced such an encounter as he'd witnessed between Dirk and Joseph.

"What so important about the job I have now?" Andy asked. "Not sure heaven shoulda picked me."

"You're strong in stature, Andy Strapp, but also strong in humility," Joseph said, looking Andy directly in the eye. "And because people underestimate you." Andy smiled and wiped his face with a towel as he thought about Joseph's words.

Andy was by no means dumb, but he knew his agricultural upbringing, southern drawl, and lack of patience for meetings gave people room to believe he wasn't very deep. Being new to the world of political gamesmanship, Andy had been content to allow Matthew and Hal to be the biggest voices on city decisions. Now, however, Andy was struggling as he walked the fine line between the political system of his party and the passionate beliefs he carried. Beliefs which compelled him to run for office in the first place.

"Life has prepared you for this position, Mayor," Joseph stated. "Trust the character in your heart to lead. The Bible says when good people prosper a city rejoices. You, Andy, are good people."

"I've done a lot of dumb things in my life," Andy shared. Joseph moved from the steel squat rack and sat on the bench beside Andy, giving Andy a closeup view of Joseph's empathetic eyes.

"What you do doesn't make you righteous or unrighteous," Joseph spoke, his lips curling into a light smile. "Letting heaven stir your heart for diving love and goodness is how you live as 'good.' That mystical mixture will help you to be strong and take courage."

"I've not been too strong or had much courage." Andy looked down at the stainless-steel water bottle again and remembering his call with Hal and Matthew.

"What's the most important thing you can do for Bekering as mayor?" Joseph asked, his face changing to a serious gaze.

Andy looking at nothing in particular across the room as he thought about the question. He knew Bekering's biggest problem. The town had grown from a small rail station community to the boom of exponential growth after World War II. In the process, the affluent white neighborhoods had fled farther and farther north. It was a phenomenon known as 'sprawl.'

"We've got to contain growth," Andy said to Joseph, shaking a bit as he said it out loud. He knew men like Matthew, Hal, and other Christian Republicans around him would strongly disagree. Andy was finding it increasingly difficult not to speak what he really believed. "Our city has needed to contain growth inside its boundaries for more than fifty years. Sprawl has killed our economy for all that time." Andy watch Joseph nod and thoughtfully consider his next question.

"Why hasn't someone tried to bring this change in the past?" This time Andy's look around the room had a purpose. He wanted to make sure the few exercisers nearby weren't listening in on their conversation. He lowered his volume.

"Because containing growth ain't much of a Republican idea," Andy said in a loud whisper. "They believe the free market will always fix everything."

"You don't believe that?" Joseph asked.

"I guess I believe the whole dang thing works best when the market and government work together." Andy leaned in and lowered his voice again. "Between you and me, most times I think the builders only want to make money and don't give a darn what impact it has on the city. Everyone goes along with it because they think that's the good, conservative thing to do." Andy was surprised at the sense of relief he felt. It was cathartic to be able to share these beliefs out loud. Almost like these thoughts had been building up and in need of a release valve.

"The builders put a lot of pressure on you to approve their projects?" asked Joseph.

"Yeah, and they're willing to pay or threaten people for it," Andy said, his face tightening. "It makes me sick to my stomach what these men have done to Bekering over the years. I would be happy if the feds would come in and throw a few more of 'em in the clink. 'Operation False Zone' stopped the leapfrog development for a bit."

"Leapfrog development?"

"Yeah, a developer can buy land at lower prices outside city boundaries," Andy explained. "The developer leaps over the more expensive property and asks the city to annex their new, cheaper property. If they can get the council to vote for 'em, the land value increases a ton. But it costs the city a ton over the long haul."

"So the developer makes his money and the Bekering taxpayer is on the hook for those expense forevermore," Joseph summarized.

"And the party leaders and Christian leaders are one hundred percent behind it," said Andy with a bitter laugh. "I guess somewhere in the Bible it must say capitalism and making money makes everything alright. Most of these big developers and Republican leaders attend BCC."

"The city isn't lacking for capitalism, Mayor, it's lacking caring leaders." Andy stared at Joseph, waiting for further explanation as he placed his hand towel around his neck and held on to each side with his hands.

"The Bible actually has great love for good government," Joseph explained. "It's politics that comes from hell." Joseph tried a drink from his water bottle and finding it empty, dropped it to the ground.

"The people giving this money for influence and those taking it have violated the universal covenant of leadership," Joseph continued," And when that happens, history and the Bible show those systems begin to crumble."

"It seems my goal is supposed to be only my next election. C'mon, let's hit one more set." Joseph and Andy stood from the bench to prepare for another round of weight lifting.

"There's a proposal for sprawl on your desk now, isn't there, Andy?" Joseph asked as he put protective chalk on his hands. Andy perceived the statement came again from heavenly inspiration.

"I—I'm not sure I should talk about that," Andy said nervously.

"Sure. But, Andy... Excuse me, Mayor, this is the day you're being called to leadership for your city." Andy stared at Joseph with uncertainty. He knew Joseph was referencing the proposal he'd discussed earlier on the phone with Hal and Matthew, but had no idea where the courage would come from to take the stand Joseph was asking for.

"Maybe you're exactly the guy Bekering has been waiting for to stand against sprawl and leapfrog development because no one has been willing to do so before." Joseph leaned his arm over the weights stacked on the weight bar.

"Let me tell you a story," he said with a smile.

In a city there were two groups separated by a railroad. One group lived north of the tracks and was very well-to-do, and the group south of the tracks was very poor.

Every time people from the south side of the tracks gathered enough money to move north of the tracks, the people of the wealthier group would find a way to move farther north so as not to live next to those who were moving from the south. This made the people who had moved from the south to the north very angry, and those who still lived in the south even angrier. Each week, groups from south of the tracks would find ways to invade the areas of those in the north to steal from the extravagance there, as those folks lived much better lives than their own.

In response to this problem, those north of the tracks hired extra law enforcement in an effort to keep the south-siders away from the north end and to punish any attempting to come into their area. Soon, all the extra resources of the north-siders were going to pay for this extra security and the cost of continuing to move farther north. They noticed the more they moved north, the more poverty came to the south side, and the problems, such as crime and gangs, grew even worse. The residents on both sides of the tracks knew there had to be a better solution, but how could things ever change? This is the way it had always been.

One day a wise man in the north was raised up as a leader by his neighbors to try and solve this problem. However, the people of the north didn't know this man had grown up in the south and loved the south-siders. This wise man carried solutions to the problems of the two peoples.

"Let's have fifty families who live north of the tracks move to the south and have the people of the north provide housing for fifty families to move from the south into their neighborhoods," said the leader.

Many of the people on both sides of the tracks grumbled at this solution, but the young man was a great leader and gently pushed the people into the solution he believed was the best for everyone. He insisted there be events to mix the newcomers to the south and the newcomers to the north with those around them. Soon the people found those from the other side of the tracks weren't different from them. Those who'd moved to the other side of the tracks were able to report back to their friends that the people they'd hated were no longer unknown enemies, but were becoming friends.

Before the people knew it, there were no longer two people groups in the city, but a people who had become one. No longer was there such a great burden to pass laws for their protection, or to pay for law enforcement to solve their problems, as the people began to resolve issues out of relationship.

Joseph finished his story and Andy watched him wait in anticipation. Joseph's eyebrows raised as if to ask Andy his thoughts on the tale.

"Nice story, but has it ever really happened?" asked Andy.

"Yes, in the Bible," said Joseph. "In Nehemiah Chapter 11. Nehemiah knew the social issues of a city could not be resolved until the people of the city came together to restore it."

"Well, it's a good Bible story, but can it work in our world?" asked Andy, trying not to sound sarcastic.

"Mayor, I believe you'll be surprised by what can happen. Keep doing things the way they've been done before and Bekering's future will be the same as its past. And you, Mayor, will be miserable knowing bigger things could have been done in your term." Andy ran a hand through his blonde hair.

"That's a lot to think about, partner. I wish it was so easy."

"If you follow what God has planned for you and this city, no party will ever be able to stop you from receiving the votes of the people who love and trust you," said Joseph, pointing a finger at Andy's chest. "It will take some courage, but, you, Mayor Strapp, are more courageous than you know. You're the great leader from south of the tracks who can lead Bekering to a new future."

The two men finished their workout and said goodbye. Andy scratched his head as he watched Joseph leave the gym.

"I'll be dying to see how I get all that past Hal Beatty and Matthew McGinnis," Andy thought as he headed to the locker room to shower and change.

CHAPTER 22:
THE PASTORS' MEETING

"He told some of my people that God loved gay people," said Pastor Rand Harvey, a balding Methodist pastor seated next to Pastor Able Hackenworth. Harvey and Hackenworth were discussing Joseph with Saul in BCC's Beatty Fellowship Hall for the monthly Bekering Pastor's Mixer, a meeting Saul created and hosted each month. The Hall was a long room, built for such events, with a commercial kitchen and tile floors for easy cleaning. "I had to remind them of the Bible's clear teaching we are to 'love the sinner but hate the sin!'"

Pastor Hackenworth looked at the floor and grunted his displeasure. "Mm, mm, mm," he mumbled. Saul interrupted the conversation to kick off the meeting by saying grace for their lunchtime eating.

"Lord we thank you for the amazing weather and ask you to bless this food to the nourishment of our bodies..." Saul's voice echoed off the tile floors, tan walls, and the adjustable basketball hoops which could be lowered from their current upright positions. Saul's heart was not completely in the prayer; he was distracted by its nervous beating, as soon he would share his plan with the group to stop the threat of Joseph.

"...And help us to love our enemies and to pray for those who spitefully use us." The irony of the last line was not completely lost on Saul as he finished with the usual formal ending of a group prayer in his circles, "...and everyone said?"

"Amen!" The group responded in unison.

Saul stood at the beginning of the food line and greeted each of the all-male group members, listening in on their conversations.

"The liberal media is at it again..." one pastor in line could be heard to say.

"It's the gay agenda in our schools..." said another.

"What do you expect from government officials..." said a third. These were the topics Saul and the great majority of this group believed were God's primary concerns.

If asked, these pastors likely couldn't point to specific passages in the Bible backing up many of these political beliefs, even though it was strongly preached that everything Christians believed must be backed by scripture. The passage stated by Pastor Harvey— love the sinners and hate the sin—is not actually a verse in the Bible, but relayed so often in Christian cultural arguments that many churchgoers believe it is.

"One of my people accused me of wrongdoing when I stand in my pulpit and encourage people as to how they should vote," Pastor Hackenworth shared at the folding table covered in a red tablecloth. "It's my solemn duty to teach people to vote our beliefs."

These political beliefs tended to come more from the shared experience of Evangelical life than deep research of the Bible. Simply put, since day one of seminary, everyone around pastors like Saul believed this way and, thus, each of them believed in turn. Now, Saul and the others were attempting to dutifully pass the tradition of these beliefs onto their followers.

"Gentlemen, gentlemen!" Saul shouted and raised his hands to gather the attention of the group. "I wanted to share my thoughts on this Joseph character. I had assumed him a harmless nuisance." He looked from face to face in the room, his brow line pressed down towards his eyes to emphasize his worry. "Lately, however, I've seen even some of our best fall for his deception."

Saul watched the group of pastors nod in agreement. Difficult questions had been posed to them by their people, thanks to the ideas Joseph was spreading in his teachings.

"If marriage is between one man and one woman, then why was it OK for King David to have multiple wives?" one pastor had been asked.

"If we are commanded to honor those in authority, then why did you speak poorly of the previous president from the other party?" was a difficult question another pastor had tried to answer.

"I hear he's quite the partier, too," said Pastor Hackenworth. "Hangs out with some of the worst sinners in our town." Pastor Hackenworth placed his hands on the table and leaned forward, swiveling his head to make eye contact around the table.

"I propose we do something about this... heretic!"

Saul was pleased his fellow pastor had used one of the ultimate emotional buzzwords of Christendom to create murmuring and agreement in the room.

"We need to call him out publicly," Saul said sternly, "at the Bekering Day of Prayer in front of hundreds of our people."

"Hal Beatty's team has been doing research on him and we will shine the light of truth for our people, and the truth will set them free of Joseph and his teaching." Saul's voice had raised in pitch and volume with his climactic sentence. As he finished, he looked at his hand and saw it shake.

Saul wasn't sure why speaking of Joseph caused his emotions to run high. For some reason people liked what Joseph had to teach, and it seemed to undermine Saul and the men in this room. Perhaps, more than Saul would admit, his own son's interest in Joseph was an ongoing open wound, as well.

"What about the miracles, Pastor Saul?" asked Pastor Briner of the Bekering Mennonite Church. "How do I explain away a man who's making physical ailments disappear?"

"Are people really being healed?" Saul paused for a moment, knowing he'd also been wrestling with this very question. "Where are the doctors telling us these ailments have actually disappeared? I've seen this before, psychological manipulation. That man is no more a healer than you or me." Deep down Saul knew he believed prayer could do amazing things. He'd seen it when Pastor Anderson had prayed for Isaac and had watched with his own eyes as the young lady had been healed in the coffee chop. Since Saul had not witnessed miraculous things occur from his own prayers, his ability to believe in them had dimmed.

"With that understood, let's move forward with our plan, gentlemen." Saul clapped his hands, finalizing the agreement.

CHAPTER 23:
DON'T CALL HIM A PASTOR

"Hello everyone, apologies for being late." Christian Anderson pushed through the Fellowship Hall double doors. Pastor Anderson wasn't particularly welcomed in meetings like these, as his philosophy of ministry was different than others in the room, but he was Saul's friend and, thus, allowed to attend. His church was known for its lively music and its more progressive cultural views.

"Hi, Christian," said Saul with his big host grin. That grin faded as fast as it formed as Christian's guest followed him in.

"I invited my friend Joseph," he said. "I thought we might like the chance to know him a bit." Saul was shocked. He stood staring at the two latecomers. Saul heard a throat clear over his left shoulder and turned to see Patty working with the women in the final stages of putting away lunch. Patty gave a subtle, urgent nod towards Joseph, signaling Saul to break the awkward silence.

"Uh, yes, of course," said Saul, motioning them to seats at the table. "Joseph and I have been getting to know each other a bit lately." Saul followed Joseph's eyes around the room. The tension was palpable. Saul thought how easy it was to talk about this man from afar, with him hidden away in a back room of a restaurant. But Saul worried what Joseph might do in this group.

"Ladies can we get some coffee and snacks for Pastor Christian and Joseph?" Saul ordered, trying to calm his suddenly frayed nerves.

"Saul, don't make these women wait on us," said Christian. "We're late and can get our own food." Joseph was in his normal jeans and T-shirt, an orange one with a picture of Jesus on the cross which said, "Jesus was the first Christian to have body piercings."

Saul noticed Pastor Hackenworth rise from his seat and was happy to let the patriarch and local pastors use this moment to query the mysterious guest.

"Good [morning] Mr Joseph..." the elder man began as he hooked his dress pants with his thumbs and pulled them up.

"Why did you call me 'Pastor'?" Joseph interrupted. "I'm not a leader of a formal congregation as you men." Saul could see Joseph smile, but it was not his usual, so charming grin. Joseph's jaw was tight and seemed to portray a disappointment over the room. Saul reached for the tightening area in his chest as he sensed conflict coming.

"OK, [or] yes," said Pastor Hackenworth as he wiped his mouth with a napkin. "Then... Joseph. We were discussing the danger of our children being inundated every day with messages about homosexuality and perversion. I wondered what your take would be on this discussion."

"Discussion?" Joseph inquired, his eyes following Pastor Hackenworth as the older pastor gingerly walked the length of the table in his slow gait.

"The discussion was about a culture endorsing homosexuality and a gay lifestyle," Pastor Hackenworth said in his pastoral cadence. "Of a culture preferring to bow to the whims of the evil world than honor the word of God." Pastor Hackenworth stopped his walk and stood across the table from Joseph awaiting a response.

"I'm not sure you need my input, Pastor," Joseph responded, his smile fading and his eyes showing a new intensity. Saul could sense Joseph had come ready for a fight. "You've all determined a mere six Bible passages out of thousands give you permission to believe as you do. My input is immaterial."

"You've been interacting with The Love Coalition group at the Defense of Marriage rally," Pastor Hackenworth continued, almost as if ignoring Joseph's comment. "And you were seen at a party with Elsa Kratt. Do you think such behavior appropriate for someone who claims to speak for God?" Joseph stared at Pastor Hackenworth, then dropped his eyes to the red tablecloth. He was silent for such a long moment Saul wondered if he'd heard the question. Joseph's chest was visibly rising and collapsing rapidly with each breath.

"Sir?" Pastor Hackenworth prodded.

Joseph didn't speak but rose from his seat and walked across the room. He came to a [white]board stored in the corner and began to write. Saul squinted to read across the distance of the hall. Joseph was writing words such as "hypocrite," "glutton," "disobedient to parents," "divorced." Joseph kept writing for such a long period of time Saul finally looked at Pastor Hackenworth and urged him to speak.

"Don't you have anything to say, good man?" Pastor Hackenworth asked.

"Again, you call me 'good' when I suspect you men don't think me good at all," Joseph said as he wheeled around from the whiteboard and pointed the black felt pen towards Pastor Hackenworth. "I find it interesting you know the name of the leader of The Love Coalition, but am doubtful you have any idea who she is." Joseph leaned on a chair and drummed his fingers.

"Have any of you ever had a real conversation with Elsa? Shared any of God's 'love' with her or her friends?" Saul looked around the room and saw men fidgeting in their chairs. None made a sound. Joseph pointed towards a man at the far corner of the table.

"Do you know Elsa has been to your church, Pastor Smithson?" Joseph pointed to another pastor. "And to yours, Pastor Harvey? And Pastor Johnson, I'm sure you know she grew up in your church and her family felt they had to leave because Elsa's (Joseph throws up finger quotes) 'lifestyle' caused too much discomfort for others."

"Now, sir, the Bible commands us to teach our people the proper way," said Pastor Johnson.

"The Bible commands love for the poor and outcast," Joseph responded, "yet the unchurched world reached out to the kids bullied at school for being different. Christians felt standing against sin was more important than to have mercy on a young girl who felt ostracized by her own hometown." Joseph's eyes seemed ablaze and he stared at one pastor after another.

"In the Bible, Jesus was sick to his stomach when he saw how the religious leaders withheld grace from people," Joseph said through clenched teeth. "Please help me understand how I should not feel the same about what I see in Bekering?"

"Joseph, that's not fair. We understand the need to love people," Saul jumped in, "but homosexuality is destructive to families. We must stand strongly against it."

"Isn't divorce destructive to families?" Joseph answered brusquely. "And doesn't divorce impact exponentially more households than homosexuality? Yet somehow you're able to contextualize Biblical words about it directly from Jesus' mouth!"

The statement caused Saul to literally reel back. He knew some of the men were divorced and he looked around the room. Several of the men were staring downwards while others looked at Joseph with fierce anger.

"In the church, the divorce rate is about half of all marriages," Joseph stated, now walking the side of the table opposite Pastor Hackenworth. "Where is your campaign to pass laws against no-fault divorce? Shouldn't that be a priority if the agenda is really to care about families and not just cater to your big givers?"

Saul shook his head meekly, as he answered.

"Well, now, that's different, Joseph."

"What's different about it?" Joseph responded, turning and pointing at Saul. "Is it because no-fault divorce is a heterosexual violation of your Bible, and thus easier for you to make peace with? Yes, indeed, some of you in this room have been divorced and are remarried yourselves, and you don't think a thing about the fact the Bible calls this adultery." Saul didn't answer, but happened to look behind him. There he saw Patty and the other women. All motionless, transfixed by the conversation.

"Let me give you the grace you withhold from others and tell you it's OK you treat divorce as you do." Joseph's voice drew Saul back to the conversation. "Heaven is willing to love people right where they are in life. Yet it is sickening when men who claim to serve in God's name have decided some actions aren't worthy of grace."

"Joseph, if we don't stand up now against this gay agenda, the government will soon try and force us to perform gay marriages in our churches," Pastor Harvey jumped in, "or they'll take away our tax-exempt status."

Pastor Harvey slowed his speech and stopped altogether as Joseph eyed him with a steely glare.

"Gentlemen, were you ever promised freedom from persecution or financial difficulty?" Joseph's volume was climbing and his eyes widened. "Perhaps your tax-exempt status is too important to you. You all need to be less worried about your personal safety and comfort and be more worried one day you'll give account in eternity for the grace and love you're withholding from people!"

"I've heard about enough of this nonsense," Pastor Hackenworth shouted, throwing his cloth handkerchief on the table. "You need to read your Bible, young man."

"You say, 'love the sinner hate the sin,'" Joseph responded, "but I read in the Bible that Jesus' purpose was not to condemn the world but to reconcile it to heaven!'" Saul watched as Joseph walked deliberately down the long table, head bowed with invisible weight. "You, sir, should read the Bible's story of Zacchaeus again. A tax collector thought by the religious leaders to be unworthy of God's love. His life was transformed through the honor given him from Jesus, God's representative on earth. Zacchaeus had been told for many years by the religious leaders he was a bad person, and that didn't change him. But love and honor changed him forever. As it says in the Bible, if we only love the people who agree with us, aren't we big hypocrites?"

"Joseph, you need to settle down," said Saul, but Joseph immediately fired back.

"No! Pastor Saul! I will not settle down!" Joseph walked back to his seat and grabbed the chair back again, his breathing hard, his chest pumping. He raised his head to the men in the room. "Someday, when you visit the throne of heaven, no one will ask if you had good theology. No, you'll be asked if your good theology kept you from loving people." Pastor Hackenworth walked briskly down the table to face Joseph once again. Saul could see the robust pastor's cheeks were flushed red with anger.

"Young man," he shouted, "do you not understand your critique is coming against men who give a lot for their people?"

"Do you understand, Pastor, that maybe heaven cares about even people who don't underwrite the paychecks of these men!" Joseph's response was a shout at the top of his lungs and his voice reverberated from the tile floors in the room. Saul stood motionless, his mouth slightly agape. He was dumbfounded as Joseph yanked the chair in his hand with such ferocity it made an ear-splitting shatter against the wall behind him. Saul instinctively stepped forward.

"Stay where you are, Saul," Joseph said, his glare causing Saul to stop in his tracks. "You men have taken the gospel and made it about the things you think important, but heaven wants you to know these things don't mean much in the spiritual world! Maybe you should be as concerned about the Supreme Being as you are with who's on the Supreme Court."

With that statement, Joseph slid both hands under the table in front of him and flipped it onto its side. The table hit the floor with the sound of a gunshot and leftover food, drinks and utensils went flying in all directions.

"Dear Jesus, save us," Pastor Hackenworth prayed breathlessly.

"Like Jesus clearing the temple," Christian Anderson said with a head shake and a smile. He nodded at Saul, who still hadn't moved from the place where Joseph had stopped him. Joseph headed for the exit and hit the door hard, forcing it to slam against the hallway door stop as he left the room with Christian close behind.

Saul looked at the mess before quickly following the men to the hallway. Saul had no plan, but the adrenalin in his veins told him he needed to track them down for a confrontation. Saul pushed open the door in time to see his wife talking to Joseph. Patty must have come through the hallway doors attached to the kitchen.

"I need to talk to you," Patty said before she saw her husband come through the door. Upon seeing Saul, she looked down in momentary embarrassment, then regained her composure. "I'd like to find some time to follow up on what we discussed at the Gala."

Joseph had followed her glance to Pastor Saul. He placed his hands on his hips and took a deep breath.

"I'd be happy to, Mrs. Thompson," he answered, his temper seemingly subsiding. "But right now..." Joseph lifted his hands and then let them drop to his sides, seeming suddenly unsure of what to say.

"I apologize to both of you," said Joseph, his voice dropping as the energy seemed to seep out of him. "I hit my limit with the 'Christianity' in that room." Joseph stomped down the hallway. Christian shrugged, the left side of his lip raising, and gave Saul a nod as he followed.

Patty averted her eyes like a schoolgirl caught in her mother's makeup drawer even as she crossed her arms in defiance. Saul's shock began to thaw, and his anger took its place inside his chest.

"We'll talk when I get home," he growled at Patty and headed back to the Hall entrance.

"Gentlemen," Saul said to the group of stunned pastors, some wiping food and condiments from their clothing, "do you now see why this man must be silenced?"

CHAPTER 24:
A FATHER-SON CLASH

Dinner time for Saul and Patty was interrupted by the phone call. Patty knew immediately it was serious as she listened to her husband's end of the conversation and watched his face turn ashen. Saul used his finger to end the call on his mobile phone as he reeled back against the wall. He felt as if his knees would fail him where he not propped up.

"That was Blake Perkins," Saul told Patty in a shaky voice, his bottom lip quivering, "their son Thad has committed suicide."

"Oh, Lord," Patty responded, her hand tightening over her mouth to stifle any cry trying to escape. After a moment of thought, she spoke what she knew Saul was already thinking.

"Thad's only a bit younger than Isaac." The statement hung in the air. It indicated to Saul Patty felt the same shame-filled sense of relief their own son was alive.

Soon, Saul was drawing up his navy-blue tie as Patty checked her white blouse and smoothed her navy skirt in front of the bedroom mirror before the two headed out the door.

Blake Perkins owned a shipping and logistics company and was chairman of the Bekering Chamber of Commerce. Saul and Patty had been to their large, beautiful home a few times, but anyone could have found the house with the flashing lights of the ambulance, fire truck, and several police cruisers as beacons to guide them in.

"Oh my God," said Patty, putting her hand over Saul's as it rested on the BMW gear shift. "They must be mortified." In Saul and Patty's recent meeting with the Perkins, Blake and Alice had shared Thad's newly problematic behavior. His parents had no idea what was going on. Now it was very clear the problems in Thad's life had indeed been urgent.

Upon a[rriv]al, the two found the front door being opened by a police officer, be[hind] whom they followed. The officer walked down the hallway to the rig[ht to the] entryway, while Saul and Patty spotted the family in the den, straigh[t ahead] from the front door.

"S[or]ry t[o bo]ther you, Pastor," said Blake, approaching Saul with his hand out for [a ha]nd[sh]ake. Saul took Blake's hand and gave a look of empathy, but was sur[pr]is[ed by] Blake's business-like demeanor. His handshake was solid and his voi[c]e pl[easa]nt. Saul looked at Patty, and it was clear between them that Blake's per[son]a[lity] didn't fit the moment. "Thank you for coming."

Th[e e]n[d of] Blake's sentence was clipped by the sound of his wife Alice, who h[a]d l[et out] a wail in the front room. Patty immediately walked to meet the dis[trau]g[ht] [m]other, led by the sound of the cries to the leather couch in the den. W[hat s]he saw there caused Patty to hesitate momentarily. Alice was always per[fectly] dressed and made up. Even at the gym, her outfit would be coordi[nated wi]th her makeup and her hair perfectly styled. Tonight, Alice was a [m]es[s. He]r makeup had long since been wiped from her face by the many c[r]um[pled] Kleenex that lay in a pile around her, and she had given up any ho[pe of] [he]r hair remaining in its normal fashion. As much as Blake's actions se[emed] [o]ut of place for a grieving parent, Alice appeared understandably wrecke[d by] [this] dark night.

"Sh[e's in]solable," said Blake as he and Saul watched Patty join Alice and th[eir] [oldest] college-aged daughter, Amy, on the couch. While the women loudly m[ou]r[ned]. Blake seemed to show no signs of grief whatsoever. "I've had to hold t[he] [fort] with the police and all." Blake pointed back down the hallway throug[h w]h[ich] the police officer had disappeared earlier.

"W[hat h]a[p]pened?" asked Saul.

"C[ome with] me, Pastor, I'll show you." The two men walked the hallway, past a [di]ni[ng ar]ea into the room Saul remembered to be the atrium. Once there, [Sa]ul [coul]d see a black vinyl bag zipped up on the floor in which, Saul felt cer[t]ain, [was] Thad's dead body. Saul's eyes moved slowly from the bag on the flo[o]r u[pwa]rds until he spotted a rope hanging over the big wooden crossbe[am. The] rope had been secured to a stair railing leading up to the second flo[or and] thrown over the beam. Saul could see the rope had been cut, but sti[ll] [r]e[main]ed as an ominous clue to what had happened. One of the official[s in th]e [h]ouse was taking pictures of the scene.

"Alice found him hanging in here when she came home from Bible study," said Blake, in a voice revealing either shock or a man completely closed to his inner workings. Blake had never been one for dramatic displays and Saul judged this to be a cover for deep down pain Blake must be hiding.

"As you're aware, Pastor, we knew Thad was having trouble, but we never imagined this," Blake continued coldly as he pointed towards the body on the floor. "We also didn't know he was gay." The surprise displayed in Saul's eyes drew a nod from Blake, indicating he understood Saul's reaction.

"He left a note," said Blake as he held out a piece of paper to Saul.

"I'm sorry to have not been the son you wanted," said Thad's handwritten explanation, "and I'm sorry I am not strong enough to resist the temptations around me. Please forgive me and may God somehow forgive me."

The note explained Thad had been involved with another young man in Bekering, but when Thad, out of guilt, had decided to break off the relationship, the other young man threatened to "out" Thad to the world.

"That would be more than I could stand," Thad had written, "and more than I want to put my family through. This is the only solution for everyone." Thad mentioned every family member by name and said he loved them. Saul looked at Blake as he handed the note back.

"My son's gay," said Blake, his voice hollow. "Or was gay, I should say." Blake looked down at the body bag on the floor. For the first time, Saul felt emotion stir in Blake, but Saul was unsure if the emotion was grief or anger. Saul knew, for a family like the Perkins who treasured Christian appearances, the black mark of having a gay son was shock beyond almost anything else.

"I'm sorry, Blake." Saul searched for something else to say but had no deep insight to share. "Let's go back and check on your wife." Saul placed a hand on the man's shoulder and watched Blake, his silver-haired head staying in place as he moved to keep his eyes on his son's body bag until they rounded the corner.

"Is Thad in hell, Pastor Saul?" Alice asked through heavy tears upon their return to the den.

"Well," Saul cleared his throat and thought for a moment. "Uh, God's grace is beyond our understanding."

"He's not in hell, Alice, for goodness sake," Patty jumped in, giving Saul a stern look.

"How can that be?" asked Alice. "He was living in sin and he committed suicide..." Her voice trailed off as her daughter Amy cried and buried her face in Alice's sweater.

Saul did indeed believe Thad was in hell. Saul had written a seminary term paper claiming suicide as one of the greatest sins one could commit since there was no chance for repentance. In the moment of reality, however, that answer didn't sit well with Saul.

"Surely a God big enough to create the universe could have grace for a boy who was hurting, alone, and afraid," he thought. Still, Saul was a fundamentalist, and no hope in God's grace could change how he interpreted the Bible. Saul looked up and found his wife glaring at him. Yes, Patty was right—this was no time to deal with deep, theological questions. It was a time for comforting a grieving family.

"Pastor Saul, can we have the memorial at the church?" Alice asked, wiping her nose with an expensive handkerchief.

"Definitely, we'll have it at the church," Blake jumped in. Saul nodded, not sure how this funeral would play with the BCC crowd and board.

After a time of comforting and working through some planning, Saul and Patty headed towards the door to leave.

"What are people going to say?" Alice asked, her eyes glassy and searching Patty's for answers.

"You'll be fine, Alice," was all Patty could muster in response. Saul knew the BCC crowd would not be kind in their discussions of the Perkins in the coming days, and he could sense Patty was assuming the same. The car was silent as Saul drove.

"Do you think he's in hell?" asked Patty, breaking the silence.

"I'm not sure, Pattz," he said, shaking his head. He could hear Patty cry, releasing pent up emotion after having stayed strong for Alice.

"I don't believe in a god who would send that poor kid to hell," she said through her tears.

"Patty, it's not for us to decide," Saul said as gently as possible.

They arrived home to find Isaac in the family den, draped across the recliner, leaning back against one arm with his legs cascading over the other. He nodded his head as his mother asked if he'd heard the news.

"I'm sorry," Saul managed. Isaac didn't move, almost causing Saul to wonder if the young man heard him. Finally, Isaac met his father with hard eyes.

"Are you really sorry?"

The question struck Saul like a frying pan to the face. He was taken back not only by the statement, but by the hard emotion behind it.

"Son, I was with the Perkins. My heart's broken for them."

"How's your heart for Thad?" Isaac snapped "Maybe he needs some sympathy right now, too."

"Hold on, son," Saul answered defensively. The truth was, Saul had great empathy for Thad. And he had great emotion stirring for his own son at this moment. There was nothing more Saul wanted than to simply walk forward and embrace his boy. In recent months, however, conversations with Isaac always drove Saul to defend his own theological morays rather than to display what he was feeling in his heart. "Thad made a decision that's impacting a whole bunch of people right now, and will for some time." Isaac sat up in the recliner, placing his feet on the floor.

"Do you know why Thad made the decision he made?" Isaac said, his eyes filled with fire as he stared at his father.

"Why... I can only assume..." Saul tried.

"He killed himself because of what you teach," Isaac said angrily, pointing at his father. "Maybe if Thad had someone he could talk to he would still be alive. But he was too ashamed to tell anyone." Saul was still standing in the entryway to the den, Patty in the middle of the room to his right.

"Not fair, son. We always try to be there to talk with anyone in crisis—always. You know I'll drop everything to help anyone, especially young people."

"Yeah, you'll be there if we get a speeding ticket, or in an argument at school, but not this." Isaac was shaking. "No, Thad knew he could never have talked to his parents about this."

"His parents loved him, Isaac..."

"They loved what they thought he was!" Isaac screamed. "There were times kids wondered if Thad might be gay, but no one ever said much about it. We all knew if he ever came out, his parents, friends, and church would disown him."

Isaac's words cut Saul like a sword. He didn't want to argue. Saul decided he would act on his desire to embrace Isaac. Thad's death made Saul starkly aware of how much he loved his son.

"Don't!" Isaac's hand shot up to ward Saul off. Saul reeled back and nearly tripped over the coffee table as if Isaac had pushed him.

"Dad," Isaac said looking straight at Saul, "when I read the Bible I don't see the same things you teach. I don't see the same Jesus you talk about."

"Stop it Isaac, you don't know what you're saying," Patty spoke up.

Saul knew this exchange was painful, as many of these arguments between the two of them had been before. Her voice seemed to soothe Isaac. His posture relaxed, but his voice kept its steeliness.

"No, Mom, I know what I'm saying more than ever before. I believe God is a lot more like the heaven Joseph talks about than the God I hear about from him." Isaac's finger pointed in accusation of Saul.

"You stop talking like that right now!" The words came out of Saul's mouth in a much more violent fashion than he'd intended, and he moved towards his son out of pure instinct. Saul's father had come at him in similar ways in those late, painful years of his dad's life. Saul had come home late one night, and his father had overdone it with the alcohol he used to medicate his own inner pain each night. Saul had refused to back down that night as he had many times before with his father. Saul could remember the rage in Ralph Thompson's eyes as that first punch landed on Saul's cheek.

Standing before Isaac today, Saul wasn't aware he was mimicking family history. In this moment of confrontation, filled with a fear and anger he had never known, Saul's instincts fell back on the response he had seen in his own childhood.

"No, Dad, I'm done keeping my mouth closed," Isaac answered. "Your words set Thad up. Your goddam rules gave Thad no other choice, Dad. You killed Thad!"

Later reliving this moment, Saul would find it hard to believe it was his hand that landed the blow across Isaac's cheek. The hand seemed to have a mind of its own as it raised into the air before coming down hard on his son's face. It was a powerful, open-handed slap. A stunning moment Saul could never take back, and one that would send his son out the door.

"Saul!" Patty cried as the sound of the slap seemed to ring in the room. Isaac stared at his father, his hand instinctively going to his cheek. Saul's hand shook as he raised it to eye level, staring at it as if the hand alone were responsible for what had occurred.

The silence was painful as Saul watched Isaac's cheek quickly redden.

The adrenaline seeped out of Saul like air escaping a deflating balloon and he looked at his son in horror as he considered what to say next.

"Isaac, I shouldn't have done that," Saul quickly spoke, his brain struggling to understand if he should apologize for his actions or try to explain them. As usual, Saul found the need to justify himself to Isaac. "I don't understand why Thad did what he did, but I know God's ways are mysterious. I can't explain everything in the world."

"God had nothing to do with this," Isaac said with his teeth clenched. Saul watched Isaac's eyes look at Patty as the young man continued to rub the painful cheek.

"Thad was just a kid looking for someone to tell him he was good. Maybe that's what all of us want, but we're never good enough." Isaac paused, appearing to carefully plan what to do next. He finally rose from his seat, looking at Saul for the first time since the slap.

"I'm sorry I've been such a disappointment to you, Father Saul." Saul froze upon hearing Isaac's use of his mocking name. Isaac brushed past him, walking towards the kitchen.

"Isaac, where are you going?" Patty exclaimed, reaching towards her son. Saul watched over his shoulder as Isaac headed through the kitchen, opening the door leading out to the garage. Saul and Patty heard the door bang against the wall and then slam upon Isaac's exit. His car's engine roared to life and his tires screeched as he thundered his car from the driveway onto the street. Saul and Patty were left behind in the quiet den.

Patty's face contorted and her brilliant blue eyes were misty as she yanked an earring from her right ear.

"The Perkins lost their son. I'm not going to lose mine, too," she said, narrowing her eyes in anger. Removing the other earring she pointed it at her husband. "You've got some things to figure out, Saul!" She punctuated her statement by throwing the earring past Saul who ducked from pure reflex. The earring hit the blinds across the window behind Saul and trickled down the window sill before falling in pieces to the floor.

Distracted by the destroyed jewelry, Saul heard Patty's angry footsteps as she stomped down the hallway in her heels. Saul flinched as the bedroom door crashed a close behind her. Now completely alone in the room. Saul tugged on his shirt collar and wondered how his perfectly planned and controlled world was suddenly spinning out of control.

CHAPTER 25:
ANGST AROUND THE FUNERAL

"For me to live is Christ and to die is gain," Saul spoke into the microphone as he preached the following Sunday at BCC. Saul had to pack away all the pain of the week to share his sermon before his flock.

"What the writer of this Bible passage is saying is living is good, but in some ways dying is even better," Saul could see the crowd was less exuberant than any normal Sunday, knowing a child had been lost to one of their BCC families. "When we die, if we've given our life to Jesus and confessed him as Lord of our lives, we go to be with him in heaven, forever." Saul paused for effect as he looked out across the expanse of people in the large room.

"This week we'll have a funeral here," he said, his lips tightening in a somber expression. "We understand a group has asked the city for a permit for a vigil outside, which means the TV cameras will be here. I beg your patience as we do our best to accommodate the city while honoring the family of the deceased. Thank you for your prayers as we walk through this pain for our congregation."

Saul closed the meeting in prayer and shook hands at the exit door of the church before Hal Beatty asked to speak privately. Saul sighed as Hal led him upstairs towards Saul's office.

"Thanks for your time, Pastor," said Hal as he pulled open the office door. To Saul's surprise, the office was not empty. Hal had assembled a handful of people for the meeting including Rich Sullivan who, like Hal Beatty, was on the BCC Board, and was one of the long-time leading families in the church.

"What a surprise to see all of you," Saul began as he strode into the office. Hal interrupted in his usual frantic mode before Saul could speak again.

"We feel this can't wait, Saul," said Hal, sweeping his arm around to indicate he was speaking for entire group. "And I assure you what we're about to tell you are feelings shared by many others in the church." Saul tried to breathe to relax the tightening in his chest as he fidgeted with his collar.

"Pastor, we need an explanation as to why you're allowing such a funeral to take place in our church," said Rich. Saul released his breath as he leaned back against his desk. There were days he longed for a job where people didn't have opinions about every single task he carried out.

"Yes, Saul," Hal jumped in again, "we feel it's time for you to speak out on behalf of the church in this tragic situation. If we're not willing to speak out for truth, Saul, then who is?"

"To what 'truth' are you referring?" The words flew from Saul's lips a little more brusquely than he intended. It had been a long, painful week, and Saul could feel his fuse growing rather short.

"Well, about the homosexual lifestyle, of course," Hal said, smacking his fist into the palm of his other hand. "Holding this service at our church is a disgrace. It's an endorsement of the evil that got hold of this boy." Saul looked around the room at the men and their wives who'd come to visit him. Six couples. All prominent in the church. Saul tugged his tie as he struggled with an answer. Hal never gave him the chance.

"Pastor, you know Blake Perkins and I are friends," Hal continued. "I'd be glad to help the Perkins find a suitable venue."

"We need to make sure this moment is used to demonstrate how damaging this lifestyle is," Rich jumped in. "Thad's death is another example of how the gay agenda is after our kids." Saul could see the heads nodding in agreement around the room. Rich's wife, Anna, even stifled a soft sob and wiped her eyes with a handkerchief. Hal pointed to the newspaper on Saul's desk, the one placed there by Christy each morning.

"This is headline news, Saul. This is our moment to make a statement, not a time to go soft." Hal's statement confirmed what Saul had felt. This discussion was less about protecting children and more about politics and appearances. It seemed people around Saul were losing their ability to tell the difference between the two. With his senses a little frayed from sleepless nights and his heart hurting from his clash with his own son, Saul couldn't resist answering the group.

"I notice none of you in this room have school-aged kids at home,"

Saul noted. "The decision to host the memorial service isn't about you or me or the church. This is about a dead boy and helping his family grieve." "This is about standing for truth, Pastor," snapped Hal, "and the war culture is waging against it. You've said so yourself." Saul was stung by the reality that Hal was reciting his sermons back to him. But Saul's anger was now boiling.

"How could you people be this uncaring about a young boy and his family?"

"That boy was a sinner who reaped the consequences of his decisions," Rich shouted, bright red color rushing to his face. "We're trying to save our country, Saul."

"Why don't we at least block the protestors from coming?" Hal asked.

"We can't, Hal, Chief Gates is giving them a permit. Elsa Kratt already called to tell me they aren't protesting; their only desire is to have signs of support for the family and the boy."

"And you believe that woman," said Rich, his eyes wild and angry. "Maybe we need a leader brave enough to refuse the law when we're fighting God's battle." Rich patted his wife's shoulder to console her as she continued to cry. Saul took a deep breath to speak, but Hal cut him off.

"It's your job to tell the Perkins this service will not happen here, Saul," Hal said, no longer feigning diplomacy. "And if you can't do the job, maybe the Board needs to find someone who will."

"We're not at war with the Perkins, my good people," Saul returned Rich's loud volume. "At best, this discussion is inappropriate. At worst, it's self-righteous and I might encourage all of you to check your hearts." The faces in front of Saul registered their shock. Saul closed his eyes, breathing deeply through his nose.

"I understand what you all are trying to say," he said in a much lower tone. "I certainly understand our fight against homosexuality more than you all. But, as a pastor and as a father, I can only grieve for this boy. This fight is for another day." Saul looked around the room to see if he'd succeeded in lowering the tension. It was clear he had not.

"Pastor, we were very concerned this would be your stance," said Rich, the color filling his cheeks and forehead. "We're a Bible-believing people, and if you're not willing to stand for the word of God, we're not sure we can continue to attend here."

"Nor can we give our hard-earned tithes here if you're not standing for truth," his wife chimed in. Saul put his hands in his pockets and walked around the back of his desk, staring at the contents on its surface. He knew a threat when he heard one, and he was considering his response.

The word tithe is a Hebrew term for "a tenth," and it was generally considered standard for churchgoers to give ten percent of their income to the church they attend. For the families in this room, ten percent was a big chunk of money. Saul had to weigh the cost of what he was about to do.

"When have I ever not stood up for God and his Word?" Saul said softly. "I've devoted more of my life to the study of scripture and service to God than all of you combined. I'm going to tell you again, as your pastor, it's time to check your hearts."

"Pastor, you better do a Bible study on the word 'sin,'" Rich responded.

"And maybe you need study the Bible on the word 'hypocrite,'" Saul said, punching a finger into his desk with such ferocity that Saul felt pain shoot up through his lower knuckle. He paused a moment, realizing the gravity of what he'd said. He knew he was past the point of no return. Saul's emotion wouldn't let him stop.

"If my service to the Lord doesn't afford me the privilege to help a family through this pain and to tell these young people there's a god in heaven who loves them, then what the hell are we doing here?" Another gasp went up through the room at Saul's use of profanity. It wasn't an accident. Saul rarely used swear words at this point in his life, but when he did, it normally had the effect he desired. This was one of those times. Saul tightened his lips in a grim look and squinted his left eye lid as he continued.

"What makes me sad is you all are more concerned I used the word 'hell' than the fact people are actually going through hell in our community," said Saul. "Maybe right now is not the time for truth. Maybe, right now, it's our job to love them." He looked around the room as some of the eyes had dropped to the floor, but Hal's gaze was steady and defiant.

"Now, I'd like you all to leave, I want to go home." Saul walked back to the front of the office and opened the door, motioning to the group. Each person sauntered past him before Hal brought up the back of the pack.

"You haven't heard the end of this," he said quietly through gritted teeth, his finger pointing at Saul's face as he passed.

"Oh, I'm sure, Hal." Saul put his hand on Hal's shoulder, guiding him out of the room.

Saul closed and locked his office door. The adrenaline of the moment began to fade and the gravity of what he'd done set in. In many ways, Saul was in agreement with the arguments made by those who had left his office, but something didn't sit right with their tone. It was Saul's ongoing struggle—where was the line between loving people and hating sin? Maybe Thad didn't know any other way to live and God considered his heart as right as it could be. Saul shook his head. This line of thought went against everything he'd ever learned and known. He wished it were true. But, after years of his own teaching to the contrary, how could he possibly tell anyone differently now?

CHAPTER 26:
A SURPRISE FUNERAL GUEST

Building a casket is not an easy process. Preparing the wood alone entails drying wood in stacks for almost three months, and then heating it in a kiln for 15 days. The craftsman then spends more than a day putting the parts together before the casket is lacquered over and again until it has a brilliant, high gloss — one which the industry calls wood that, "looks a foot deep." Seamstresses then hand sew the interiors of the casket with the same skill as makers of fine clothing. After inspection, the completed casket is finally ready to ship having taken almost half a year to make.

Saul had gone with the Perkins as they chose the high-end mahogany casket which cost nearly $4,000. He knew the Perkins could easily afford such an expense but Saul assumed the choice was more about the Perkins desire to keep up appearances.

"Pastor, I know what people are thinking about Thad's death," Blake answered Saul thought. "We want to show how much we loved our son." As usual, Blake Perkins was one for logic over emotion.

"How are you doing with all of this, Blake?" Saul tentatively asked. Blake ran his hand through his graying hair and leaned back against the corner of the mortuary hallway wall.

"How am I doing?" he said, his nostrils flaring. "I found out my son was gay from a suicide note and my wife can't stop crying all night from nightmares of our only son in hell. How do you think I'm feeling, Saul!" The response was raw and more honest than Saul expected. He watched as Blake quickly straightened himself from the outburst, adjusting his sports coat on his shoulders.

"But it doesn't matter much how I'm feeling," Blake continued, his voice changing back to his normal, emotionless tone. "What's important is we make sure every detail of our son's funeral is perfect. Then we'll move on from all this."

Saul watched Blake turn the corner of the mortuary that day with amazement. It appeared Blake wanted a good funeral show and then to forget about this part of their lives. Maybe Blake was in shock, or maybe there was part of this man glad his son was gone—this way, dealing with the mark of a BCC family with a gay child wouldn't be an ongoing concern. Saul wiped his chin, struggling to process how a family leader in his church could have such a void of compassion for his own flesh and blood. Saul hoped he was wrongly interpreting Blake's emotional status.

The day the casket was delivered to the church for the funeral was an appropriately gray and rainy day. The church was overflowing with flowers from well-wishers but attendance at the event was low.

The Love Coalition was holding a silent, candlelight vigil in Thad's honor outside the church.

"We mean no disrespect to the Perkins family or the Bekering Christian Center," The Observer quoted Elsa. "We simply want to show love for Thad in a way that encourages others to come forward, rather than make a decision similar to Thad's." Elsa went on to explain her group would allow no signs for the event expressing anything other than love for Thad and to offer support to marginalized young people. "This is not a day to protest," she told the newspaper.

Saul and Patty arrived at the church, walking under their umbrella. The Coalition huddled under umbrellas behind the "Thou Shalt Not Cross" tape put in place by Chief Gates' men. The well-wishers who braved the scorn of some of their fellow parishioners somberly walked past the scene and into the church with occasional glances at the group of silent protesters. The group was holding signs with slogans such as "We Will Always Love You, Thad," "Love Is Always God's Lifestyle," and "Thou Shalt Love Your Neighbor." There was another sign with a hotline number for young people to call for support in a crisis such as Thad's last days and hours.

After entering the church and heading to Saul's office, Patty stood looking out at The Love Coalition.

"I wonder if those people love their kids as much as we do," she said. "Or are they monsters advancing an evil agenda?"

Saul sat at his desk and looked at the back of her head. He felt her statement was a shot at him. The two hadn't spoken much since the day of the slap. Isaac hadn't returned home, leaving occasional messages with Patty that he was staying with friends. Saul had spent a great deal of time in recent days in his son's empty room crying on Isaac's bed. Saul and Isaac had quarreled before, but Saul felt this time an irreparable chasm had formed between them.

"Patty," he said, but she raised her hand to stop him.

"Not today, Saul," she said, walking past him to the office door. "Let's get through the day."

Through the open door, the sound of an organ drifted into the office. Saul looked to the closed-circuit screen behind his desk to see people trickling into the sanctuary and taking their seats. He saw Alice and the Perkins family enter the room and heard her cries as she raced to the open casket at the front.

"My baby," Alice moaned as she laid her hand on Thad's chest. Saul could see Alice was despondent, despite the dark veil covering half her face. She was a mother in mourning, the exact opposite of her husband, who was leading their daughter to her seat.

Saul pulled on his shirt sleeves to straighten them beyond his jacket as, once again, his emotions would have to be contained to perform his pastoral duties. He studied his notes. The Perkins had been adamant there was to be no reference made to the contents of Thad's suicide note, nor the circumstances of the end of his life. Saul added a couple notes before a knock at the open door caused him to close his leather binder.

"Pastor, it's time," said Dave Tomlin, the funeral director in charge of the event.

"Yes, Dave," Saul nodded as he tucked the binder under his arm and followed Dave to the sanctuary. From his stage seat beside Sally Redgrave, one of the best singers in Saul's church choir, Saul could see two large, smiling photos of Thad situated on either side of the casket. One in his high school football uniform and the other a recent photo of Thad as a member of a wedding party. Thad was a handsome young man with thick, wavy brown hair, and the pictures were perfect for the occasion. In fact, Saul noted, everything was indeed perfect, as Blake had hoped.

Only Alice seemed to be throwing a wrench into Blake's plans. Her voice was heard easily across the room as she now slumped over her son's body.

Blake came up behind her, taking her by the arm and tugging her towards her seat where she slumped next to Patty.

Sally opened the program with a song. Saul had honestly hoped Sally's song would last forever. When she finished, Saul felt he had to swallow a softball to speak. He cleared his throat and adjusted his tie, gathering his thoughts.

"Thaddeus Montgomery Perkins was born into this world on August 20, 1998. He left the world too short a time later." Saul looked up from his notes and noticed Isaac had entered the sanctuary. Saul took a step back and leaned against his special podium for a moment, unable to contain the emotions raised by seeing his own son at a young man's funeral. He bit his lower lip to hold back his tears. Any one of the seventy people in the audience would have assumed Saul was emotional about the ceremony itself. However, the relief he felt, initially, at seeing his son, now was turning to seething anger. He was angry with Isaac for mocking him. He was angry with Joseph for filling Isaac's head with strange ideas. Most of all, he was angry with himself. There must be something wrong with him making it so difficult to relate with his son. Saul breathed in a deep breath in order to continue his funeral duties.

"Second Corinthians Chapter five, verse eight tells us 'To live is Christ, to die is gain,'" Saul spoke, stretching to speak from authority behind his pulpit. Isaac took a seat amongst the many empty seats in the back of the sanctuary. "In dark days like these, we look to scripture to give us a measure of reassurance." Saul looked again at the Perkins family. Did he really have any assurance to give them?

"Our Lord says in his word, he will have kindness on us, everlasting kindness, and His compassion will never fail us." Saul self-coached to keep a somber voice without lacking energy.

"Isaiah fifty-four, verses eight and ten say, 'though the mountains be shaken and the hills be removed, yet my unfailing love for you will not be shaken nor my covenant of peace be removed.'" Saul was reading from his notes now, trying not to think about the words for fear of his voice failing. "That's the God we lean on for days like today."

"The great old hymn says, 'Just as I am without one plea but that thy blood was shed for me!'" Saul's voice raised as he settled into his default preaching rhythm. He began to believe he could make it through the service. "None of us will stand one day with a single defense in front of a God who is absolute justice, but we will all have to throw ourselves on the mercy of that heavenly court..."

"What about me, Pastor?"

For a moment Saul's brain could scarcely register a voice had cried out in the room. His thoughts were jumbled for only a few seconds, but it seemed almost an eternity in the room. Saul finally focused on the sight of a young man approaching the front of the sanctuary.

"What did you say, young man?" Saul inquired as he looked down from behind the podium.

"What about me, Pastor Thompson," the young man responded, before his arms were grabbed by a church security officer. The officer had a look of a professional security worker, complete with the curly wire leading from his ear down inside his jacket to some hidden communication device. An armed security team was always in place since Saul first received death threats and bomb threats messaged to the church.

"No, Damon," Saul said to the security guard. "It's fine, let him go." The security guard quickly released the young man, who Saul judged to be about Isaac's age, perhaps a bit younger. The young man pulled his shoulders free to straighten his jacket and the oversized shirt and poorly tied tie around his neck. Saul thought he might have seen the young man in the church before, but he couldn't place him.

"I'm sorry, young man, this is not an appropriate time to speak. The family has asked all comments and eulogies be held until the reception after this memorial," Saul collected his thoughts in time to calmly explain. As always, his job was to provide safety to the people at the event, a role he took very seriously.

"Isn't this a church, Pastor?" the young man said, nearly spitting out his words in anger. He had tears in his eyes and snarl on his face.

"Yes, it is, son."

"Then tell me, is there forgiveness for me?" Saul studied the young man for a moment and considered where this all might be going.

"There is forgiveness, young man, for whatever you've done. There is grace for everyone."

"Really? Even if I'm the reason Thad is dead?" the boy said. Suddenly the snarl left his face and he broke down in tears, leaning against the theater style seat to his left. Saul was shocked at how young he suddenly appeared. A small chorus of voices could be heard from the small crowd in the cavernous room. "I'm the guy Thad was breaking up with. I was his boyfriend and I loved him. Is there really forgiveness for me?"

With a wave from Saul at the pulpit, the security guard standing next to the young man quickly began to usher him towards a hallway exit as the cries of Alice Perkins and those of her daughter echoed through the room. Alice lurched forward and, again, fell on her knees at her son's casket.

"Get the hell out of here you son of a bitch," yelled Blake Perkins as he dragged Alice back to her feet. "You killed my son!" Saul caught a glimpse of the young man as he was whisked from the room. He saw pure shock on the boy's face. Saul was momentarily frozen as he looked back and saw Isaac had left during the chaos of the moment.

"Folks! Folks, please calm down," said Saul bellowing into the mic on his cheek as he regained his composure. He waved to the organist who began to play somber music and Saul reached into his suit jacket to mute the wireless microphone transmitter on his belt. He walked off the stage and approached the Perkins, putting a hand on each of their shoulders.

"Blake! Alice! Listen to me, I need you both to find your way back to your seats. You don't want this service to end this way." Blake looked at Saul with wide eyes. The anger seeped from his face and, for the first time, Saul witnessed actual sadness in the man's eyes. Saul patted him again on the shoulder and motioned for Blake to help get Alice to her feet.

"My team will hold that young man and I can deal with him after the service," Saul said in his most reassuring tone. "For now, it's about honoring Thad." Alice looked up at Saul and put a handkerchief to her mouth. Standing this closely to her, Saul could see the mascara streaks behind her black veil. Blake took her by the arm and the shoulder and nodded.

"Today is about remembering the best of Thad," Saul finished before heading back up onto the stage, unmuting his belt-loop transmitter.

The rest of the ceremony continued as normal as possible.

"Lord, we ask your blessing on the Perkins family and for all of us who are grieving," Saul prayed in a closing prayer, which, mercifully, brought the proceedings to an end.

The weight of a mahogany casket was about 400 pounds empty. It wasn't an easy task for six of Thad's Bekering City College football teammates to bear the weight as they slowly moved down the church's center aisle to the waiting hearse destined for the graveside memorial.

Saul returned his mic and exited the stage and was led by his security team to a side room where the interrupter of the service was waiting. The team informed him the young man's name was Peter North.

"Hi, Peter," Saul said softly as he entered the room. He immediately noticed any defiance the young man had displayed in the service had completely evaporated.

"I'm the reason, Pastor," Peter said tearfully. "I'm the reason Thad is dead."

"That's not true, son," Saul said, taking a seat next to Peter. Suddenly Saul was filled with compassion for the young man, a compassion he seemed incapable of for his own son. "As sad as this all is, Peter, Thad made his own decision."

"We'd been seeing each other for a couple months," said Peter, his eyes staring at the table. "I loved him, but he felt guilty. It pissed me off." Saul reached out to put his hand on the young man's arm before pausing with his hand midair and finally lowering it back down to the table.

"The bible says the wages of sin is death," he said to Peter, his voice clearing and growing stronger. "You were both playing with fire."

"He told me, Pastor. He told me, and I wouldn't listen," Peter said, self-loathing twisting his features as he patted the table in front of him.

"He told you what, Peter?" The boy straightened up and looked directly at Saul.

"Thad told me if I outed him he would kill himself." Peter's voice held an icy pain causing Saul to shiver, as if he was hearing Thad's voice from the grave. "He told me his dad would completely disown him for his feelings and it would kill his mom. He said he couldn't face that..." The young man's voice trailed off and his eyes looked towards heaven. "I'm the reason Thad is dead. I hope he'll forgive me." Saul wondered for a moment if Peter was referencing forgiveness from Thad or from God. He couldn't help but think this seemed to be the kind of question everyone was asking these days.

"It's going to be fine, Peter, let's pray for you." Saul said a quick prayer and stood from the table. "Let's call your parents and get them down here." Saul motioned to his team to take care of the details as he reached to open the door. Saul needed to hurry to meet the funeral team and the family at the cemetery.

"Pastor Saul? Can God really forgive me? Can he really forgive my sins?" Saul paused at the door. He also struggled to know exactly how God handles human behavior.

This week Saul had gone back to some old seminary books and found, in the fourth century, Augustine, a noted Christian theologian had asserted suicide to be a sin. By 563 A.D., the church prohibited funerals for any suicide, regardless of the circumstances, and by 1284 churches refused to bury suicide victims in a consecrated cemetery.

Could the grace of God be "amazing enough"? Saul knew his teaching week-in-week-out provided little room for a god displaying such grace. Today, however, seminary lessons weren't enough for Saul.

"I surely hope God can forgive your sins, Peter. We all wish for a god with a big heart." Saul exited the room, quietly snapping the door behind him.

CHAPTER 27:
HEALING A MOTHER'S HEART

"God works in mysterious ways," Saul shared at the graveside service, repeating a saying Patty had heard far too many times over the past few days. The whistling wind competed with Saul's words as a storm threatened Holy Saints Cemetery of Bekering. Patty mentally urged Saul to wrap it up.

"I know God is here today to touch the hearts of the living so we can grieve well and continue to live."

Patty sat on a white wooden folding chair wearing her overcoat even though Saul still had only his simple suit jacket. The casket next to Saul was poised above a hole in the ground on burlap straps, soon to be lowered, the expensive box never to be seen again.

"I believe Thad would have wanted us to honor his memory by living life to the fullest," Saul preached, "So, ashes to ashes, dust to dust, we commit you, Thaddeus Montgomery Perkins, to eternity, amen."

"Amen," answered the crowd in unison.

The family and crowd of friends moved from the graveside as rain lightly began to fall. A huge tent on the cemetery grounds had been set up to house the wake.

"Get inside, Amy, quickly," Patty said as she hugged the Perkins daughter near the tent entrance.

"Why are all these people here for this show, Mrs. Thompson?" Amy asked, here eyes swollen from intense crying. "It's all a stupid front for my parents to hide the shame of their gay son!"

"Let people grieve as they need to, dear one," Patty urged, keeping her arm around her as they headed into the tent. "No parent should outlive a child. No one can ever know the pain your parents are feeling unless they have lost a child of their own."

Amy eyed Patty in way that seemed she realized this hinted of a backstory. Patty was relieved, however, that Amy didn't inquire further.

Patty sneaked a look over her shoulder and saw members of The Love Coalition standing in a loosely formed group with the rest of the attendees, no longer encumbered by the "Thou Shalt Not Cross" tape. Their signs were set to the side, Patty guessed out of respect for the Perkins and the event. She even noticed some members of the group were shedding tears.

"Hi, Mom," rang out a familiar voice inside the tent. Patty saw Isaac and walked to him, arms open for a tight embrace. The tears she'd kept at bay broke free, partly because she hadn't seen Isaac for three days, and because her son's face was streaked with his own tears.

"How are you, babe?" she said, touching Isaac's cheek with the back of her hand. Isaac's eyes were swollen and red.

"I've been better," he whispered.

"It's not easy to lay a friend to rest. I know that for sure. Don't be afraid to let yourself mourn in whatever way you need."

Holding her son, Patty looked around the event and saw it was well planned, with space heaters and the plastic sides of the tent unfurled to the ground, creating a comfortable atmosphere despite the weather. Patty asked Isaac to walk with her to get Cokes for her and for Alice. As they approached the bar, they saw Joseph stationed against the tan tent wall on the grass floor, working for the North End Grill catering team, supplying food and beverages for the event. His normal T-shirt had been replaced by a white collared shirt with the North End Grill logo slightly hidden under his black apron. Joseph's normal jeans had been replaced by black slacks for this somber job. The three exchanged pleasantries.

"Frightful day," said Joseph. "Anything I can do to help?"

"I don't know. I'm not sure what's up or down right now." Isaac said quietly before relaying to Joseph the story of his recent altercation. Patty could see the hurt in Isaac and the empathy in Joseph. Patty was glad Isaac had Joseph as a resource. After all, Patty and Saul had not done well in supporting their son through this hard time.

"I don't know why God lets life get this crazy," Isaac said. "For Thad or for me."

"I am convinced there is justice and mercy in this world, and in the next one," said Joseph. "And that is true for Thad. Today, Thad is whole, I believe."

"But isn't suicide, like, the unpardonable sin?"

"Nothin is unpardonable, no one is ever irredeemable," responded Joseph. "Even the Christian story is of a God who will go to the endless lengths to save the human treasures on earth. We may all see a time of purgatorial type fire, but, in the Bible, fire almost always represents purification not punishment. Can you imagine calling someone a "good father" when they are willing to set their children on fire? And Christians say their God not only creates the fire, but will stoke if for a million billion years to torture his creations?"

Isaac's face crumpled, his tears pouring forth.

"Then why would God allow Thad to do this?"

"God had nothing to do with this," said Joseph, his voice unwavering but calm. "This was completely the work of darkness and human hatred. The only thing that was from heaven was a connection to Thad's spirit at the end."

"You saying Thad is in Heaven?" All three turned to see that the question came from Alice Perkins standing nearby.

"Mrs. Perkins," Joseph gave a slight bow and offered her a seat. "The Bible says no one can be plucked from Jesus' hand. I believe Thad loved well. Though his life in this world ended tragically, his relationship with the divine spirit of heaven did not."

Patty thought Alice might cry, but as she rubbed her eyes with an overused tissue, it seemed there weren't any tears left.

"I was told you're someone I might want to talk to," said Alice, looking desperately at Joseph with eyes showing days of tears and stress. Joseph offered her a soda, which she sipped before setting the plastic glass on the table. Joseph served a few other waiting patrons, then came to the end of the bar at the table where Alice and Patty were seated, next to which Isaac was standing.

"My son is dead," Alice said, "and I wish I were dead, too." Joseph took hold of her hand and knelt next to her.

"Thad doesn't want you to be dead," Joseph answered. Alice looked at him for a moment and then broke down with tearless sobs. She reached into her purse, but couldn't find a handkerchief. Patty reached in to help and discovered a silk one that Patty thought had to be very expensive. She placed it in the hand of the grieving mother.

"Does he hate me?" she asked, choking on her words.

"Oh, my dear Alice," said Patty as she leaned in to give her friend a hug. She looked at Joseph, showing a plea for help.

"I assure you, no son could ever hate a mother like you," Joseph finally responded. "If you're talking about God, I can also say with certainly, nothing of heaven is mad at you."

"But my son killed himself, Joseph," she cried. "My little boy. My sweet little boy." Patty felt her own mother's heart tug as Alice leaned her head against Patty's shoulder.

"When I think of how scared he must have been," she said, "how alone he must have felt..." her voice trailed off.

"Alice, I know this is horrible," Joseph said, stooping slightly to look into her eyes, "but I also know there is goodness in the heavens. That's why I'm certain you can still connect to Thad and you will see him again. Always, when mother's lose children, they can rest assured their connection remains."

Joseph looked at Patty as he finished the sentence. Patty couldn't hold back her own emotions now as she realized Joseph was talking about her, as well as Alice. Patty reached a hand and clasped Isaac's next to her.

"Alice?" Joseph said in his fatherly tone as he took her by the shoulders and looked into her swollen eyes. "You knew, didn't you?"

The statement caused Alice to slide back in her seat.

"You knew your son was gay and you loved him even though it didn't fit your theology. You're such a good mom." Alice looked dazed. Patty thought Joseph must have had another one of his magical moments, sensing a person's secret.

"If only I had talked to him," the grieving mother said as she covered her face in the handkerchief.

"You did the best you could," Joseph said with the deepest kindness in his eyes. "God knows it and your son knows it." Alice hugged Joseph, her demeanor seeming to Patty to be much lighter as she walked away to tend to guests.

Isaac lightly kicked at a piece of grass below his foot as Joseph turned his attention to him.

"One thing this day should symbolize to you, Isaac, is life on earth is short." Patty was amazed by how much empathy she saw in Joseph's twinkling eyes. "I wouldn't let this go on too long if I were you."

Joseph ... ...cted attention towards the other side of the tent where Saul stood ... ...various family members and friends of the Perkins.

"I think ... ...u need to go talk him," said Joseph. "He needs you, and you may not know ... t, but you need him, too."

"I agree ... ...th Joseph, son," Patty said, squeezing Isaac's hand before releasing h... You should give your dad a chance to make it right. He really does love y... Isaac stared at the grass floor of the tent.

"I don't ... ...w, Mom," he answered without looking up. "I don't have any idea what to ...."

"Tell him ... ...at," said Joseph. "Be honest about what you're feeling but let him know y... ...e still his son. All of us are softer to family at funerals." With one last loo... ... his mom, Isaac walked towards the other side of the tent. Patty watch... ...s she took a sip of her soda.

"Patty, y... ... haven't grieved the son you lost," Joseph said with a soft glance at her.

"You m... ... .. the baby I miscarried?" Patty asked in a soft, high-pitched voice.

"Yes," ... ...h said. "Healing is coming to you." Tears began to pour out of Patty. She f... ...t warmth flooding her heart.

"I've al... ...s wondered," Patty said as she stared at the distant tent wall, "can the ba... ... lost be alive in heaven?"

"A ... ... a connection between a child and a mother is never lost," Joseph k... ... responded. "If you made a spiritual connection with the potential lif... ...side of you, then your love has that child alive and well today — in heav... ...d in your heart. It's time to heal, Patty, and stop blaming God for losing th... ...regnancy."

"I have ... ...er felt the same since that baby died. I want to feel normal again, Jose... ..." she whispered.

"You will ... he said with a soft smile. "Your journey is beginning in a new way, and y... ...d your husband are going to see great healing come into your lives." Patt... ... Joseph stop and look across the tent. Patty's eyes his and they both watch... ...saac approached his dad.

"Healin... ...ill come," Joseph said, "but it very well may still be a little rough for ... ...le." The two were startled by a shout from across the tent.

"Are yo... ...dding me?"

It was ... ... , and he was screaming at Saul.

CHAPTER 28:
LOSING A SON AND LOSING CONTROL

"I'm trying to say it's time for you to come home, Son," said Saul. "Your mom is worried sick." Patty had hurried across the grass to listen in on the discussion between her husband and her son. Saul stood with his back to the tent, palms raised as if pleading for understanding as he spoke. Isaac's eyes jerked up quickly, with a dark look that made Saul flinch. Isaac was wearing a polo shirt and khaki pants. An attempt to dress up for the occasion that made Patty remember him as a less-assured young boy. It was clear any affection he'd brought to this moment had just disappeared.

"That's what you have to say to me right now?"

"Well, yes. You can't stay with other people anymore. It's a big imposition on them." Patty's eyes worked back and forth between her two men, wondering if she should stop this ever-more public exhibition or simply let it play out.

"You've got to be freaking kidding me, Father Saul!" Isaac's ponytail trembled, the title coming from his mouth dripping with head-shaking sarcasm. "Keep your voice down, Isaac," said Saul, "we're at a memorial gathering." Isaac looked at Patty and gave a smug smile.

"Mom, can you believe this guy?" said Isaac with a caustic laugh. "After what happened the other day? Now he tells me I'm imposing on his friend?" Isaac crossed his arms on his chest, symbolizing a block of any connection to his father.

Patty's heart sank. She knew deep down Saul wanted to throw his arms around his son and apologize. However, she'd watched, time and again, how Saul was incapable of showing unqualified affection to his own child.

"Isaac, that's not what I meant," said Saul, his voice softening.

"Oh, it's exactly what you meant." Isaac pushed past Saul before Saul grabbed his son's arm. Now Patty could see Saul's eyes narrow in anger.

"Isaac, don't embarrass me like this in front of my people."

"That all you care about, isn't it, Father?" Saul held Isaac to quiet him as he looked around to see what funeral guests might overhear their argument. "What are you going to do? Hit me again?"

This made Saul drop his grip. Saul put his face in his hand which rested atop an arm crossed his body.

"You care more about who might have overheard what I said than you care about me," Isaac spat out. "That's what it's always been about—how I make you look." Isaac gave a dismissive wave towards Saul.

"I'm done! I'm moving out of your house and this God-forsaken town!"

"No, Isaac! You don't mean that," cried Patty. Saul was prepared to protest when the scene was interrupted by loud voices. Patty watched as Saul struggled to decide to stay and work on this moment with his family or fulfill his duties as Pastor at this event.

"Get out of here, you freaks!" came a shout. Patty recognized Hal's voice and a chorus of others in some sort of argument.

"Pastor, come quickly," yelled Blake Perkins at the tent entrance. Saul took one last look at his son before running past Blake and out of the tent. Patty looked at Isaac for a moment.

"Go on," Isaac said, motioning his head towards the tent opening through which Saul had disappeared. "You better make sure he doesn't get into more of a mess." Patty touched her son's arm and then walked briskly to the edge of the tent. As she exited, she saw Hal and his circle of people. They hadn't come to the funeral but were confronting The Love Coalition in the distance at the graveyard.

"Saul, be careful," Patty said in loud whisper as she walked to her husband's side. He looked at her with emotion-filled eyes. It was clear he was unsure what to do next.

Night had fallen, but the bright fluorescent lights of the cemetery gave Patty the ability to see that The Love Coalition, who had stood courteously during the graveside service, were now grouped together in a park across the street from the cemetery, holding a silent vigil. They held candles, which they had to cover with their hands to keep them burning in the light rain. They held their signs from the funeral.

Hal's group had made their own signs. "God created Adam and Eve, not Adam and Steve," and "Your lifestyle is YOUR choice, not God's!"

"You have no right to be here," yelled Rich Sullivan, standing next to Hal.

"We do have a right to be here. This is public property and we aren't doing anything to disrupt the service," said Elsa. "Unlike you."

"You're disrupting everything by being here," yelled Hal. "I don't care what the Chief or Pastor Saul say. Someone has to stand for truth around here."

"I'm not going to argue with you now, Mr. Beatty," said Elsa. "I don't want to disrespect this poor family or Thad's memory."

"I'll show you disrespect," spouted Hal, his comb-over hair now askew and sliding across his forehead, covering his left eye. He reached for the sign with the hotline phone number. "Somebody DOES care" it said in white lettering on the green background. Hal grabbed it from a young man's hands, ripped it from its wooden support, and threw it to the ground.

"Holding such a sign is disrespectful. Or don't your 'kind' understand such things?" Patty could see Elsa look at the ground and rub her temple. She was clearly measuring her response to Hal's offensive statement. She straightened up, towering over Hal, and stared down at him.

"You've persecuted us Christians long enough, Ms. Kratt," Rich Sullivan jumped in on the conversation. Elsa took a deep breath.

"You call it persecution," Elsa answered in a low, slow voice, "I call it a human response to people who are real jerks." Hal took a step towards Elsa and pointed a finger inches from her face.

"You better be careful who you call names..." Hal never finished the statement. One of the men in Elsa's group, a young man in his twenties, jumped on Hal's back with his arms around Hal's neck and wrenched him back from Elsa, pulling Hal to the ground.

"No! Keith," Elsa shouted, reaching for the two men, but she couldn't stop them from tumbling into the muddy grass. Patty looked at Saul who hesitated for a moment, then took off running towards the group.

"Saul! No!" yelled Patty, but it was too late. She watched as her husband ran into the fray and grabbed the young man to try and pull him from on top of Hal.

"Always the pastor," she murmured, feeling the increasing rainfall. Patty looked to her right and saw Joseph and Blake had come out of the tent and were standing beside her.

"Gentlemen, this is my son's memorial!" Blake yelled.

"Hal! Stop this!" yelled Saul.

"Get back, Saul, you've made your choice," said Hal, finally pushing the young man off with help from Saul. Hal scrambled to his feet, trying in vain to use his hand to repair his hair. "You did nothing to protect the church. Somebody had to do something."

"Not like this, Hal!" Saul said, his voice cracking. "Not like this." Patty could see her husband's emotions welling up. Then she saw Hal's arm recoiling—Saul, who was distracted, did not.

"Saul!"

Patty's shout was too late. Hal had a crazed look in his eyes as his clenched fist came down hard, connecting squarely on the side of Saul's temple. The punch caught Saul totally by surprise and sent him reeling to the ground. Patty rushed forward along with several men, including Joseph, who grabbed Hal and held him back from further aggression.

"Hal," said Blake, the steeliness in his voice not to be questioned, "you and your people need to leave." Blake looked around the circle. "In fact, all of you should leave." The skies broke even more and the rain came in a downpour. People scattered for shelter. Hal tried to regain respectability as he stood and pulled his jacket back into place.

"Blake, I truly do apologize," said Hal, "so sad to hear what happened to your—boy." Blake stared daggers at Hal.

"Get out of here, Hal, before I lose my temper," the father said, his fists clenched at his side.

"I'm going," Hal said as he wiped his face with a handkerchief retrieved from his jacket. He stopped and stood over Saul, who was still on his back soaking in the rain and the wet ground.

"Pastor Saul, I wasn't going to share this with you now," he said, still wiping his face with the handkerchief. "I might as well let you know we're calling a special board meeting to have a vote of censure as per our bylaws. I suspect the meeting will not go well for you. Enjoy the rest of the day with your—friends." Hal tossed the handkerchief towards Joseph who watched it hit his chest and fall to the ground.

"Maybe those freaks can help your husband up," Hal said as he scurried past Patty. Patty saw Hal lean in to Joseph heard him whisper.

"You punk," Hal growled, his hand grasping Joseph's shoulder to pull his ear even closer to Hal's mouth. "You think you can mock me in public and get away with it? I know who you are." Hal released Joseph's shoulder and looked him straight in the eye.

"And soon everyone else will know, too." Hal smiled an evil grin and, after giving Joseph a patronizing tap on the shoulder, he walked away.

Patty knelt in the mud to slide her hands underneath her husband's shoulders. Joseph took Saul's hands and together they assisted Saul in getting back to his feet. Once upright, Saul sprinted towards the tent, his feet trying to navigate the slippery field in an effort to properly finish what he'd started.

"Isaac's not there, Saul," Patty correctly alerted her husband. Isaac had left in the middle of the melee and the moment was gone. Patty watched Saul slouch into a chair near the corner of the tent and accept a towel handed to him by a waiter. As he tried to dry his normally perfect hair, Patty didn't know whether to hate him or pity him. Saul had chosen, once again, being right over his relationship with his son and Patty wondered if the Perkins weren't the only parents who'd lost a son that day.

CHAPTER 29:
CHANGES IN BEKERING

Isaac was looking forward to Joseph's storytelling group today. He was carrying the weight of conflict with his father, the sadness of Thad's funeral, and had become aware of negativity being spread around town about Joseph. Isaac's friend Tank had struggled with Joseph's message and Isaac's search for new ideas. Tank's religious upbringing and his father's rigid influence had caused Tank to refuse now to even speak to Isaac—Isaac's first experience of rejection caused by a Christian worldview that convinced people it was their godly duty to tear away from relationships out of line with their ideological views.

"I need some good news today," Isaac said out loud with a slap on his steering wheel as he drove towards the North End Grill.

Entering the restaurant, Isaac saw Joseph standing with the group near the hallway entrance to the back room. Isaac wondered why they weren't inside.

"It's locked," Joseph said to Isaac, who noticed his friend's T-shirt of the day. It was black with a picture of Jesus on the cross with the words, "Jesus was stretched for love; we should be willing to be stretched too."

"We're trying to find Mr. Abraham to get it open." Isaac ran both hands through his long hair. It was clear something wasn't right. The back room had never been locked before.

"Joseph," said Mr. Abraham as he came out of the kitchen, "there'll be no more meetings." Mr. Abraham's face was wrinkled in worry and his voice quivered as he spoke.

"What?" The group reacted with confusion. Isaac, who was carrying a week's worth of pent up emotion, let loose.

"This is bullshit!" Isaac yelled as he leaned forward and pointed an accusing finger at Mr. Abraham. Joseph raised his hands to quiet everyone.

"Calm down, there has to be a simple explanation".

"Joseph, I can't have you here anymore," said Mr. Abraham. He was wearing his regular cloth apron over his black collared polo shirt with the North End Grill logo. Joseph had said Mr. Abraham must have a hundred of those shirts, as he wore one every day. Or at least he had seven of them. "And I need to give you this."

Mr. Abraham handed a white envelope to Joseph. Isaac immediately knew it was a pink slip. The end of Joseph's tenure as a North Point Grill busboy.

"Who're you working with, Mr. Abraham? Hal Beatty? My father?" Isaac jumped in again, his face flushed with anger. "We can fight this!" Joseph gently placed a hand on Isaac's chest and pushed him away from the restaurant owner. Isaac started to protest one more time, but was stopped in his tracks by the look Joseph was giving him.

"We can fight this," Isaac pleaded with Joseph.

"No, we won't fight this, Isaac," Joseph answered firmly but in a calm voice. "People with an empowered identity know how powerful it is to turn the other cheek, rather than to get into the mud with the pigs." Isaac was amazed that Joseph showed no sign of animosity or fear, but rather seemed the perfect display of calm in a storm.

"I love your passion, Isaac. Thanks for caring about me," Joseph stated, smiling at his young friend.

"I understand, Mr. Abraham, I don't want to hurt your business."

"You're a good man, Joseph," said the shop owner who paused, choosing his words carefully. "I don't know what to say, but... he holds my lease." The group responded with groans.

"Why would Beatty want to do this to you?" Isaac asked Joseph after the group finally dispersed. Joseph grabbed his jean jacket off a peg on the wall and slipped it on.

"Because the mindsets in Bekering are strong. People don't like to give up the comfort of the status quo—they particularly don't like to have their deeply held beliefs challenged. Even if the status quo is unhealthy and dangerous." Joseph motioned for Isaac to sit down with him at an empty table.

"It's like the story of the scorpion and the frog..."

One day a scorpion and a frog stood on the side of a river, both needing to reach the other side. It was the rainy season, and the river was running high and was dangerous to cross.

"Why don't you give me a ride across the river since you can swim?" said the scorpion.

"No, the water is too high and too wild. I won't even be able to see where I'm going," responded the frog.

"I'll sit on your back and serve as your eyes to see where we're going. I can guide you."

"But you're a scorpion. When you get on my back, you'll sting me, and I'll die."

"Why would I want to hurt you?" the sly scorpion replied. "We'll both be in the water, and if I sting you, I'll die too."

The suggestion made sense to the frog, and soon the frog invited the scorpion to climb on as the two entered the treacherous water and began to swim. A short way into the trip, the scorpion raised up his tail and stung the frog three times, paralyzing him.

"Why'd you do that?" the frog asked before both creatures sank to the death awaiting below the waters. "Now we'll both die."

"I'm a scorpion," answered the culprit, "it's what I do."

Joseph smiled at Isaac and motioned for them to stand and head for the door.

"You see, Isaac, when a person allows religion to have a place in their lives for some time, and their relationship with Father God isn't deep, they become more dangerous than someone with no religion at all. They can't help it—it's what they do." Isaac watched as Joseph took one last sad look back at the North End Grill.

"Time for us to go," Joseph said, motioning towards the exit. Isaac could see the hurt on his friend's face as they walked in silence to Joseph's car. Joseph leaned against his car door and stared into the distance.

"A person with a political mindset can miss what God is doing" Joseph said, finally breaking the quiet. "A political mindset allows a person to justify bad things for a good cause. Remember, it was the religious leaders who stood against Jesus. Jesus was loved by those 'bad' people of the world." Isaac nodded in understanding.

"So, I don't completely blame people like Mr. Beatty," said Joseph as he pulled his keys from his pocket, "he's been fed this church belief system so deeply, by people like your father, cable news channels, and political leaders, he can't tell his right hand from his left."

"How does someone get out of this belief system?" Isaac asked as he shielded his eyes from the bright sun.

"Repentance."

"Like repenting of sin?"

"Sort of," said Joseph, reaching to unlock his car door. "Remember 'to repent' actually means to change your mind and go in a different direction." Joseph unlocked and opened the groaning car door, clearly in need of some lubricant on the hinge.

"You may not know this, Isaac, but the word 'Bekering' means 'repentance'" Joseph said with a laugh as he climbed into his humble vehicle. "I came here suspecting this was a town in need of just that."

"That'll never happen here," said Isaac, sliding his hands into his pants pockets and slumping his shoulders.

"Don't be so sure," Joseph answered, closing his car door and leaning out the window as the car roared to life. Isaac could see Joseph suddenly had a gleam in his eyes, as if he remembered a deep secret. "I've seen repentance before. I've watched elected officials from both parties apologize for hating one another. It's a powerful, beautiful thing." Joseph gave a short laugh.

"Don't lose heart," he yelled as he sat back in his seat and the car started to pull away. "When it gets darkest, light is about to come."

CHAPTER 30:
A CHANGE AT THE DAY OF PRAYER

"Saul, what if we didn't go," Patty said. She was watching herself in the vanity mirror on the passenger side of Saul's beloved car as she inserted an earring.

"Patty, you know I have to go to the Day of Prayer," Saul answered as he drove towards the North Bekering Shopping Center. The Bekering Day of Prayer was the annual Super Bowl of the Bekering Evangelical community. It was the day the Evangelical churches of Bekering would come together to ask God to bless their city. Saul wasn't sure what the day held, but he put on his uniform anyway—the navy-blue suit and his red, Republican power tie.

"Saul, I'm telling you things aren't right since your fight with Hal." Saul looked at Patty from the corner of his eye and could tell she was genuinely concerned.

"Hal's a Christian and a sensible guy," Saul assured his wife, even as he rubbed his bruised temple. "We'll put this all behind us for the good of everyone at the event."

"Or he'll punch you again."

Saul laughed but quickly realized Patty wasn't. Saul was actually quite worried, he just didn't want Patty to know it. Saul had driven by the venue the previous night and watched Hal's crew putting everything in place. The normal, last-minute planning meeting, in which Saul, as MC, was always involved, didn't occur last night. At least Saul didn't know if it had occurred.

As they arrived at the venue, Saul noticed the tension in his wife's face.

"I'm not going," she said suddenly, sitting back in her passenger seat and staring forward across the parking lot as Saul chose a parking space. "I don't want you to go either."

Saul took her hand and leaned in to kiss her cheek. He saw her eyes glistening with moisture, almost giving her the appearance of a scared young girl.

"It's alright," Saul said, "we have to go." Patty pushed him away.

"No, you have to go," she said. "I don't have to at all. I'm done trying to please these self-righteous people. Leave the keys, I'll sit here in the car." Saul looked at his watch. He didn't have time to argue.

"Saul," said Patty, as Saul opened the door to exit the car. "Someday this is going to have to be about you and me and our family, not about the church, town, politics, or anything else. We need to get back to 'us,' or we're going to completely lose track of one another." Saul felt the importance of the conversation she was laying before them, but it was like an itch he couldn't reach as the press of time precluded any immediate follow up. He blew her a kiss and headed towards the event entrance.

The venue was actually a grass field near the North Bekering Shopping Center transformed into a veritable outdoor conference center. This was another event previously held at the Bekering Convention Center downtown, but two years ago, Hal had become chairman of the planning committee and had moved the venue here. Red, white, and blue bunting adorned the stage. Rows of white chairs to seat nearly one thousand people from local Evangelical churches stood in neat lines in the audience, and the sound system and video screen were in place.

"Hey, Pastor Saul," said Christian Anderson, reaching to shake Saul's hand as the two walked through the entrance. "Another day of celebrating God and the Republican party?"

"Come on, Christian," Saul frowned, "give me a break. Today's not the day for your kidding."

"Oh, rough day? Sorry to hear that," Christian said with a look that Saul interpreted as truly empathetic. Even though Christian would joke with him, Saul appreciated that he could be real with Christian and didn't have to try to live up to any expectations. The two men stopped at the check-in table and, as Christian received his seat assignment for the stage, he looked at Saul with soft eyes and his lips pursed as if in consideration of what he wanted to share next.

"Don't you ever get worried, Saul, we're too closely tied with political ideology?" he asked. "After all, the Bible does say, 'if MY people will humble

THEN SE...S, THEN he will heal our land. God was telling Bible followers to repe...t...'sinners' or Democrats.'"

Sa...l s...l at the woman behind the desk and walked forward. He assumed h... ...uldn't need a seat assignment, nor the pass hanging from a yellow ...any... with the words "Bekering Day of Prayer."

"I ...ou ... worry too much, Christian," Saul responded, "we'll be praying for Go...'s ...ng today."

"I know ...at's the stated purpose," the younger pastor answered, "but even the i... ...f having Matthew McGinnis and Hal Beatty MC-ing rather than a pas... Saul blinked as he looked at Christian, trying to hide his surpris... H... ...t on his smile as he spoke.

"Hal? ...ing today?"

"It's w... I heard," Christian answered, his face displaying that he unders...o... ...shockwave he'd sent through Saul's body. "I thought you'd've known."

As Ch... ...n headed off to greet another group of pastors, Saul couldn't help reach ... ...p to his face, as if trying to make sure it didn't reveal the queasi...ess ...ng in his stomach. Saul had wondered why Matthew hadn't been li...hti... ...his phone with last minute details, but he'd refused to believe a chan...e c... ...have been made behind his back.

Sa...l tu... and headed behind the stage in a forceful power walk to find Matth...w. H... ...otted Hal coming his direction. Saul took a deep breath and tugged at h... ...llar. Time to make amends.

"Hal, n... ...o see y—" Saul was cut off mid-sentence as Hal brushed by him, nearly ...cking Saul backwards. Hal didn't acknowledge Saul's presence. Anna Ston... ...l's assistant, trailed in his wake. She looked back at Saul and shrugg...d h... ...oulders in dismay at Hal's rebuff.

"W...hat i... ...e world," Saul thought as his mind burned through numerous possibl... sc... ...os of what was taking place. He found Matthew backstage standi...g wi... ...group of volunteers.

"M...tth... ...what gives?" Matthew looked at him for a moment and heaved a sigh. He h... ...ed his clipboard to a worker next to him and guided Saul by the arm to ... ...orner of the stage.

"S...ul, ...'s been a change," Matthew said in a hushed voice. "With what's goi...g ... at the church and the board, the committee felt it might be better ...ou n... ...MC today's event."

"What're you talking about, Matthew? This has been in place for months."

"I'm sorry, Saul," said Matthew, turning to walk away, clearly wanting to keep this exchange short. "The committee made the decision."

"You mean everyone caved to Hal," said Saul, grabbing Matthew by the shoulder to stop him.

"We all agreed to this, Saul," said Matthew through clenched teeth, "now let go of me." Saul was stunned by the animosity as Matthew harshly shoved away Saul's hand. This was Saul's show. It was his plan to make today Joseph's comeuppance. Apparently, Saul's encounter with Hal at the funeral had truly changed everything.

"Matthew, how did Hal get power over this? This is supposed to be a spiritual event to pray for blessing our city."

"Don't be naive, Saul," Matthew said with a stern look. "You of all people know this event — and even our church services — stopped being spiritual years ago."

CHAPTER 31:
JOSEPH'S COMEUPPANCE

"Welcome everyone to the Bekering Day of Prayer," a voice shouted over the speaker, "brought to you today by Beatty Development and the New City Bekering Housing Development." The people began filing into the venue and Saul headed for the stage but was stopped by a security guard who asked to see his VIP badge.

"You know me, Fred," Saul said to Hal's familiar employee, "I don't have a badge."

"Pastor Saul, I apologize, but I was told not to let anyone on the stage who wasn't in the program or didn't have a badge." Saul sighed.

"Fred?" Saul pleaded with his acquaintance. The security guard hesitated, then checked his clipboard and pointed to a seat in the back row.

"That seat is empty, Pastor," Fred replied, looking around to make sure nobody was watching the interaction. "You can sit there, please don't tell anyone I allowed you through."

Saul settled in the back row next to Christian. Saul thought about leaving, but felt it important for him to stay and observe what might occur. Saul shielded his eyes to look over the crowd. He spotted Joseph in the front row, as planned. Saul could see Joseph had his hair fashioned into a man-bun today and his white T-shirt said, "God loves everyone: terrorists, immigrants, presidents, televangelists..." underneath the list, a bigger font displayed, "and even Christians."

"Welcome everyone to this amazing day," said Matthew into the microphone as the program began. His voice boomed over the large crowd.

"What a great day for Bekering, amen?"

"Amen!" The crowd responded in unison.

Matthew announced, again, Hal Beatty and his New City Bekering Housing Development as the major sponsor of the day. Hal stood from his front row seat and shook hands with Matthew while stepping to the mic.

"Like you said, a Day of Prayer being led by a political leader and a developer?" Saul whispered to Pastor Anderson.

"I'm excited to have you all here at this beautiful shopping center, today," said Hal as he stood at the front of the stage, "and to have you here, on this great piece of land, where one day, the Good Lord willing, we will see the dream fulfilled of a new city, with the building of the New City Development I will call the 'North Bekering Estates.' Some of the most beautiful housing you'll ever see in Bekering." The crowd politely applauded. Hal began to vigorously explain the voting process and the mayor's role in it. Several people in the audience loudly voiced their support for Hal and the approval of the development.

"I wonder when the Bekering Day of Prayer will actually have a moment of prayer," Pastor Anderson whispered to Saul. Saul watched as Hal waved towards Mayor Strapp, who was strategically seated behind the mic stand in the front row on stage.

"Mayor, I am grateful you're a praying man and will hear from God on this project," Hal said, pointing towards the mayor while wearing a pasted-on grin. The crowd clapped for the mayor and Andy stood and acknowledged the applause before quickly settling back in his chair.

"Wow, Hal must think he's brilliant, putting the mayor on the spot like that," Christian said to Saul with an eyebrow raised in disbelief. "Beatty clearly thinks the mayor won't have the guts to vote against the Bekering Christian community." Saul quickly glanced at Christian and gave a nod before turning his attention back to the show.

"Also, today," Hal continued, his shrill voice booming, "we want to acknowledge a young man catching attention as he has ministered in our town." Hal looked to his right and motioned to where Joseph was sitting

"Joseph is right here in the front row. Please stand up and be acknowledged, Joseph."

The crowd applauded as Joseph slowly rose, looking suspiciously at Hal. Joseph pivoted to give his trademark smile and a slight wave to the crowd before turning his eyes back to the stage.

"Here it comes," Saul heard a pastor in front of him say to another. "Wonder if this guy has any idea what's about to happen." Saul leaned in for a clear view of Joseph. He suddenly felt less excited about his plot as he watched it from an outsider's view.

"To tell us more about Joseph, let me introduce Pastor Abel Hackenworth of the Stanton Avenue Christian Church." Hal held out his arm welcoming Pastor Hackenworth to the microphone.

"Thank you, Mr. Beatty," said Pastor Hackenworth, buttoning his suit jacket as he prepared to speak in his normal, sing-song preaching style. "Now many of you have had the pleasure of listening to Pastor Joseph's teaching and ministry. Perhaps you have even heard talk of miracles he has performed. Well, your pastors want you to know we are not fooled by all the soft words and so-called miracles."

Saul quickly shifted his gaze from Pastor Hackenworth to Joseph. He had a difficult time gauging Joseph's reaction. Joseph looked stoic, only his eyes betraying a clear sadness.

"We've seen men like this before come through towns like ours," the pastor stated, looking down at Joseph, "men like this come with evil intent to harm our people." Saul could hear a buzz working its way through the crowd.

"This is wrong!" Christian Anderson shouted as he jumped to his feet, causing Saul to jerk his head to so hard towards Christian he wondered if his neck would hurt tomorrow morning. Saul was shocked at Christian's courage. "Joseph has done nothing but encourage the people of our town. And he's been brave enough to say things many of us have felt for a long time."

"Sit down, Pastor Anderson," said Hal from his front row seat giving the pastor an intimidating stare.

"This is flat out wrong, Hal Beatty."

"Sit down, immediately, please," said Hal coldly, "or I will have you removed from the stage."

"Saul, do something," Christian pleaded, turning to Saul, "you know this isn't right!" Saul wasn't going to do anything. He was wallowing in his own struggles. Saul ashamedly looked away from his friend and back at Joseph.

"Will any of you guys stand with me against this?" the young pastor asked, his eyes moving back and forth among the others on the stage.

The crowd appeared to be growing uncomfortable, and not just from the glaring morning sun. Few pastors would meet Christian's gaze as Ha; beckoned for two security guards who quickly appeared on the stage. Seeing the gutless response of the other pastors, Pastor Anderson headed towards the stage steps.

"You don't have to remove me, I'll leave. I want no part of this." Christian walked down the steps to a smattering of boos from the crowd. The other pastors looked at one another, but none was willing to do anything more than shake their heads.

"Let's get this back on track," said Hal, twirling his hand forward in a circular motion, signaling for Pastor Hackenworth to continue.

"Yes, uh— forgive us the disturbance," said Pastor Hackenworth in a hurried fashion. "As I was saying, our pastors have queried Joseph as to his credentials to ensure you people are being kept safe with good, biblical teaching. Our findings? Well, Mr. Joseph isn't a minister at all."

"Our findings?" Saul mumbled to no one in particular. Saul leaned forward with his palms on his knees, trying to catch his breath, almost as if he'd been punched in the gut. This event was becoming an ode to Hal's personal vendettas, and everyone was falling in line.

"No, people, our Joseph is no minister." The pastor's tone became sinister. "He's only a man. A busboy. And what's more, he's not been honest with you about who he is. Our Joseph grew up in Bekering and left when his family moved away many years ago."

Sounds of "oh my" and other exclamations could be heard throughout the crowd. Hal focused his stare at Joseph, who seemed to be calmly focused on the sky behind the stage.

"Why did your father leave town, Joseph? What secrets are you hiding from all these good people?" the pastor cajoled. "Why haven't you told people you are from Bekering?"

Saul was unsure what these questions were all about. He'd simply planned for the pastors to tell people Joseph was not a credentialed minister and to speak of heresy. This additional information must have come through Hal's research team.

"I heard from Matthew McGinnis that Joseph's father was run out of town for something illegal," said a pastor seated in front of Saul.

"Let me tell you folks," Pastor Hackenworth's voice dropped attempting to underscore the seriousness of the matter, "Joseph didn't want you to know his secret because his father was literally run out of town in scandal. This Joseph is the son of a scandalous contractor who had to leave town. Joseph is not someone who does supernatural acts. He's simply the son of a defamed Bekering peddler." The crowd began to murmur even more. Pastor Hackenworth looked down at Joseph with incredulity.

"What is it, Joseph? Why have you hidden this secret?" Everyone looked at Joseph.

Joseph didn't move but stood with the same austere look on his face as he remained silent. Saul watched as Hal motioned to his security leader to be on notice.

"This man talks about being connected to heaven, calls our Lord 'The Divine,'" said Pastor Hackenworth. "He has no reverence for God. No awe or fear of God talked about in Scripture. Joseph, do you not fear the Lord?" Saul saw Joseph had closed his eyes and appeared to be praying. He continued to show no sign of answering the accusations coming from the stage.

"Do you not have a word to answer these charges?" Pastor Hackenworth continued with a hearty laugh. "Apparently the storyteller has nothing to say." The rotund pastor barked another deep-toned laugh. The crowd chattered loudly now, and Saul could see the uproar begin to grow.

"Watch what happens now." Hal had turned around and was alerting the pastors and leaders behind him. "My employees out there will get things stirred up." Hal was right. What began as a murmur was now a low roar, continuing to grow.

Boos burst out in the crowd as Joseph stood unwavering. Hal pulled Pastor Hackenworth back from the microphone, giving room for the crowd's discontent to grow. Hal cupped his hands to his mouth and joined the chorus of boos as they crescendoed.

"Who are you?" yelled someone in the crowd.

"What did you come here to do?" yelled another.

"You are a FAKE pastor!" Suddenly the audience began to chant.

"Fake! Fake! Fake!"

"Who are you, Mr. Joseph?" said Hal, stepping up to the mic to lead the chants. "Nobody wants some fake from the outside coming to Bekering and telling us how to live."

"Fake! Fake!" Saul could hear the chant gaining steam as Hal led the yelling into the event sound system.

"In my day we would have taught this man a lesson and made him pay for his sins." He stared Hal with a big grin. "We'd have handled a man like this and then run him out of town on a rail!" Saul's mouth was agape as he looked at Hal in disbelief. Was Hal calling for physical violence against Joseph?

Just as Saul had feared, a man lunged over a row of chairs at Joseph before audience members and a security guard held him from falling on his face.

"Fake! Fake!" The chants were louder now and being shouted by an overwhelming majority of the people in the event area. A cup filled with soda and ice came from somewhere in the crowd on a high trajectory and landed squarely on the side of Joseph's head, exploding in a wet mess over Joseph's face and hair. The sticky substance ran down the sides of Joseph's head, causing his long hair to unfurl from the man-bun and stick to him. The soda was followed by a full water bottle landing at the base of Joseph's neck, temporarily causing him to lose his balance and sink to one knee.

"Behold your miracle worker," Hal shouted into the microphone.

"Oh my God," said Saul, sitting up on the edge of his chair. His plan had been to call Joseph out and expose him, not to incite a riot. He jumped up and waved his hands. "Please everyone, this is not how we do things."

Saul was too late and without a microphone. He was also too far away to stop the older man in the jean jacket who'd come around and thrown his shoulder into Joseph, knocking him from one knee to his back with full force.

Saul watched in horror as the mob mentality gave people permission to be their worst selves. He was stunned at how easily the fear and anger of his people could be worked into a frenzy.

Joseph was a drenched mess as an increasing number of items were thrown in his direction. He scrambled back to his feet and Saul could see him looking at the faces Saul knew as BCC regulars. He saw Joseph lock eyes with Tina Bettz, Isaac's young friend, whom Saul had seen at Joseph's storytelling events. Tina was standing directly in front of Joseph, with an angry, shriveled face, shouting along with the crowd.

Suddenly Joseph looked up at Saul who could see heartbreak in Joseph's eyes. There was nothing Saul could do but slink back to his chair, overwhelmed with shame at what Bekering and his political followers had become.

Another man came running at Joseph. Saul recognized Tank Cook, Isaac's former friend, who looked intent on inflicting physical harm.

"Watch out!" Saul heard someone yell, but it was too late. Tank threw a hard right hand to Joseph's face, knocking him once again to the ground. Saul was shocked to see that a police officer standing by did nothing as Tank launched onto Joseph and landed several more blows. When other officers finally pulled Tank back, Saul realized it was Myles Cook, Tank's father who had stood motionless as this violence took place.

Saul put his hand over his mouth, sickened by scene.

"You're all good, God-fearing people in a God-fearing town," shouted Hal, his smile revealing his enjoyment of the moment. "Thank God for these men on this stage and our officers who will protect this city from interlopers like this man."

"God had nothing to do with this," said Saul to no one in particular as he watched Joseph being dragged by the officers behind the stage.

"Fake! Fake! Fake!" Hal again chanted along with the crowd, and many of the pastors on the stage.

"Wow, it didn't take much to stir the people up against the guy, did it?" said a pastor sitting slightly down the row from Saul.

"Yes, it's a shame," groaned Saul. "A shame we Christians are so easily manipulated to look more like the whitewashed tombs of the Bible than look like Jesus." Saul had the revelation that this was a natural outcome of the political and religious division he'd created and nurtured in Bekering.

CHAPTER 32:
LOVE THINE ENEMIES

Saul slowly slid from his chair and walked to the stairs in order to exit unnoticed as he slowly slid out of his chair.

"How'd you like the event, Saul?" smirked Hal who had approached before Saul could leave. He stared at Saul like a cheap jewel thief who'd gotten away with the crime. Saul looked at the ground and gave a pained laugh as he wheeled to leave without responding. Saul's progress was stopped by Hal's big paw as he pulled Saul close enough to smell the coffee on Hal's hot breath.

"You learned a lesson today, Pastor," Hal whispered in Saul's ear. "Mayors and pastors come and go but I will always run this town." Saul shook his shoulders free and headed quickly out of the venue.

"I saw Joseph dragged out," said Patty in a panic as Saul arrived at the car. The engine was running and the air conditioning had continued to run to keep the car interior cool. "I asked Joseph what happened but he didn't even look at me. Was this your idea?"

Saul plopped into the driver's seat as the two sat with only the car's AC making a sound.

"What happened to Joseph?" Patty demanded. "Is he going to be alright?"

Saul looked coldly towards his wife.

"I really don't know," he said, his skin tight against his cheekbones. "I'm not sure if anything will be alright."

"But..." Saul cut his wife's sentence short as his hand slapped down on the steering wheel in a moment of intense rage.

"I don't care about Joseph!" Saul barked and then his anger evaporated like a bright firework disappearing in the air. "I think I lost everything."

Patty didn't move. She was afraid of the violent reactions she had witnessed from her husband in the past week, but she was even more terrified to see his sorrow.

About to apologize, Saul heard a tap of knuckles on his window. He was surprised to see Elsa Kratt standing beside his car.

"Hello, Pastor Saul," said Elsa as Saul looked up at her through his descending automatic window. "Forgive me for bothering you. I need to share something."

"I—I'm surprised to see you here," stammered Saul.

"I do like to see what's happening in my city," she responded, "so I bought a ticket." Elsa placed her palms up against the roof of the car and leaned in to keep the glare of the sun from her eyes.

"Of course. Good," Saul answered. He saw Elsa's eyes move to Patty and give a smile. "Where are my manners, this is my wife, Patricia."

"Patty, please," Patty responded, reaching across Saul to offer her hand in greeting to Elsa.

"Please, forgive me for bothering you," Elsa said as she shook Patty's hand. "I've desired to apologize." Saul's head twisted in shock. He looked at Patty to see if she was as surprised as him.

"Apologize?" Saul answered, turning back to Elsa. Saul's brain quickly catalogued the times he'd encountered Elsa and remembered the anger he'd felt towards her. He remembered sermons referencing those meetings. Even with this history, Elsa had always been civil to him. He wondered why she would feel the need to apologize.

"I've been in many arguments and struggles with you," Elsa stated, "and I've felt a great deal of anger towards you."

"We've had our moments," Saul responded with a light smile, trying to lighten the lead weight of guilt he felt in his gut. Elsa agreed with a smile of her own.

"A friend recently pointed out to me that I've never once asked you to sit and share what you see in our city. Maybe we could've found something on which to collaborate, for the good of Bekering." Saul tried to hide what he was feeling but was betrayed by his fading smile.

"Wow, so wonderful and kind of you," said Patty. "Isn't it, Saul?" Saul stared at his wife in silence for a moment before realizing he needed to speak.

"Yes. Yes, of course, it is," he said, trying to smile nonchalantly. This was a moment grace would have served him well, but grace never seemed to replace Saul's need to feel righteous. "You understand, Ms. Kratt, the things we disagree on are vast. I don't see how they don't overwhelm anything we might have in common." Elsa's head bobbed back as her smile became a look of surprised confusion.

"We're both human beings, for one," said Elsa, her tone filled with disbelief, "and we both love this place. Why can't we find ways to put aside our differences?"

"Because—well, because we can't," said Saul, "I can't." There wasn't great conviction behind his words as he stumbled on. "What you're saying sounds nice, but my Bible is clear your life choices make it impossible for me to collaborate with you. I can't endorse your lifestyle."

"Oh, this is so crazy, Pastor Saul," Elsa argued. "If we do a fundraising drive together for a good Bekering charity we both believe in, how is that an endorsement of anything other than caring for people?"

"Don't get me wrong," said Saul, "in many ways I think you're a very fine person..."

"Saul!" exclaimed Patty, placing a hand on her husband's shoulder as if to will him in another direction.

"But I'm clearly evil and bound for hell?" Elsa retorted. Her face grew serious and she leaned closer to the open window.

"Now, let's not get emotional, Ms. Kratt," said Saul, raising his hand as if to stop the conversation from proceeding.

"How can you not get emotional?"

"Me?" Saul responded, his brow furrowed in confusion.

"If I were you I'd get emotional at being trapped by crazy ideas and that those ideas led to the beat down of nice young man today." Elsa shook her head.

"That trap has you all so close-minded, you can't even have normal thought and introspection around issues," she said, her volume increasing. "Trapped by trying to please selfish, dishonest men like Hal Beatty in the name of your religion."

The silence hung heavily between the two.

"I may have overstepped my bounds," Elsa stated, bringing her volume back down to her normal level, "but, am I wrong?"

Saul sat staring at his steering wheel.

"No dear, you're not wrong," Patty finally chimed in, leaning towards Saul to make eye contact with Elsa.

Without warning, a car stopped in the lane in front of where Saul had parked. A window rolled down and an elderly lady said something to Elsa. Saul couldn't hear what was said and leaned towards the window for a better vantage point from which to hear.

"I'm sorry?" said Elsa in the direction of the woman's car. A man whom Saul assumed was the woman's husband was driving the car.

"I said you're a horrible person," the woman shouted, leaning out her own window, her face scrunched into an angry sneer. "You ought to be ashamed for the things you do and say." The woman pointed an accusing finger at Elsa as her husband accelerated and drove away from Saul's car, leaving a fog of dust behind. Saul cringed at the exchange.

"Pastor, I'd love for you to answer something for me," Elsa finally spoke as she tucked tight and pulled her white T-shirt taught over the waistband of her jeans. "How could Jesus love a thieving, traitorous tax collector, an outcast person with a very contagious skin disease, a prostitute and a woman from a different culture..."

Elsa looked down at Saul; he felt like she towered over his car.

"...but Jesus' people—your people—can talk to me like this? Heck, even you are afraid to be seen in public with me."

"I'm no afraid, Elsa. I simply can't collaborate with you." Elsa backed up from the car door and squinted in the sunlight.

"I pity you, Pastor," she said. "You're the one trapped in a lifestyle." Saul looked at Patty as Elsa walked away.

"I can't turn my back on truth," he said softly. Saul put the car in drive and he and Patty headed home in silence.

"Why can't we?" Patty finally asked as they were halfway to home.

"Why can't we what?" Saul responded, turning the wheel of the car to follow The Loop.

"Why can't we love Elsa as she is?" Saul looked at his wife, wondering if the question were rhetorical or if she wanted an answer. Saul decided to leave the question unanswered as he drove home deep in thought.

"She's better than we are," Patty finally spoke again into the air. Saul continued to drive in silence, having nothing he could say to prove her wrong.

CHAPTER 33:
A FRUSTRATED DRIVE

It was Saturday afternoon in Bekering, two days after the Day of Prayer event, and the town was still abuzz. Joseph had not been seen since leaving the North Bekering Shopping Center and everyone assumed he'd left town for good in humiliation. If anyone was saddened by this, not many were willing to admit it.

Isaac hadn't come home except to pick up a few belongings when Saul was not around. Isaac's absence hung as a great sadness over the Thompson home and was a weight on Saul as he tried to prepare for tomorrow's sermon.

"I need something," he spoke into the air. Saul knew there was a good chance it would be his last sermon at BCC, as the special board meeting had been slated for Tuesday.

"Aaaagh," Saul groaned in the silence of his home study. He tossed his reading glasses on the desk and decided to pass some time in front of the TV in the den.

"Welcome to Fox News—Fair and Balanced," came the audio through the speakers in front of the TV monitor. On the screen was one of the young, attractive female news hosts on Saul's favorite cable channel. The network always seemed to have a female host in a short skirt sharing the news from a couch or behind a plexiglas desk. Such sexualizing of women would normally irritate Saul, but because this station provided the "true" news, sympathetic to his beliefs, Saul was much less critical of how it operated. He sat in his favorite chair as the TV droned on.

"The Democrats' evil plot to overthrow the President continues," said the woman. "We have the exclusive details of this conspiracy…"

"Nah, let's check out something else," Saul mumbled as he clicked the remote.

"…Developer Hal Beatty and Republican party leader Matthew McGinnis have pressured the city council and mayor on this week's New City annexation vote," said the Channel 5 reporter's voice over the video. "And that pressure has stepped up as the mayor's support for the project seems to have wavered. Beatty says a vote of support for his new development is critical for Bekering."

"Any opponent of this project is an opponent of jobs for the people of Bekering," Hal said as he was being interviewed, "and is against progress for our city."

"Are you including Mayor Strapp as someone against progress of the city?" asked the reporter into his microphone. "He says he may veto the approval if it's passed." The reporter tilted the mic back towards Hal.

"I believe the mayor will make the right decision," Hal said with his best smile, "as will the rest of the council." Saul felt that familiar queasy feeling in his stomach as he watched Hal revel in his influential position.

"So, that's it, Saul?" Patty's voice rang out. Patty had come into the room and was standing with a tense stare and her hands on her hips. "That jerk is on TV with his fat grin and we lose everything?" She started to speak again but then put her hand over her mouth and stared into the kitchen. Her silence enveloped Saul like a fog.

"What do you want me to do, Patty?" he asked.

"I want my son back," she shouted, her emotions erupting like a bottle blowing its lid, "and I want you to be the leader of our house, not Hal Beatty." She headed towards the kitchen.

"Forget this, I'm getting a drink."

"Honey, don't" he pleaded, but she was already around the corner and the clink of the bottles resounded from the kitchen cabinet. Saul suddenly needed to be out of the house. He grabbed his keys and headed for the car.

The Thompson's one financial extravagance was Saul's BMW convertible. He loved to let off steam by driving at high speed around town. Saul jumped on Highway 95 and saw the needle climb past ninety. He headed back onto Beatty Road and sped towards town, pressing the accelerator again as he gave a yell and smacked his steering wheel with his fist. Saul was feeling a lifetime-worth of frustration well up. Hadn't he done enough? Saul was startled by the red and blue lights in his rear-view mirror.

"Perfect ending to a perfect day," he said looking up into the mirror. After receiving the ticket and a stern warning to slow down, Saul drove aimlessly until he looked up and saw the church.

"What the heck," he said as he parked and headed inside.

CHAPTER 34:
SAUL'S SEARCH FOR ANSWERS

"God, you saved a wretch like me, but now I feel you've left me to fail." Saul folded his hands and he leaned on the seat back in front of him. He felt the turmoil in him. His emotions fluctuated from anger, to fear, to being absolutely puzzled at how his well-planned life had come to this situation. "Oh, God," Saul moaned as he absent-mindedly tugged at the white shirt collar which peeked out from his yellow sweater.

He let his eyes sweep the BCC sanctuary. In the dim lighting of the one bank of lights he had turned on, Saul noted the opulence of the room. The rich tan and gold trim of the paint, the decorative, sound-absorbing pads on the wall and the elegant risers on which the choir would stand tomorrow morning. There was the expensive, water-consuming, heated baptistry behind the top-of-the-line drum cage and the expensive in-ear monitoring system awaiting their music team. Three enormous video screens hung above it all.

Saul had worked feverishly nine years ago to raise the money for all this and it was everything he'd dreamed it would be. Every detail thought through with excellence. It was built with Saul's belief such a room properly displayed God's splendor and showed God not to be a beggar. Tonight, however, even the plush theater seat couldn't ease Saul's pain.

"Everything here was built for comfort," he thought, "but there's no comfort here for me." His normally well-kept black hair was askew, and Saul's regular impish grin was replaced by a tight-lipped grimace.

"I guess I'm the one who has always supplied the answers here, perhaps that's been the problem." Saul's stomach rolled with a hungry grumble, but he was too distraught to realize he hadn't eaten for most of the day. He was much more aware of the torment in his soul than that of his stomach.

"Haven't I done enough for you, God?" Saul pleaded, his voice strained as his prayers were now spoken out loud. "Why have you forsaken me?" Saul slid from his seat and climbed to the acrylic podium on the platform as if to give a sermon to the empty seats facing him.

"God's game," he spoke in a tense voice as he began a hopeless talk, "is to use people up and then abandon them when he's done with them." Saul slammed his hand down onto the pulpit to finish his point.

"Ladies and gentlemen, I stand before you as a testament to this truth. Amen?" There was no response other than the echo of his own voice.

"My son! My job! My reputation!" Saul screamed, his voice cracking from the force of his anger. "I'm losing everything, God, and you're nowhere to be found!" Saul's face was red with anger as his accusations continued.

"Maybe I'll tell them the truth about you. I'll tell them you're the kind of God willing to take everything from a man and leave him to die, like you did my..." His head dropped, the tears leaving his eyes and landing in a splash on the pulpit. He made no effort to stop them.

"...Like you did my father," Saul said in a low voice, sobs pushing their way out from deep inside of him. "God? Do you even care?"

"I promise you there is care for you." The voice came from the back of the room and startled Saul. He looked up and saw Joseph coming down the aisle. Joseph looked different. He still wore his jeans and had on a T-shirt. This one said, "You can tell me to go to hell, but I'm going in a different direction!" Despite his normal attire, Saul sensed a different atmosphere around the young man. New age people might call it an "aura." To Saul, Joseph was... different. Saul wiped his face to feign composure.

"I thought you left town," he said as Joseph approached and sat in the second row.

"No, I headed out to spend some quiet time connecting to heaven. My purpose here isn't complete." Saul looked closely at Joseph and was surprised he had no visible markings from the scuffle from two days ago. Saul might have imagined a swollen eye or at least a few cuts and scrapes would still with his head crooked to one side.

"I think it's good you're finally getting honest," said Joseph.

"Good that I'm screaming at God?"

"Look at the Psalms," explained Joseph. "Those are some pretty salty accusations. No truly omnipotent god would be afraid of that." Saul stared at the back of the chair in front of him. Joseph's voice lowered, taking on a more serious tone.

"Listen to me, Saul. It's a great day because it's the next phase of your life. You have great influence in your community and that influence is not ending now," Joseph laughed and hit the seat back in front of him so hard it made Saul jump. "In fact, it's just beginning! You, Saul Thompson, are the reason I'm here. You are the answer to Bekering's prayer."

Saul studied Joseph's kind face and soft eyes before breaking out into laughter.

"You really are crazy, Joseph," Saul said through his cackles. "God has thrown me on the scrap heap."

"Not at all," answered Joseph. "You're just being nudged to a bit of repentance."

"That's a pretty dang hard nudge," Saul chuckled, "but I'm sure I need to repent. I'm a sinner like so many others." Joseph looked at him with a smile but didn't respond.

"What?" Saul asked in discomfort.

"You've simply missed the goodness of heaven in all this."

"How?" Saul felt his anger return as he was chided again by this young man. "I've followed everything I know to do." Joseph smiled again for an awkwardly long moment, giving Saul's impetuous anger a moment to recede.

"You know I'm going to have to tell you a story, right?"

"I guess that's your job," Saul answered with a smile of his own. It was the first time he had authentically smiled all day.

194

CHAPTER 35:
A HARSH GOD

"This story is called 'The Investor and the Dividends,'" said Joseph. "There was a rich leader of a successful investment business whose responsibilities were taking him away for an extended time..."

"Here's an allotment of investment money," said the Boss to three of his workers. "While I'm gone, I want you guys to keep the business moving." The Boss went away and when he returned, he checked on the workers. The first worker was the Boss's best guy.

"I wanted to kill it while you were gone," said the first worker. "I invested aggressively and doubled your money. Man, I love this business!"

"Great job," said the Boss. "I'm putting you in charge of ten departments."

"I'm still learning the business, Boss," the second worker said, "but I did my best and have a fifty percent return on your money."

"Awesome," said the Boss. "I'm going to put you in charge of five departments.

The Boss called in his third worker. This guy was always tough. He was a stickler for the rules, hassling his co-workers and constantly working on things which didn't expand or advance the business. The Boss had decided this was the last chance for the third worker.

"I know how important your money is to you, Sir," the third worker said with the false humility of a man who assumed his superiority to the others. "They were risking your money and I became concerned. I put my portion in a drawer to ensure at least some of your money would be here when you returned." The Boss looked at the third worker, disgusted.

"I gave my business to you and you didn't do the work of the business. You were more interested to watch the others fail than doing what I'd asked you to do. Did you really think I needed you to protect my money?" said the

Boss. "I could have put the money in the bank myself and gained a little interest and saved the cost of your salary. You've misjudged me. I love when my workers risk investing the things I give to them. If we fail while trying to grow the company, I'll absorb that loss. But you are so sure I want to bring punishment for failure that you're unwilling to have any hope of success. I'm giving your investment fund to the first worker and your days here are over."

"The Parable of the Minas," said Saul, referring to the Bible story Joseph had modernized. "I've taught on this story many times. The first worker represents Christians who do the work they're supposed to do and the third worker is someone who does nothing. They hide their testimony of Christ." Joseph's smile faded a bit and he looked at Saul almost with pity in those kind eyes.

"You see, Saul, you've totally missed the meaning of that story." Saul sniffed for a moment, feeling a bite from Joseph's reply.

"Then why don't you enlighten me to the true meaning?"

Saul's caustic response caused the young man to stop for a moment. Saul thought Joseph might respond negatively, but he continued with grace. "The first worker represents someone who's come into the full relationship with God as a father. In this relationship a person is empowered to do the work of God."

"I think you just repeated what I said," Saul responded.

"No, your answer was about doing work," Joseph pushed back. "The values of heaven are for people, not for fulfilling tasks. We ought to be about the work of our Christian life from our love for him. Not out of some duty to him. We can only work from love if we know how to love ourself." Joseph leaned back in his seat, studying Saul for a moment.

"The first worker understood the Boss's true character, the third worker did not." Joseph leaned in towards Saul. "The third worker is you!" Saul's eyes grew wide and his face darkened.

"Come on," Saul argued.

"You, Saul, don't understand the character of your boss," Joseph said, his look growing more somber. "You follow a harsh taskmaster, not a good father."

"But God can be harsh," Saul retorted. This caused Joseph to rise from his seat and motion for Saul to follow.

Joseph led Saul up the long aisle to the gold-gilded foyer. The room was filled with commissioned paintings from several local artists.

"What do you see in this picture, Saul?" asked Joseph, directing Saul to a huge painting near the building's front exit. The painting was probably four feet in height, but still was swallowed up in this large entryway and missed if one wasn't intentional to study it.

"It's the Bible story of 'The Woman Caught in Adultery,'" answered Saul. Prior to this moment, he'd never really noticed the painting.

"Do you see in this picture any thing of heaven that is harsh?" asked Joseph, smiling as he viewed the portrait. Saul looked as well. It depicted Jesus writing with his finger in the dust, squatting in front of a terrified woman who was on her knees, barely covered in tattered clothes seemingly ripped from her. Her hair was a mess, everything about her was frantic. She was desperately looking at Jesus, as if understanding he was her only chance to be saved from the death she was due by the law of the religious leaders.

You couldn't see the faces of the men surrounding them in a circle, only their feet and the bottoms of their fine robes. Saul could see Jesus was looking at the woman even as his finger was engaging the dirt. He had a look of caring and safety in his eyes. Not unlike... well, not unlike the look he'd seen on Joseph's face tonight.

Saul noticed Joseph's smile as he pondered the painting.

"Well, I guess I don't see a harsh God," Saul finally answered with an awkward grin for Joseph. Saul was feeling his beliefs being chipped away as Joseph gently challenged him. "Jesus is going to chase away her condemners."

"But didn't she sin?" asked Joseph with a hint of a mocking tone.

"Well, yes. She did sin."

"Then why is God letting her get away with it?" Joseph asked now tilting his head slightly to the right as he seemed to ponder his own question. "He's not," said Saul. "Jesus is going to tell her to go and sin no more."

"Yes, after putting his own life on the line for her and he's totally forgiven her," Joseph said as he pivoted from the painting to Saul and raised his finger to make his point. "That's your harsh God. Not only does heaven forgive, as with this woman, but even risks life and reputation for those who deserve punishment. Doesn't sound very harsh to me, Saul."

Saul didn't answer. He looked back at the painting.

"Saul, which group are you?" Joseph asked, again gesturing to the portrait. "The rock throwers? Or with Jesus in giving the woman freedom to move on with her life, without a religious beat down?" Saul crossed his arms, pivoted and leaned against the wall next to the painting.

"I've been pretty harsh, I think," Saul said looking down at the foyer's plush red carpet. "Like the men in the picture."

"Because you follow a God who is harsh, you have to be harsh to others," Joseph said. The empathy in those eyes moved Saul and he felt his emotions coming to the surface. Saul moved to sit on a bench nearby, staring off across the room. He felt his world was going sideways from the conversation.

"But when heaven gives generously," Joseph continued, "you can see the divine as loving—not harsh. Like the second worker in the story, someone not of your same belief, yet they've captured heaven's heart in ways you can't see. Like Elsa."

Saul's head whipped around as Joseph sat down next to him.

"Elsa? But she's a sinner…"

"Saul," Joseph responded placing a fatherly hand on Saul's shoulder. "Are you going to be one who throws rocks at Elsa, or one who stands against her condemners?" Saul looked down at his hands as he nervously rubbed them together.

"There are people in Bekering who don't ever attend church yet carry more divine love for this city and its people than a lot of Christians I've seen." Saul could see that nudge to repentance in Joseph's eyes, but Saul wasn't fully on board.

"But if someone is living in sin," he asked, "how can they capture divine love?"

"Come on, Saul, don't you see it yet?" Joseph prodded, "you've missed the whole story. You need to understand a new definition for 'sin.'" Joseph leaned forward.

"You think sin is about a list of rules and some god with a naughty or nice list, like Santa Claus. This is why you accuse God, because you don't understand the nice list is for those who live in relationship with others, and the naughty list is for those who try to impose rules on themselves and others."

"And it's also why you believe that god punished your father," Joseph shared with a look of compassion in his eyes, "and believe you were left alone to suffer the consequences of that punishment."

Saul couldn't quite compute what he'd heard. He wrestled with his emotional response to Joseph's mention of his father and Joseph seemed to recognize it.

"Saul, the goodness of heaven was there, in the backseat of the car with you in elementary school." Joseph's voice was soft, his shoulders relaxed. It appeared Joseph no longer wanted to prove a point but wanted to share in a gentle way.

"What—how could you possibly know about that?" Saul stammered. "Oh, yeah. God—uh—heaven tells you things." Joseph was quiet as the suppressed memory flooded Saul, feelings hidden for a long time now exposed by this stranger. Saul's nature was to resist these feelings, but the tears were coming.

"God was making us pay for Dad's sin," Saul said as he parsed through his memories. "I don't understand it, but God works…"

"God works in mysterious ways?" Joseph interrupted. He sighed deeply. "Saul, once again you've misjudged…"

"I've misjudged the goodness of heaven, I know, I know," Saul responded facing towards Joseph and waving his hands. "You don't know what it's like to have your father's pride stolen from him."

"Actually, I do, Saul." Saul stopped for a moment.

"Oh yes—your dad. The contractor."

"He was railroaded out of town by people like Hal Beatty because he wouldn't play their crooked game." The two sat for a moment staring ahead.

"Bad things don't happen to people for good purposes," Joseph spoke up. "But bad things do happen, but we know the love and goodness and wisdom are there for us even in the bad things."

"I can't believe that," Saul said softly as his back stiffened and he leaned forward on the bench. "There's no way goodness was with us as my father's life fell apart."

"You were taught that bad things happened because God is mad and thus you thought your father losing his job was his fault for offending your harsh god. But, it wasn't God's fault or your father's fault that he was fired." Saul shook visibly as he processed what was taking place. He looked at Joseph, desperate for help for the pain welling up.

"You believe there can be divine mercy for the woman in the painting, but not for you, Saul?" Saul wanted to answer but stopped. He looked at the woman in t   ainting across the entryway. Saul's spirit broke and the tears were j   heartfelt cries as Saul buried his face in his hands. The pain he'd ke   n for many years rushed to be free, and Saul was afraid now that it   ed, it wouldn't stop.

"My d   came a monster," Saul said through his sobs, the tears falling on his   nts leaving droplet marks on his thigh as he felt the full, deep pain of his

"I   my dad was in HELL!" Saul moaned, slapping his hands on his thig   ooking at Joseph was fire in his eyes. "Oh God help me!"

Saul re   d a torrent of loud wails and cries letting out years of pain. He marveled J   was willing to simply sit with him in silent support.

"If the   you've worked so hard for were here right now," Joseph said when   spoke, "what would you say to him? Be completely honest."

"Why   ou allow my dad to be hopeless and die?" Saul said without thinking,   est tightened, "It wasn't fair. And it isn't fair what's happening to me now."

"S   he most honest thing you've said in a long time," Joseph said softly, and   divine is happy you two are speaking again."

Saul sl   d back, suddenly exhausted. Joseph smiled.

"Your   ng is happening, and it's happening fast." Joseph looked around the   n once again.

"You've   your job was to protect others from the wrath of your harsh god." Saul   d thinking for a moment and nodded his head in agreement. "What you   y should be doing is the business of heaven, risking investment in people."

Said cl   his eyes and nodded his head. Something told him Joseph was right. Saul   d his head in his hands before sitting up and speaking.

"Ch m   sh, I've believed something untrue for so long." Saul moved his eye   in thought. "And it's clouded my view of God and my purpose here or   d in Bekering. But God's not punishing me, he's…"

"You c   y it," smiled Joseph.

"He's   ad at me." The two men laughed together.

"Dad?"   oice came from the other end of the foyer. Saul was stunned to see Isaac   Patty.

"Isaac?   at're you doing here?"

Patty s   d and gave him an encouraging nod.

"Mom called and asked me to help her find you," Isaac said, fighting back emotions. "I told her I didn't care, but she was worried…" his voice trailed off.

"Son?" Saul rose and moved towards them. There was a moment of tension, then Isaac ran forward and grabbed his father in a tight embrace, their cries overlapping.

"Please forgive me, Son," cried Saul. "If…"

"I know, Dad," said Isaac, his tears flowing. Patty walked over and joined in and the three were entwined together.

"Thank you, Jo-," Saul turned to thank the bearded young man, but Joseph had left the family alone to reconnect.

CHAPTER 36:
A NEW SERMON

The parking lot at The Bekering Christian Center this Sunday was a snarl of traffic for each of the three services, well beyond the norm. People must have sensed there would something to see, like a car accident drawing gawkers. Saul was headed to his office after the second service and was surprised to find it unlocked.

Hal was inside along with Matthew McGinnis, Mayor Strapp, and two members of the city council—Council President Evan Brown and Member Ines Duarte. Saul sighed, realizing Matthew and Hal had moved forward with their plan to hold this shady meeting. Saul reached to tug at his collar but realized he wasn't wearing his normal suit and tie today. He awkwardly dropped his hands to his side.

"Guys, you need to leave," said Saul.

"But Saul..." responded Matthew. Saul held up his hand.

"Gentlemen, it's Sunday morning and this meeting is illegal." Saul pointed defiantly at the door with a flourish. "You're lucky I don't turn you in."

"My bad, Pastor Saul," said Andy, who bolted for the door. Saul could tell Andy was happy to leave, having likely been strong-armed in the first place.

"Fine! Let's get out of here," said a grim-faced Hal. "We apparently are not welcome in our own church."

"OUR church, perhaps, Hal, but MY office," Saul responded.

"For now, Pastor," Hal spat, leaning towards Saul in a menacing posture. "For now."

Saul's blood ran cold as Hal and the group left. Saul reached for the door to close it and pushed the cell phone number to call his wife.

"Pattz, you won't believe what just happened..."

"You deserve the highest praise..." sang the worship team as the band broke out in loud music to the delight of the unusually large crowd. For those paying attention, today was different at BCC. Saul was sitting with his family during the music service, not in his office or on the stage, as was his usual routine.

"Here we go," he whispered as he took Patty's hand. Saul could see Patty was already teary-eyed as the music began. "It's going to be fine. Father is with me today."

After the music, announcement of upcoming church activities, and passing the plates for the offering, it was time for Saul to speak.

"Good morning, everyone," Saul greeted as he walked up the steps to the pulpit on the stage.

"Good morning," voices rang out across the seats. Saul could hear the whispers as he worked his way up the steps. He wasn't in his power suit, but a sweater and khaki pants and the people were taking notice. His typical microphone—the one normally on his cheek—wasn't in place. Instead he'd chosen to hold a microphone in his hand. Saul was surprised how humbling it felt to be without his normal tools of authority.

"I'm honored you're here today." Saul took a long look around the room, taking it all in, perhaps for the last time. "It's ironic. I've always wanted all of Bekering to come to BCC, and here you are. I wonder what brought you all today?" A light laugh went through the crowd. Saul smiled as well, strangely at peace. He studied his notes on his iPad which was sitting on the pulpit.

"It's a great day to be at BCC, and it's a great day to be a follower of God." Normally the BCC crowd was boisterous in response to Saul's teaching, but today it was strangely quiet. Saul's eyes raised up to the balcony where Joseph sat in the front row with Becky Townsend and her friend Ruby. Joseph gave Saul a nod.

Saul's gaze then dropped directly in front of him where he saw Hal, Matthew, and their circle of followers. Hal sat in his navy suit and bright blue tie, arms crossed, glaring at Saul. Saul decided to avoid eye contact in order to avoid distraction by any response this group might exhibit.

"If you have a Bible with you, turn to the New Testament book of Mark chapter four." If Saul had any doubts of his plan, this would be the moment to shift. Saul willed himself to stay calm and plow ahead.

"This passage says, 'he who has ears, let him hear.' I urge you today, my friends, to ask God to give you ears to hear, because it's one of the most important prayers you might ever pray." Saul went on to read to the end of the chapter.

"'…To you has been given the secret of the kingdom of God,'" Saul read from his large, black, leather-bound Bible, "'but for those outside everything is in parables, that they may indeed see but not perceive, and may indeed hear but not understand.'" Saul closed his Bible with one hand, holding the mic in the other.

"And on the reading of God's word we say…"

"Amen!" It was only a handful of voices answering in the crowd, where normally nearly all would respond.

"Jesus was pronouncing that people around him were suffering under an ancient mindset—a curse, if you will," Saul began to explain. "This mindset went into effect when people forgot who God really was in their lives and in the lives of those around them." Saul wasn't in his usual cadence, and his Midwestern accent wasn't kicking in. Today wasn't a show. No, today was a day of transparent, honest sharing with his people.

"The mindset meant these people could read scripture or hear good teaching, but their hearts were closed off to understanding anything other than what they'd always known." Saul paused to take a breath.

"You see, when we begin to believe we know everything that is right— in other words, when we become religious—we cut off our ability to understand God's heart for the world around us. Then it becomes easy to be self-righteous. It becomes easy to ignore God's command to love people. It becomes easy to ignore God's command to not only love people like us, but to also those with whom we disagree." Saul reached down into the stand of the pulpit to take a sip from a plastic water bottle placed there for him each service. Sometimes, in a stressful situation, one's mind can take a funny turn, which was currently happening to Saul as he pondered the merits of a reusable water bottle in the future. He focused his thoughts by looking at Patty to his right. Seeing her smile empowered him to confidently continue.

"I stand here today to say I have been the unhearing, self-righteous person." Audible murmurs could be heard around the room at Saul's shocking revelation. If it wasn't already clear, it was now impossible for anyone not to notice something different was happening today.

"I've been your Senior Pastor at the Bekering Christian Center for twenty-two years, and I've done my best to lead this church where I believed God would have it go. I thought I knew what was right. But I have to say, my people, I've been wrong." Gasps and more murmurs could be heard around the room. People looked right and left to see how others were reacting. Saul peeked at Hal and Matthew as they exchanged smiles.

"Like the people described in this passage, I've been deaf and I've been blind to what the Father God was doing for a long time," said Saul, feeling strangely free without the urge to tug at his collar. "God had to bring someone to show me that even I didn't truly understand the character of God." Saul looked up at Joseph, who wore a broad smile.

"I tell you, folks, God is not a harsh God, eager to punish sinners. No, He is a good God, slow to anger and full of love. Full of love for his people, and full of love for our enemies." Saul looked around the silent room. He saw many people shifting awkwardly as Saul lifted his voluminous Bible into the air.

"I promise you, my beliefs in this book haven't changed, not one bit. I still believe every word. But my understanding of how God wants me to live out those beliefs—well, that's completely changed."

"Oh my!" someone said in one of the rows closest to the stage.

"Today, my friends, I repent," Saul said with passion, his voice cracking slightly as he began to fight back tears. "Today, I am changing the direction of my life." Saul paused again and walked out from behind the pulpit to the top step of the stage. He scanned the crowd, trying to look directly at as many people as possible.

"I repent today," said Saul, picking up his cadence slightly. "I repent of my belief that God wants politics and a political party to be his answer to the problems in our world."

"What is this?" Hal grumbled loudly in the front row.

"I repent of my belief that religious rules can bring God's answers to Bekering. The belief that I had to get laws passed to make people better was no different from the Pharisees' belief that good religion could bring the Messiah to Earth."

Saul paused for a moment, letting his words germinate in the minds of those listening. He noticed that every seat in the room was full, and people were standing in the back of the room. He took another deep breath and continued.

"A of to I am convinced God doesn't want to take over the government to change our country. There's no messiah coming to be president or judge to solve our issues. I know now this has never been God's plan." Saul paused and smiled

"But while Father God might not want a take over of government, I am convinced his people serving with his love can change everything. His love can bring transformation to our city, our state, and our entire country." Saul felt his emotions running high, but he kept the tears at bay.

"I repent because I've allowed men in this church to believe it's OK to do immoral, corrupt acts in the name of a good end." Saul looked at Hal. "God can never bless our morally fuzzy behavior, no matter how good our intentions." Hal tilted his head forward and squinted his eyes, staring back at Saul, unable to speak. This time Saul didn't avert his eyes.

"I'm not scared of this bully anymore," Saul resolved in his heart.

"I repent. I totally ignored the Bible when it says, 'the meek shall inherit the Earth.'" Saul walked back on stage and slapped his Bible down on the pulpit. You could hear a pin drop in the room. "People, I haven't been very meek." Saul looked down at the top of the pulpit and leaned against it with one hand.

"I was never afraid of offending people in these political battles," Saul continued. "I thought the taunts and disagreement were scars of valor. I was blind to the fact my battles were hurting people and driving them away from God rather than drawing them in. I will never again put partisan whims ahead of God's heart."

"He's gone totally insane," Hal blurted in a voice heard across the room.

"Not insane, Hal," Saul said with a grin at his Board Chair, "and also not blind." Hal stood to his feet.

"This is preposterous, Pastor," he shouted, pointing at Saul, his face turning such a shade of red Saul thought it was almost a shade of purple. "You need to step down..."

"Sit down, Hal, and let the Pastor speak." The voice was Andy Strapp who was sitting one row back and to the left of Hal. "If you don't quiet yourself, this country boy's gonna to take care of things out back."

"The nerve," Hal mumbled as he meekly sat in his seat. Saul smiled and made a downward motion with his hands to calm the moment.

"There won't be any need for violence, folks," Saul said calmly. "But thanks, Andy." Silence hung in the air like a heavy fog. Not even a baby's cry could be heard in the room.

"Folks, I hurt my family, and I want to apologize to them before all of you here." Saul's voice gave way as he looked down at Patty and Isaac, each smiling through teary eyes.

"I bless Bekering," Saul continued.

"Amen, Pastor!" said an elderly lady in the front of the room. For the first time in the service, Saul had a word of encouragement from the seats.

"Thank you, dear sister," he said, pointing to the woman. "I have loved this city but I haven't been as involved with seeking justice for the welfare of all as we're commanded to do in Jeremiah 29:7. Today I say Bekering, you're a great city, and we'll no longer try to change you with a message of anger and fear, but will pursue hope for everyone in the city, and not just the wealthy and powerful, in hopes that we'll leave Bekering better for our children and our children's children."

"Amen!" A couple voices this time. Saul wasn't necessarily prompting the room to join in audible agreement, but he was warmed by the small growth in support.

"I bless my opponents," said Saul, "some who may not fit my belief system, but still love people and love our city as much as I do. I will not declare you enemies, but rather human beings created by God, like me. This will enable us to sit together and find common ground."

"Amen!" Elsa shouted from the balcony, catching Saul's attention. He hadn't realized she was in the building. Saul watched as people whispered or shared knowing looks as he shared her smile.

"Listen to me, people," Saul spoke again, grabbing the attention of the room. "I bless those in Bekering who are not as well off as some of us may be." Saul was slowing his speech now.

"I declare prosperity in Bekering is not only for the few who happen to live in the right part of town. God's hope is for our entire city." More affirmations. Saul leaned forward and made sure to catch Hal Beatty's eye.

"I will lead you, my friends, in doing work for the benefit of generations to come, not to selfishly serve only our own generation. Years from now, our children's children's children will say this generation sacrificed to build a better city and a better state for them."

"Amen!" said a large portion of the crowd.

"Young people. I will do what I can to make sure you always know you have somewhere safe to turn when wrestling with the questions of life."

"Preach it, Father Saul!" Isaac chimed in making Saul laugh. Tears of joy began slipping from Saul's eyes and rolling down his cheeks. He loved being able to smile with his son.

"Now, let's get real," Saul said, grabbing a handkerchief from his pants pocket to clean up his face and pointing towards Hal and the group in front. "I might not be your leader after this coming week. Honestly, I might have earned that pink slip." This statement caused a new round of murmurs.

"So, let me say thank you for all these shared years. Whatever I do from this point forward, I will do with my eyes wide open and my ears tuned into what God has to say. I will never let men guide me in the wrong direction again." Saul looked around and heaved a deep, satisfied sigh.

"God bless you, Bekering Christian Center, and God bless our city and everyone in it." The people sat glued to their chairs as Saul finished and the keyboardist began to play on the stage. Saul walked down the steps and grabbed Patty's hand as they headed for the foyer to greet people on the way out. Everyone seemed unsure of what was to happen next.

"Praise the Lord!" shouted Joseph in the balcony.

"Praise the Lord!" the people responded, standing up from their seats. As he walked to the back of the room, Saul felt a peace and freedom he had never experienced before. The pressure, and the need to tug on his collar, were gone.

#

"You and your friends can yell whatever you want, Saul," Hal snarled, meeting Saul in the foyer and placing a hand on the back of Saul's neck, "it's not going to save you."

"You don't scare me anymore, Hal." Hal stopped.

"What'd you say?"

"I feel sorry for you, Hal," Saul said with an empathetic grin. "I pity you for being stuck in a lifestyle where you believe money and power make right. You're the saddest man I know and I'm so sorry I was a weak pastor and didn't tell you before."

Hal sniffed. He looked confused as he saw the people staring at him.

"Like I said, he's gone crazy," said Hal to Matthew. "We'll find out who's sad this week."

"Have a blessed day, Hal," Saul responded sarcastically, opening the door and gesturing for Hal to exit.

As Saul watched Hal head down the steps towards the parking lot, he heard a grunt as Hal looked up to see Michael Brookes from The Observer standing outside, along with a photographer.

"Mr. Beatty, can you respond to an accusation that you held a secret meeting this morning, violating the Bekering Public Meetings Statute?" Brookes held out a small recorder.

"Get the hell out of my way," answered Hal tersely brushing past and trying to avoid the photographer who was snapping photos.

"Can you answer allegations you've coerced or even offered money in exchange for votes on your New City project?"

"Can't you leave a man alone at church!" Hal shouted. He grabbed one of his associates by the collar, almost pulling the young man off his feet, and whispered into his ear. "You get inside and make sure the council members and Mayor Strapp go out the back exit."

Saul leaned outside and watched the photographer follow Hal and his wife all the way to their car, snapping pictures even as Hal fired the engine and roared away.

"Saul, I thought you said you weren't going to turn us in?" Said Matthew McGinnis, peeking through the door but avoiding being spotted.

"I didn't," Saul said in a plea of innocence. Matthew quickly scooted away, likely searching for another way out of the church.

"I wonder how The Observer found out about the meeting?" Saul said to Patty as he reached to shake the hand of a parishioner.

"I wonder," said Patty with a big smile, holding up her cell phone with a cheeky grin." You're so gracious, hon. Me? I'm a little more vengeful."

"What am I going to do with you!"

Saul and Patty enjoyed shaking hands and greeting all. A heavy week lay ahead, but their hearts were lighter than they'd ever been.

CHAPTER 37:
THE BOARD MEETING

"I think the case is pretty simple."

Saul sat at a folding table covered in a black table cloth and positioned on the stage of the BCC Beatty Fellowship Hall. Hal was standing just a few feet away and speaking in his role as "Chairman" of the BCC Board. The board had affirmed last year they wouldn't "cave" to political correctness by calling Hal's position the non-gender specific "Chair."

"By his own admission, from the pulpit this Sunday," Hal continued, "Pastor Saul has changed his beliefs and acted out of those changes." Hal was dressed professionally in a black suit and the same solid blue tie he had worn on Sunday, reading from a prepared text. Saul and Hal were facing an audience of twenty-seven board members and about a hundred others who had come to observe the open meeting.

Saul noted there were women in the room, but none served on the board. This was part of the denomination's long-held tradition: women were not allowed in leadership positions, other than teaching children. Patty had always refused to come to these board meetings, but tonight was different. She was here to stand with her husband against men she deemed "massive hypocrites and women-haters."

"Now, that's not necessary," Saul had told her. "They don't know any better."

"I know," she answered, "but their ignorance doesn't make it right." Saul always appreciated Patty's unique way of pointing out hard truths and he very much appreciated her presence in the front row on this night.

"With his egregious and heretical behavior, Pastor Saul violated the terms of his work agreement as Senior Pastor." Hal shook his fist in the air to emphasize each word.

Saul was somewhat amused at Hal's appearance and demeanor. Dressed to the nines and on his best behavior, Hal was pulling out all the stops to play the victim for tonight and pointing to Saul as the evil in the room. Joseph was right about how religion "looks so good as it does such bad."

"Hmm. Good slogan for one of Joseph's T-shirts," Saul snickered. He looked up in time to see Patty giving him a visual scolding and Saul grew serious once again.

"Pastor Saul has refused to pronounce homosexuality as sin, denigrated our own church members, and this past Sunday was teaching strange theology. Brothers, I don't believe we have any choice but to call for a vote of no-confidence for Pastor Saul and ask the executive committee to begin proceedings for his removal, as authorized by our bylaws."

"I'm the Christian being thrown to the lions," Saul imagined, stifling another smile.

"Let me add," said Hal, looking up from his script with an orchestrated look of pain on his face, "I have served here for fifteen years. As much pain as it brings me and my wife, I must stand for truth. If Saul Thompson remains the Senior Pastor here, we will have to go elsewhere and take our tithes with us." A smattering of applause rattled around the tile floor of the room that bore Hal's last name. Saul was aware it was Hal's close associates doing most of the clapping.

"Now we'll proceed with public comment," said Hal, turning to sit down and wiping what Saul judged to be a crocodile tear from his eye.

"I've loved Pastor Saul for years, but if this is how it is, my family can't stay here," said Myles Cook, the police officer.

"Like the others, we would have to leave and take our money elsewhere," shared Rich Sullivan. The next half hour was filled with several more members stepping forward and making similar declarations into the microphone.

It was painful. These were Saul's friends, people he and Patty had loved for years. Saul noticed, however, he wasn't crushed as he would have been in the past. The old feelings of shame were gone.

"This is important for you all to see," said Matthew, who was also representing the board, calling for a display to be put up on the video screen.

"This is a check we received in the offering on Sunday." Saul looked up and saw the name of the family was blacked out, but the large amount in the money line was still visible.

"As you might read in the signature line it says, 'no tie, no tithe.'" Saul could see someone had placed this check in the offering plate without an actual signature, making it impossible for the church to deposit the check.

"Another obvious sign," Hal bellowed, "that allowing Pastor Saul to stay on would be very damaging to the finances of our church, even as we're in the middle of fundraising for our children's center." Saul could see heads nod in the crowd.

"As required by of our bylaws, the accused..." said Hal, his face beaming with false sympathy, "...I mean, Pastor Saul will have a moment to defend himself before the vote." Saul stood slowly as Hal was seated in his chair.

"Thank you, Mr. Chair, for allowing me a moment to speak in my own church at a meeting of the board of which I am President," Saul said looking straight at Hal. Hal didn't return his gaze but looked out at the audience.

Saul paused for a moment and looked at the screen.

"'No tie, no tithe,'" Saul repeated in a voice displaying the irony of the statement. "If that's not the most unbelievable thing I've heard in a church business meeting, then my name is Uncle Sam." Saul shook his head in disbelief.

"I shared my heart on Sunday," he said, returning his view to the audience. Saul was wearing a light green sweater and khakis, which stood in stark comparison to the more formal business attire of many around him. "I assure you all in the strongest terms, I will not try to save my job by turning away from what I shared Sunday." Saul looked down the line of board leaders on the stage; disbelief shone on each face. They truly believed Saul would come hat-in-hand to save his job.

"Many of you have been my friends and co-laborers for years, and to you I offer my view." Saul paused to look around the crowd. "If what I've seen on display tonight is what I've taught you as Senior Pastor, then I don't deserve to be the spiritual leader in this place." Whispers swirled around him like fallen leaves picked up by the wind.

"Yet, if the board is willing to see our church change, then I'm fully with you. However, if this church is not willing to change to something in alignment with the goodness of heaven today - rather than politics and religion — and from stupid messages on checks like this"—Saul motioned to the screen once again—"then you won't need the executive committee. I'll resign."

Saul grabbed his cellphone, motioned to Patty as he descended the stage steps, and the two headed for the door hand-in-hand, leaving a stunned audience behind.

CHAPTER 38:
NO LONGER A PASTOR

The leaves crumbled beneath Saul's gloves as he cleaned the gutters of the BCC parsonage. Perhaps it was a bit odd for Saul to be on this ladder when his job, and his occupancy of this house, was in peril. Saul, though, needed the distraction.

"Prominent Bekering Pastor to Resign" said the front-page headline of The Observer, along with news about the big New City annexation vote. Someone had leaked the news about Saul and the BCC board meeting to the paper and Saul's fate had been announced before it had even been told to him.

Saul's cell ringtone sprang to life and he tapped his Bluetooth earpiece while standing at the top of the ladder on another windy Bekering day.

"Hey, you saw the headline," Saul said as he answered a greeting from Joseph.

"Yeah, I did," chuckled Joseph. "Wanted to see how you're doing."

"Oh, as good as can be expected," Saul answered as he scooped another healthy portion of leaves and dirt.

"Remember, you're not defined by a job. You did something powerful with your sermon on Sunday." Saul was grateful to Joseph. This was the only check-in call he'd received.

"Your repentance can change this city." Saul realized Joseph was trying to raise his spirits and he decided to let it happen. A smile crept into the corners of Saul's mouth.

"Thanks Joseph. What does your goofy T-shirt say today?" He heard Joseph laugh on the other end of the call.

"It says 'God loves Cans—PeliCans, MexiCans, RepubliCans, and people who Can.'" Saul punched his Bluetooth to end the call and tried to push fears of joblessness from his mind.

"Heaven, I hope there is something new for me now, Father God," he said out loud. "Please don't let me end up like my father." Saul wiped his brow, unknowingly smudging dirt on his forehead.

He went back to his task, using a handy tool called The Gutter Scoop he'd purchased at Bekering Hardware and Goods a couple years ago. He listened to Dirk Rogers through the KBEK web app on his phone.

"Thursday's the big day for the New City annexation vote," said Dirk through Saul's Bluetooth.

"Yes, it is," said Hal, Dirk's guest for the show.

"Guess this is why Hal hasn't served my pink slip yet," Saul thought.

"Now, Hal, I have to ask," said Dirk's voice through Saul's earpiece, "did you really pull the mayor and two city council members into a meeting in Saul Thompson's office?"

Saul sat his tool on the edge of the roof. He was stunned to hear Dirk challenge Hal with a difficult question knowing the amount of sponsorship money Hal spent with the station.

"Well, I was told we weren't going to talk about that," Hal stammered. "It's fake news from The Observer."

"Would you agree such a meeting would be a violation of city statutes?" asked Dirk. "And hasn't our city been known for corruption through our history?" Saul let a breath loose and stared across the horizon.

"Well, whaddya know." Saul leaned against the roof, astonished at what he was hearing. This was definitely a different Dirk.

"Are you calling me a crook, Dirk?" Hal shot back. "How would you feel if I never buy a dime's worth of advertising on this station again?" Saul was motionless on his ladder, eagerly awaiting Dirk's answer. After a moment's pause, Dirk responded.

"So, you're not denying the meeting occurred, you're just threatening me and this station." A terrible noise came over the airwaves which Saul discerned was the sound of Hal's headset and microphone hitting the KBEK remote desk. It sounded like a roar of thunder and then the shrill whine of feedback from the broadcast. Saul put his hand to his earpiece and scrunched his eyes in pain from the harsh sound.

"That might be the end of my job," said Dirk, "but it's time we dig into truth a little more here on KBEK. We'll be back with Mayor Strapp next." Saul laughed out loud, pulling off his dirty gloves and setting them on the edge of the roof by his gutter tool. Something amazing had happened. KBEK never before had challenged the status quo of Bekering, KBEK WAS the status quo.

"Wow, can the mindset of a city or a people group really be transformed?" Saul's ringtone interrupted the thought and the KBEK commercial break.

"Pastor Saul, how are you today?" Hal's chipper voice seemed out of place for this type of conversation and for the conversation he just ended over the airwaves.

"I just heard you on the radio," Saul said sporting a large grin that Saul imagined Hal could almost hear on the other side of the call.

"Hmph," Hal huffed, his chipper demeanor fading before turning to a more professional voice. "Pastor, as Chairman of the Board of Directors, it is my difficult duty to make this call." Saul was amazed at Hal's ability to compartmentalize in his life. He had completely compartmentalized his dramatic radio performance.

"The board overwhelmingly passed a vote of no-confidence last night and recommended the executive committee begin proceedings to remove you as Senior Pastor. I'm sorry."

Patty exited the front door, likely drawn by the sound of Saul on the phone. Saul gave her a grim head shake, confirming the news they'd expected. Patty put her hand to her mouth and looked away.

"Your sympathy means a great deal, Hal" Saul answered, the right side of his mouth twisted upwards in a sarcastic smirk.

"Let's keep this professional, Pastor," Hal answered sternly. "You mentioned a desire to resign, last night, so I led the board to agree to a severance payment if a deal can be struck for you to leave on your own. This would save our people the pain of a protracted battle, of course."

"Very generous of you all, Hal," Saul said coldly. "Yes, I'll be true to my word and step down if the board feels the church can't change."

"Thanks for being honorable, Saul," Hal responded, sounding relieved. "We'll have the attorneys begin the paperwork right away."

"Knowing your thoroughness, Hal, I'm sure they've already begun." Hal had displayed his disdain for Saul at the board meeting, but Saul fought his urge to return the feelings towards Hal. Saul wouldn't give Hal that power in his life and his face lit up with the freedom from Hal's dominance. There were no more stomach knots and tie tugs.

"Take care, Pastor," said Hal. "Oh, and I'd appreciate your prayers for my city vote..." Saul didn't let Hal finish the sentence. He disconnected the call, descended the ladder and approached Patty.

"Well, now begins a new chapter of our lives."

"Those sanctimonious pigs!" Patty answered, her voice filling with rage and her eyes with tears. "You've given your life to those people!"

"We're not defined by that job, Pattz," said Saul, putting his arms around her shoulders. "We've had twenty-two good years with BCC. We'll bless them and trust God to take care of us."

"We'll lose our house." Patty tried to hold back an anguished cry, her eyes turning to look at the beautiful BCC owned house that had been her home.

"I'm not who I was before, babe," Saul answered, a soft smile playing on his lips as he leaned back to wipe a tear from Patty's cheek. "We're not the same. We can have peace in the middle of this."

CHAPTER 39:
TWO REPORTERS AND AN IDEA

"God, what do you have for me now?" Saul asked out loud as he mindlessly flipped on the TV to the Channel 5 Noon News. He had forgotten about his ladder, his gloves, and gutter tool outside.

Alone, no longer feeling the need to stay strong for Patty, Saul put his head in his hands and let his heartbreak loose.

"What happens now?" Saul knew the denomination would never place him again in a senior role, and he knew a long history as a pastor wasn't great resume material for a man in his fifties looking for a job in the non-church world.

Saul was to leave that thought lingering in the air as he was again interrupted by his cell ringtone.

"Hi, Pastor Saul, it's Michael Brookes from The Observer," said the voice as Saul pushed the Bluetooth button.

"Hey, Mike," said Saul with a quick gust of breath, greeting the reporter with familiarity.

"Saul, hate to bother you, but you know I have to call for a quote," said the reporter. "Now that it's official." It had been just minutes since he'd spoken to Hal and already the news was "official."

"Mike, I love to help you, I respect the work you do." Saul knew Brookes to be an honest man who worked hard for his stories and had a real desire for truth. Saul had observed how people treated the reporter and the pain it caused Brookes as every story not fitting a partisan viewpoint was dubbed "fake news." Saul agreed with Michael's recent editorial describing the danger to democracy when elected officials and civic leaders, like pastors, undermined the credibility of media outlets and their followers blindly believe them.

"There is no such thing as 'the media,'" Michael had written. "There is no conference call everyday to synchronize our stories. We're all a bunch of small, privately owned businesses trying to sell enough advertisement to stay in business."

"Mike, there isn't anything I can say as my employment status is still in process," Saul told the reporter.

"Between you and me," Brookes responded, "Hal Beatty called me last night with the scoop you'd resign today. I think he's trying to curry favor as I continue to dig into his illegal meeting." Saul was about to end the conversation when Brookes jumped back in.

"Hey, any quote for me on Hal's project?" said the sharp reporter. "You going down for the council meeting?" Saul's own concerns had kept him from thinking about civic matters. In the past, Saul never missed a council meeting with a big vote.

"Mike, I think Patty's call from the church Sunday is all our household can do to help you there," Saul said with a slight smile.

"I won't forget your help, Saul." Saul looked up and saw Channel 5 was talking about the annexation vote.

"Mike, I gotta go."

"...the report in The Observer said Hal Beatty and several of his colleagues had an illegal meeting," Saul heard the reporter's voice over the video on the screen. "One local activist thinks this alleged violation should be enough to stop the matter." Elsa Kratt appeared on the edited TV video.

"Can you imagine this local developer had the mayor and two council members in his pastor's office days before this important city vote?" Elsa said in the interview. "Those two council members should be required to recuse themselves from the vote." Saul nodded absentmindedly before suddenly realizing, to his amazement, he agreed with Elsa Kratt.

"Local opposition leader Elsa Kratt isn't opposed to the measure because of what she believes was an illegal meeting," the reporter continued, "she feels the proposed annexation is bad for Bekering."

"Research has shown repeatedly sprawl development is bad for a city's economy," said Elsa. "The research is undeniable. These developments are major factors in the concentration of impoverished areas in a city. They also create a racially and economically divided city, which Bekering has been for too long."

The reporter appeared on the screen holding a microphone with the words "Channel 5 News" on the plastic mic flag. She was standing on a sidewalk with Elsa's downtown Love Coalition office in the background. "Ms. Kratt is calling for Bekering citizens to voice their concerns at tonight's council meeting." Saul could see people in front of the office holding signs saying "Sprawl is NOT progress" and "We Love Downtown Bekering."

"Patty," shouted Saul, clicking off the TV and jumping up from his chair, "I have to go." It'd been years since Saul had nothing to lose. He wasn't going to waste an opportunity now. In moments, Saul was at the building he'd just seen on TV and he was being led into Elsa's modest, disheveled office. Saul could see Elsa lean back and blink as she realized who'd just walked in. He was also sure she was surprised by his messy, unbuttoned appearance.

"To what do I owe the pleasure?" Elsa asked. Saul tried to quickly organize his thick head of hair with his hand, but he feared he was unsuccessful and gave up.

"I'm so sorry how I've treated you," he started, "I'm ashamed." Elsa accepted his apology and Saul continued.

"I saw you on the news," he said with the beginnings of a smile. "I think we might have found something we can do for the city together."

CHAPTER 40:
THE VOTE

"We can't keep doing business the way we have," Mayor Strapp spoke in Bekering's City Council Chambers. "My dad used to say, 'no matter how pretty the pig, when it gets fat, it gets slaughtered.'" The crowd laughed at Andy's rural euphemism.

Saul and about fifty other Bekering residents sat listening to the Mayor's arguments for the contentious vote set to take place. Saul had cleaned up after meeting with Elsa, and donned his usual suit and red power-tie. Patty was seated beside him in the front row as they watched Andy share at the public podium.

"The point my pop was making is no matter how right something seems, when it don't work anymore, you get rid of it." Andy was speaking looking up at the city council members and staff seated on the chamber dais. "Fifty years ago, our old leaders opened the door to unchecked growth and we've reaped the crap from those dumb decisions." Again, Andy's informal manners drew scattered laughs through the crowd.

There had been much speculation that Andy would stand against Hal's annexation vote, and now that reality was unfolding in full view of the council, the public, and Hal, who was seated just to Saul's right. Saul put his fingers to his lips, marveling at Andy's courage to step out and do what was right. Saul wondered if he would be able to display similar bravery.

"Trust me, I want our developers to make money—lots of it," Andy stated, leaning forward to aim his lips at the small microphone on the thin metal rod attached to the podium. "I'm not the sharpest tool in the box, but even I'm learning that local and state governments can work with builders. We can work in ways that bring a profit while still benefiting all our community. This would raise the economy for us all and just makes darn, good sense." Andy turned to the audience, projecting into the room without the microphone.

"I promise it can be done!" The small crowd applauded for Andy, but Hal and Matthew—seated on Hal's other side—did not.

As Andy turned back to face the council, Saul's eyes travelled up to the big silver letters on the wall, saying "The City of Bekering." Underneath were the words "In God We Trust." Evan Brown had brought the proposal for adding the second statement to the wall, even though he was not known for a strong Christian faith and was an infrequent visitor at BCC. Matthew had pushed the vote and pushed his people, including Andy, to support the idea as a wedge issue for future elections. Behind huge support from the Evangelical conservative community, the proposal passed, despite a surprising last second protest mounted by a group of pastors.

"We would prefer the council actually listen to God and not bother with taking God's name in vain by putting his name on the wall," Pastor Christian Anderson had argued.

Today, it was evident to Saul that Andy was living in Christian's statement. Andy was following his faith, even at the risk of his political career. Just as Joseph had encouraged him, Andy was doing right instead of bowing down to Matthew, political money, or any man-made party or ideology. Joseph was right: political mindsets can be changed.

Andy leaned heavily against the podium and Saul could see the mayor's hands shaking as he worked through his notes. Andy cleared his throat and finished with all the authority of an experienced statesman.

"I stand against the passage of this annexation because it is flat out wrong. It violates our city plan and it's bad for the people you and I represent. And we represent all of Bekering, not only those who live up north." Applause erupted behind Andy, causing Evan Brown to pound his gavel and call for quiet.

"Not a big crowd supporting Andy," Saul heard Hal say to Matthew as the two scanned the crowd. Saul and Hal both knew council members got skittish when there was a big contingency disapproving of a vote.

"Be careful, I'm sure that group is planning some big show," Matthew cautioned.

"I've got three votes in my pocket," Saul had heard Hal whisper. "Two votes are locked in for the other side." Saul knew the math Hal was reciting.

Three members were voting yes, two were voting no. It was up to Council Members Ines Duarte and Jack Hansen to be the deciding votes. If both voted yes, the tally would be a five-to-two vote which, by city law, would preclude Mayor Strapp from vetoing the approval. If one voted against the annexation, then Andy could send the proposal back with a veto, which would then take five votes to override. If both voted no, Hal's proposal was sunk.

Saul watched as Hal locked eyes with Council Member Duarte, who quickly looked away. Hal had contributed handsomely to her campaign, of which she had likely been reminded by Hal in Saul's office.

"We're about to wrap up the public comment segment on this issue," said the council president as Mayor Strapp took his seat. "Is there anyone else wanting to comment?"

Saul reached for Patty's hand and squeezed tightly.

Suddenly, all four sets of the room's double doors popped open and humanity began pouring in. Each person wore a bright, neon-orange T-shirt saying, "We Believe in Downtown Bekering."

"Here we go," said Matthew.

What happened next didn't meet Matthew's prediction. The group filtered into the room in silence, not with loud chants. Each respectfully took a seat or, once the seats were full, lined the room and sat or leaned against the wall. Patty waved over Saul's shoulder, causing him to turn and see Joseph and Isaac entering the room, sporting the same neon-orange shirts President Brown had raised his gavel, anticipating the noise of those arriving and his gavel now stood frozen in mid-air as the council president was unsure how to react to the group's less-than-defiant entry.

"I would like to speak," said Saul, his voice echoing in the silent room as he walked to the podium looking up at "In God We Trust" on the wall and took a deep breath. Was he ready to trust God in going against what he'd known for a long time? Saul didn't need to tug at his shirt collar now. He was ready.

The council members eyed one another. Saul knew they were surprised to see him.

"For the record, please state your name and occupation." "Mr. Council President, my name is Saul Thompson, a citizen of Bekering—currently unemployed... Saul could imagine Hal behind him, glaring with fire in his eyes.

"I am opposed to this proposal and ask today the council members vote against it," Saul calmly said into the microphone. The room buzzed.

"Quiet please," said President Brown. "You have two minutes, Mr. Thompson."

"I have watched for twenty-two years as this city has grown north and north and more north," Saul continued. "Heck, my church was part of that migration... well, my former church, I should say." Saul reached for his tie. Not to cinch it up, but to pull it loose. Yes, a person can have their mindset transformed and Saul was about to give a unique demonstration of such.

"I have watched people—good people, mind you—but people blinded by the thirst of profit and partisan ideology do things normally unacceptable or not part of their character." Saul pulled his tie completely out of his collar and sat it on the podium. He reached and began to unbutton the top button of his shirt collar.

"As a close associate of Mr. Hal Beatty, I would put him in that category," Saul continued, resisting the urge to look at Hal's face. "I can tell you with certainty Mr. Beatty misled this council during its approval of the North Bekering Shopping Center. He never planned for a farm on the land he is now asking to be annexed into the city limits."

"Preposterous!" Hal shouted, and the room chattered in response to Saul's statement.

"Order please," said Evan Brown, giving a slap of his gavel to the block of wood on his desk.

"You can't let him go on like this, Evan!" Hal shot back.

"Hal," said the council president, pointing his gavel directly at the developer, "you need to sit down." Saul had resumed unbuttoning his shirt, causing council members to look at one another in confusion.

"That being said, today's vote is about more than an overzealous developer," Saul stated, his voice ringing through the speakers. "This vote is about something like me repenting of what I've done to get this city in the mess that it's in. And in making a change in my life, I want to show others what it looks like doing the hard work to see our city transformed. I encourage all of you to do the same." Saul pointed a finger and ran it right to left to point at each council member.

Another button unbuttoned. Saul could see he was televised on the big screen above the seats and to the public on cable TV. The council members strained to see what Saul was going to reveal underneath his shirt.

"When our leaders seem coerced to benefit a small subset of our population and subvert good planning put into place to help the city thrive," Saul finished with the last button and pulled his shirttail free, "it sucks the will out of the people to believe something better can happen."

"With all due respect, dear council, I ask you to overcome the long-time, conservative mindset of our city and vote 'No' today, because it's just the right thing to do." Saul slid his button-down shirt off to reveal the same bright orange, "We Believe in Downtown Bekering" T-shirt being worn by Elsa's group.

"I ask this because I believe in Downtown Bekering and I love my city." Shrieks of joy broke out in the crowd and wild applause erupted all through the room. President Brown sat momentarily frozen, unable to pound his gavel.

Saul placed his dress shirt on the podium, turning to give a full displaying of his T-shirt to the audience and to Hal and Matthew. As the response continued to ring out, Saul couldn't stop the smile from overtaking his face. He rubbed his face and fought to reign in his emotions to finish what he had to share.

"Please everyone, let's respect our council president," Saul spoke into the microphone. "We're not here to win a fight and bully; we're here to plead our righteous case. Council members, we respect and trust you to lead our city." The room grew quiet as Saul grabbed his clothing and headed back to Patty. Saul could see the council members in deep thought.

"He's trying to punish me for having him fired," Hal screamed, standing and pointing at Saul. This seemed to break the shock from Evan Brown and he pounded the gavel again.

"Mr. Beatty, this is my last warning for you."

It was time for the vote. There was silence as the city clerk read the proposal, including the parcel number given Hal's land and asked for the vote.

"An 'Aye' vote is for approval of the annexation. A 'Nay' vote is opposed," the clerk spoke into her microphone. "Council President Brown, how do you vote?"

"I vote Aye," Evan answered. A smattering of applause from Hal's supporters filled the room.

"The council president votes Aye," the clerk noted.

"Council Member Selleck, how do you vote?"

"I vote Nay!" the elected official answered emphatically. A muted applause followed this vote. Evan Brown again gave a rap of his gavel on to the block of wood.

The vote continued and soon the screen behind the dais showed three affirmative votes, two negative votes, as anticipated with Duarte and Hansen yet to vote.

"Council Member Hansen, how do you vote?" asked the clerk. A crackle of anticipation filled the room as all awaited this key vote. Saul felt Patty grab his hand as they listened.

"Um, it's a very difficult decision," Hansen responded. "After hearing Mr. Thompson's thoughtful plea, I believe I, too, have some repenting to do. I have decided to vote Nay." People jumped to their feet shouting. Hal looked at the floor, his mouth pressed in a tight line. The veto-proof vote he wanted was no longer possible, and the entire outcome rested on Member Duarte.

"Quiet please!" said Evan Brown, pounding his gavel so hard the block of wood flew from the desk and landed on the tile floor in a loud clatter. A bailiff retrieved it and the room quieted for the final vote.

"Council Member Duarte, how do you vote?" asked the clerk. The room focused on the young Hispanic woman who'd recently been elected. She looked at Saul and he could see her turmoil. She leaned forward to speak once but still seemed unable to form words. She looked at Saul again and, after a moment's hesitation, Saul watched her countenance change as she arrived at her final decision.

"Mr. Council President, may I have a short discussion with you and the city attorney?" This caused a clamor behind Saul and Patty. Saul had to admit, this was good drama. He watched Ms. Duarte share an unheard conversation with the two men.

"Well, uh, it seems there's an issue here," said Council President Brown. His face was grim as he looked at Hal. "Council Member Duarte has asked to recuse herself from the vote in light of recent contact with the public regarding this issue. The city attorney will review this contact to see if anything inappropriate has occurred." The room buzzed and Saul watched Michael

Brookes begin to type furiously on his computer at his seat in media row, just to the left of the public lectern. Other media members scattered or jumped on their phones. Saul looked at Patty, eyes wide open in amazement. They'd made Bekering history.

"We have three affirmative and three negative votes," Evan continued, "with one recusal. Therefore, I declare the vote a tie and the annexation is not approved. This meeting stands adjourned."

"You'll never get elected again," Hal cried out, Matthew grabbing him by the shoulder in an effort to calm him down. Hal's face was a dark shade of ruby red as the crowd's raucous applause rang out behind him. It wasn't a full rejection of the measure, as they'd hoped, but for the first time anyone could remember, Hal had come before the city asking for action and the city hadn't met his demands. That was reason to celebrate.

"Four weeks and I'll be back with my votes in hand," Hal said leaning over Matthew towards Saul.

"And my friends and I will be here fighting you all of the way," Saul responded, pointing his finger defiantly at Hal's face.

Saul took a deep cleansing breath and smiled. He'd stood against the mindset of his own people and watched change occur. He sensed his life's purpose was unfolding before him.

CHAPTER 41:
A DRIVE TO THE PAST

"Oh, Lord, help me," Saul groaned as he and Isaac lifted the heavy box onto the back of the borrowed Chevy pickup. Isaac laughed.

"The Lord isn't here to help," he joked. Saul clapped his son's shoulder as they continued to move the Thompson family belongings from the BCC parsonage. Saul and Patty were moving to a small condo downtown and Isaac had found an apartment of his own.

"Ever hear of a moving company?" Isaac teased as they loaded a heavy armoire.

"I'm unemployed, kid. You work a lot cheaper," said Saul with a smile as the prepared for their third trip to the new home. It was going to be a long day.

A vehicle pulled into the driveway and Saul recognized Ted Freeman, the banker, pulling up. He was wearing his modern-framed glasses but was not in his usual formal attire, sporting jeans and a baseball cap instead.

"Pastor, sorry to interrupt..." Ted hesitated for a moment, taking his cap from his head as Patty came through the garage to see who'd dropped by.

"What is it, Ted?" asked Saul, wiping his shirt sleeve across his brow, Ted clearly had something important on his mind.

"Would you all take a ride with me?"

Isaac parked the loaded pickup inside the garage and they piled into Ted's SUV. Saul looked at Patty in the back seat from his front seat vantage point. She gave a confused smile and shrugged her shoulders. They were on an adventure together, Saul thought, and this definitely qualified.

"Pastor, some people aren't happy with the way you were treated," Ted shared, keeping his eyes on the road.

"You're very kind, Ted," said Saul with a pat on his friend's shoulder, "but you don't have to call me 'Pastor' anymore."

"I'm not so sure Hal Beatty gets to decide if you're a pastor or not," Ted said, giving Saul a serious look, "I believe that's God's job."

"We're going downtown," Saul heard Isaac say, pointing ahead of them as Ted turned the pickup off the highway.

"Are we going to the old church?" Patty asked from the back seat. Ted didn't answer but soon the original Bekering Christian Church building was in view.

"Here we are," Ted said dramatically. He smiled for the first time on their journey as he pulled into a spot in the small church parking lot. Saul felt a mix of emotions causing a shiver as he looked at the old building.

"Looks like it's been abandoned a while," Saul said climbing from his seat, "but it's still a pretty church."

"Oh, it sure is, hon," said Patty joining him in front of the stairway entrance to look at their former church home. The two panes of stained glass had endured a fair share of rocks, the white paint was stressed, and the yard was filled with weeds and dead grass, but Saul could feel what this place had once meant to him. Patty agreed.

"You remember, Saul?" Patty asked, her wistful eyes looking up the short stairway, but seemingly seeing days gone by. "We were dreamers. Ready to change the world, not babysit some crabby church people."

"We connected with the neighborhood," Saul said with a stare, his mind racing with memories. "We barbecued right in this yard to try and draw people to our small group."

"Why don't we go inside and take a look?" said Ted. Saul swallowed hard as he grabbed Patty's hand and they began the climb.

"Is that music? Or am I hearing things?" Saul said as they neared the door.

"Go in and find out," Ted encouraged them, no longer hiding his big grin. The shabbily painted double doors creaked open and Saul couldn't believe what was inside.

"I'm trading my sorrow…" sang a small ensemble of musicians up on the stage, "I'm trading my shame…" A band inside was playing an old worship song. Patty laughed excitedly.

"Honey look," she said, "our people!" Saul could see a small gathering of people inside the dark building. There didn't appear to be electricity as the only light was the morning sun coming through the windows.

"I guess it's Pattz," Saul answered as they stepped carefully onto a rotted rug in the foyer. Saul felt excitement bubble up, maybe there were still some heavenly surprises to be had for him.

"I see you, Saul!" said Joseph, who was in the sanctuary doorway to greet them. His cool blue T-shirt had a smiley face and said, "Today is a GOOD day (like every other day)!"

"You are the answer to Bekering's prayer!" Joseph motioned for them to enter. The music continued to play, and Saul, Patty, and Isaac walked through the old foyer past the swinging doors into the church's sanctuary. The doors had been propped open with old hymnals.

"Hey everyone, it's Pastor Saul and Patty!" Saul looked around the room as his eyes adjusted to the darkness. He couldn't believe what he was seeing. Was his recent change of heart really making an impact on people?

"Look, it's Frank and Alice Perkins," said Patty as she clasped hands with Alice. As they moved forward, people on both sides of the ratty aisle grabbed Saul's hand and hugged Patty. Saul could identify the faces of BCC parishioners and many others.

"Pastor, I'll never forget you standing with me," said Andy Strapp. On the other side of the aisle, Saul spotted Dirk Rogers, the KBEK Radio host, and Becky Town send.

"This is my daughter, Esther," she said. Saul greeted Esther and Becky's friend Ruby. As Saul turned, he suddenly found himself in Elsa's embrace. He stiffened for a moment, then put his arms around his new friend.

"Maybe this church is something we can collaborate on for the city," Elsa said in on Saul's ear. Saul stepped back, hands on hips and looked around in confusion. "Church? Here?"

Ted climbed onto the stage as the music quieted. "Pastor Saul, Patty, please come to stage." The steps groaned as they stepped up. Saul hoped the stage would hold. As he looked out over the group, Saul eyes filled with tears, a regular occurrence these days as his heart softened.

"Pastor Saul, you said you'd lead with your eyes and ears open," Ted said loud enough for everyone to hear. "We're ready to follow a pastor like that." The group erupted in cheers and whistles.

"Oh, wow..." Saul answered. Both hands went up through his hair. "In this dusty old place?"

"Why not, Saul?" said Patty, jumping in. "Why not start over?" Ted pointed to a man approaching the stage with a set of keys in his hand.

"This is Frank Smidt," said Ted, "he owns the place."

"Pastor, if you want it, the building's yours," said Frank, holding out the keys. Saul shook his head in disbelief. "Downtown needs a good church and I want to help make that happen." Mr. Smidt smiled and since Saul seemed frozen in place, he grabbed Saul's hand and put the keys in it.

"I'll take the healthy tax write off, of course," Smidt said as the crowd laughed.

Saul felt himself momentarily wobble on his feet, nearly overcome with the moment. He leaned over and whispered to Patty.

"Maybe God isn't mad at me, after all," Saul leaned over and whispered to Patty.

Gathering his balance, Saul stepped back into the call of his life. Ted was right. Hal didn't get to determine if Saul is a pastor. With a dramatic motion, Saul held the keys aloft to a round of cheers. Soon Saul raised his hands for quiet.

"I'm not sure I deserve this honor," he said. "But... it would be pure joy for Patty and me to lead this group, in this building!" People screamed and Saul had to quiet them again.

"But this time we do it differently," he said. "We will be about investing in people, with relationship, not politics and religion."

Wild applause broke out again and the band kicked into its music. Excitement filled the air. Patty gave grateful hugs to those on the stage.

Ted leaned over to ask Saul a question.

"Well, Pastor, what'd we do now?"

"Actually, Isaac and I could use some help moving boxes..."

CHAPTER 42:
TIME TO CHANGE THE WORLD

"Where you taking me?" Joseph asked. He was a passenger in Saul's slightly used Buick Enclave SUV with Patty in the back seat. The convertible BMW was now gone in a budgetary decision.

"It's not a 'place,'" Saul joked as he eased the SUV down a long side street, "it's a new start."

Joseph's red T-shirt displayed the words "In hell it will be hard not to burn your hamburgers." The shirt had a picture of flames and the devil holding a burger on a spatula.

"How's the church doing?" Joseph asked.

"Well, it's not really 'doing' at all," Saul responded.

"The people all agreed, we didn't want to do church anymore, so…" Patty chimed in. Saul watched Joseph smile at Patty. She was a new person having come out of a period of counseling for alcohol abuse.

"You look great, Patty," Joseph said, reaching to clasp her hand.

"I feel great," she responded.

They turned the corner and Saul watched Joseph's eyes grow wide.

"Whattya think," laughed Saul, "the 'church' has been completely transformed."

"Just like Saul," Joseph laughed. They parked and exited the vehicle and showed Joseph what used to be an old, rundown white church, that had born the scars of downtown's Bekering's demise, was now a Phoenix rising from the ashes.

"Well, Holy Heaven," mused Joseph.

The group of visionary souls had breathed new life into the old church. They had stripped away the old paint and decay and coated it with a beautiful muted green with light gray trim, giving the building a contemporary but natural appearance.

The windows, fogged and cracked the last time Joseph had seen them, were replaced with large, clear glass panes that would maximize natural light and provide unobstructed views of the newly tree lined grounds.

And just above the brand new exterior doors was a sign — "Bekering Spiritual Healing Center."

"OK," laughed Joseph, "I can see you definitely did not decide to start another church."

They headed inside and the old wooden pews were replaced with comfortable chairs, bean bags and large pillow arranged in various patterns.

"This set up will fostering a sense of community and inclusivity," said Patty. "For spiritual gatherings, yoga class and discussion groups."

The high, vaulted ceiling was adorned with delicate, hand-painted murals depicting scenes of spiritual significance from various spiritual practices. In place of the pulpit, there stood a serene meditation space with cushions and candles.

"The choir room off the stage has been converted into a library and reading room with books on spirituality, healing, and self-discovery," Saul stated excitedly.

"I'm blow away," said Joseph. "You've changed the atmosphere here from somber and religious to warmth and a palpable sense of serenity. This will truly help bring healing here to Bekering."

"Now you gotta see what's down the hall," Saul exclaimed as he and Patty led Joseph into a hallway smelling of new paint with mod designs of all kinds of colors.

Saul pointed to a door on the right and ushered Joseph in. He watched Joseph's face shine as he entered a room similar to the North End Grill back room.

"We call it 'Joseph's room for story-tellers,'" Patty said in a low voice as there was activity going on in the room. Joseph put one arm around her and the other around Saul.

"This is why I came to Bekering," he said. Saul wondered if Joseph was talking about them, or the room named after him.

The room contained about twenty people sitting on the chairs, pillow and the floor listening to Isaac, who was speaking from the small stage.

"...I ran for city council because I'm convinced heaven loves good government," Isaac said to the crowd, looking up to give Joseph a wink. Isaac had recently cut his hair shorter and dressed slightly more professionally after his recent successful run for office. His tattoo, however, was clearly visible.

"I'm not trying to take over the council and make it do 'Christian' things, as others have." The group, filled with people of all ages, seemed locked on Isaac's every word. "If people who claim to follow the teachings of Jesus will serve with excellence, there'll be blessing to enable those people to positively influence our world—and we won't have to be big jerks anymore."

The crowd laughed with Isaac and he soon wrapped up today's premier "Bekering Downtown Church Cultural Discussion." Isaac showed a poster of upcoming events such as artist evenings and tech training to be held at the still-being-renovated building. As the guests cleared out, the family stood by the front exit and Saul could see the satisfaction on Joseph's face. Suddenly, Saul sensed a little sadness, as well.

"Well, guys, it's time for me to go," said Joseph.

"No, stay a little longer," prodded Saul, "we'll grab some chairs, have some coffee and chat."

"I don't mean 'go' from this room," Joseph responded. "I mean my time in concert Bekering is finished."

The Thompsons looked at each other with concern.

"You all will now carry the message of heaven for Bekering," said Joseph, propping his shoulder against the wall before realizing the paint was still a bit wet and left a mark on his shirt. "I'll always be with you in spirit and, like this paint, you'll always be with me."

"Joseph, I have to ask..." Isaac searched for the right words. "Are you some sort of angel or something?"

"Definitely not an angel," Joseph cackled with his familiar smile. "I'm more like one who comes alongside."

"That term is 'Paraclete,'" said Saul, "the name the Bible gives to the Holy Spirit."

"Yep," answered Joseph, "something like that."

"Wait! I almost forgot," Isaac said suddenly. "We've gotta show you something." He asked his parents to come help him move some boxes in what looked like a storage room. Patty located the right one among all the stacks.

"You're gonna love this, Joseph," Isaac said as he pulled a yellow T-shirt from a box filled with similar shirts. Isaac held it up to display the "God is NOT mad at you" print on the front.

"We can... sell... these." Isaac's sentence fell flat as he and his parents looked around the empty room. They went out into the foyer with no luck. Joseph was gone.

The three stood silently in the entryway for a moment, perhaps pondering what their encounters with Joseph had meant to their lives. But not for long. Bekering was ready to be transformed, and there was a lot of work to do.

EPILOGUE

Joseph smiled with satisfaction as he drove down the highway. His father might have been run out of Bekering, but now he had nothing but gratefulness for the chance to be part of its transformation.

"Love that goodness of heaven," he laughed to himself.

"…God is not an old man, and God does not belong to Republicans…" sang the Gungar song on Joseph's car sound system. "God is not a flag, Not even American. And God does not depend on a government…"

"I doubt some of the people here will like this song much," Joseph laughed out loud.

Looking to his right, he saw the sign announcing the name and population of his next destination. He saw the social clubs and churches welcoming visitors to the town and he had a familiar question: What will they do now that Joseph has come to town?

ACKNOWLEDGEMENTS

This book could not have been written without the amazing support of so many people, including my friend Dan Robinson, who continually was telling me I would write a book. Thanks to Dan's wife, Louise, for loving me as I worked on this book and for the love of their two special kids, Isaac and Ruby (each of whom has a character named after them in this story).

To my partner in crime Bob Prater. Thanks for cheering me on for this book and for always challenging me to change the world with what I have in me. I believe that's true, and I love you for thinking it. To Wayne Jacobsen who encouraged me to keep writing and assured me he would tell me to stop if the work wasn't good. To editors Rakel Sampson and Laura Thomas and my friend Joaquin Alvarado who gave me such great input in making the story a better experience for the readers. Toby Delaney gave me a book cover to help the book feel real to me before it was completed. I can't thank all of you enough.

To the gang at Jeffrey Scott Agency - Natalie, Jessie and Marcus and, of course, Bruce. Thanks for believing in me and giving your time and expertise.

Finally, I want to say how much I love my family. Sydney and Samuel, my two children, thanks for being great people. I love you both so much and am amazed at who you are. To my partner, Ashley, what a journey we're on for our household mission to be part of positive transformation for our city, state and the whole world. I have no regrets walking this life with you. Thank you for being my champion on this project and in my life. I wouldn't be who I am without you.

There are so many more I could thank but to all of you — you probably know who you are - I'll simply say my life is full because of my relationship with you. Thanks for being part of seeing me through to my best self.

I love you all.

Made in the USA
Monee, IL
04 February 2024